Also from Indigo Sea Press
by Dorothy McMillan

Deadly Urges
Vile Acts
Soul Crossed

indigoseapress.com

The Gray Green Underground

By

Dorothy McMillan

Stiletto Books
Published by Indigo Sea Press
Winston-Salem

Stiletto Books
Indigo Sea Press, LLC
931-B South Main Street, Box 145
Winston-Salem, NC 27103

First Stiletto Books edition published
December, 2015
Stiletto Books, Moon Sailor and all production design are trademarks of Indigo Sea Press, used under license.

For information regarding bulk purchases of this book, digital purchase and special discounts, please contact the publisher at indigoseapress.com

Cover design by Stacy Castanedo

Manufactured in the United States of America
ISBN 978-1-63066-267-7

This book is dedicated to the love of my life, my husband Al, who has continually encouraged me through many dark days and never let me give up. It is also dedicated to my wonderful children, Debra, Michael, and Kimberly, the cream of any mother's crop. And, of course to my grandchildren, and great grandchildren.

My deep and abiding love also goes to Ray Bradbury who kept me from abandoning my writing at a very discouraging point in my career, and who continued to encourage me for so many years.
You're deeply missed, Ray.

ACKNOWLEDGEMENTS

A sincere thank you goes to my wonderful and helpful beta readers who often struggle through rough drafts of my work without a complaint.
Al McMillan, Debra Harvey, Ann Snow, Trina Williams, and Kimberly Harris. And my gratitude goes to my agent, Mike Hamilburg, for taking me where I needed to go all those years ago.

"Mankind! Judge of all things, feeble earthworm, depository of truth, a sink of uncertainty and error, the glory and the shame of the universe"
-Blaise Pascal

Preface

If by chance you run across an old stone castle in a wild little Southern California canyon, the first sight of it will give you a creepy, skin-prickling sensation.

Surrounded by dark whispering forests, the giant stone edifice has languished there for over a hundred years. Built by a small hunchbacked man named Hagan Poole, it is a strange place that can easily hold dark secrets.

Hagan Poole apparently suffered a heart attack, and died there. His ashen bones lying in a tangled heap were discovered sometime in the 1990's. He left no heirs.

A local couple purchased the strange place from the state, and turned it into a hotel. The Hotel Grande. However, most customers found it far too roughhewn and uncomfortable, and the endeavor failed after a few short years.

The giant stone citadel sat alone for many years with its hallways collecting enormous tangles of hoary spider webs. Slimy gray-green fungus and powdery white mold oozed from the blushing Tutor brick that lined the stone walls. The entire place reeked of a syrupy dampness and a putrefying mushroom smell. Abandoned and forlorn, the Hotel Grande languished silently. Forgotten.

Forgotten, that is, until twenty-eight year old Isabel Warren received the unexpected phone call from her dead husband.

Chapter One

The loud bleating of Isabel Warren's cell phone gave her no warning of what was about to happen. A delicate humming-bird of a woman with amber hair and a sprinkling of pale freckles, Isabel casually flipped open her cell phone. "Hello," she said, wondering if it might be one of her fellow teachers wishing her happy holidays. She was only twenty-seven, and already a widow, so their sympathy for her sometimes showed up in nice little ways.

"Issy . . . it's Jorge," said a deep, rumbly voice.

"Jorge who?"

"Jorge Warren. Your *husband*, Issy!"

A bizarre shiver slithered up Isabel's spine like an icy snake. Her cell phone became slippery in her hand and she almost dropped it. It couldn't be Jorge. After all, Jorge was dead! Dead for the past four years! As dead as Tutankhamen! She had wept at Jorge's memorial, and sent his powdery ashes to the Brighter Day Memorial Park. Who on earth would call her and say such a cruel thing?

Jorge now resided in a cherry-wood box all tucked neatly into a cold marble wall. He was resting peacefully in perpetuity a few yards away from an alabaster fountain spraying water out of an angel's mouth like a mist of tiny white diamonds. Therefore, the voice that now rumbled inside her ears couldn't possibly be her dead husband's. Nevertheless, it sure as hell sounded like him! Her hands began to tremble and she fought to keep the phone to her ear. Her whole body went icy damp.

"Issy," the voice said in a raspy tone. "I need you! I need your help desperately."

"Listen you! What kind of sick hoax is this?" She started to slam the cell phone on the floor, wanting to stomp on it . . . to crush it, but something wouldn't let her. "How could you do something so unkind?" she said, close to tears.

"I know this upsets you, Issy, my suddenly turning up like this."

"Upset me!" Isabel said in an ear-piercing screech. "My husband's been dead for four years! Why should I be upset if he suddenly called me?" Her legs abruptly lost all sensation. She felt certain she was going to collapse in a heap on the floor.

"I know, I know," he pleaded. "However, what I did four years ago had to happen. I had to play dead! I promise I'll tell you everything when I see you. Issy, please!"

"No!" she yelled. "If it's really you, I don't want to see you! You're dead to me! I want it to stay that way!"

"Issy, I'll explain everything . . . you'll understand."

"No! I will never understand why . . . you were dead and now you're not!" Then with a jolt she suddenly realized how much she needed an answer. If it was true, she needed to know why Jorge had played dead, and why he was suddenly resurrected. She slowly let out a long sigh. "Okay then, explain!"

"It is complicated!" His voice turned harsh. "I've gotten involved in some nasty shit. Otherwise, I would never have come to you!"

To Isabel his words began to sound like something out of a bad movie. It started out about how he still loved her. Now it sounded more like a threat. This had to be a dream . . . a twisted nightmare! Nevertheless, fighting the thought of it, she knew that the voice was Jorge's. Absolutely!

A hot blast of anger hit her. "How can I possibly help you?" she growled. "I can't help a dead man." She heard Jorge give a groan, then silence. "Jorge?" More silence. "Damn it Jorge! I guess you've gone and died again!" She tasted anger in the back of her throat, all sharp and metallic. Anger felt better to her than the icy shock and fear she'd first felt.

"You're a biologist, Issy. That is why I need you!" Jorge finally said in a tense voice.

"I'm a biology *teacher*, for God's sake! I teach high school biology! You were the biologist, Jorge, spending your entire time mutating DNA and creating God knows what! Until you died, you son of a bitch!" She spit out the words as if they tasted bad. "How could you be so cruel?" She swallowed some of her anger, almost

3

choking on it. "Okay, so if you didn't die, so where the hell did you go? I know we were almost divorced but even so I still loved you, even if you were impossible to live with. Or to live without, considering how much time you spent in Japan."

"I love you, Issy. But right now I need you!"

"Then tell me why?" she whispered, fighting back tears. "Why?"

"Because my whole life is going down the drain. I put myself in danger . . . and you as well."

"Me? Because of something my dead husband did?"

"It's too complicated to tell you right now."

"I'm sure it is," she said, her breath short and wooden now, making her feel strangely numb.

"Listen Issy! I'm working at a place called the Hotel Grande. I'll explain everything if you will just shut up, and meet me there."

"The *what* hotel?"

"The Hotel Grande."

"I've never heard of it?"

"It's a huge old place up Angeles Crest highway."

"I've never driven that road," she said, and told herself there was no way in hell she would consider going. "You mean it's in Eaton Canyon?"

"No! You just take highway 2. You'll hit Red Box, but just keep going until you reach a turn-off called Jump-off-Jimmy Creek Road. The Hotel Grande is on a piece of homesteaded land at the end of that road. You can't miss it. The place is an unusual stone structure, like a gigantic castle. It was closed up for years, but it is back in use now."

"No thank you, Jorge!"

"I will meet you out front." His voice was demanding. "There's a parking area by the front entrance. If you beat me there, just tell them you're looking for . . . for Joe Watson, the name I go by now. Can you remember that?"

Isabel started to answer, but stopped, anger burning her lungs.

"Issy, damn it, answer me! I'm called Joe now, not Jorge, can you remember that!"

"No!"

"For God's sake, Issy, do not mention my real name. That person is dead. He has to stay dead!"

"Listen, you . . . you back from the dead Jorge!" she said, gritting her teeth to protect herself from the bizarre situation. "I have a lot of things to take care of. Even if I agreed to meet you, I couldn't until later this week."

"Tonight Issy! *It has to be tonight!*"

Isabel stood in stunned silence feeling as if some sort of inexplicable hallucination had trapped her. She shook her head, hoping to shake away the idea that she was actually talking to her dead husband.

"It's the holiday break at school for you," he said. "You don't teach again until the first or second week of January, right?"

Isabel closed her eyes. Was Jorge really not dead and gone to ashes? His husky voice suddenly gave her the willies. A heavy surge of both disbelief and fear flooded over her. "Jorge, I'm not going to go running up the mountain roads. It's December! It's cold. It's supposed to snow above 4,000 feet. I don't have chains for the Jeep and I don't think I have a warm enough jacket. So get someone else!"

Isabel's legs went weaker as she thought about possibly seeing Jorge again. She'd pictured him as a specter for so long, just a ragged piece of mist, until the memory of him had finally faded. Now out of the blue, Lazarus had arisen! At that moment she hated him and loved him, both emotions so fastened together fighting for control, she could not separate them. He certainly wasn't the best husband, but he hadn't been the worst either. Not quite anyway.

"The place isn't high enough for much snow," his said. "It's in a little valley at about 3,000 feet. Just meet me there!" he demanded. "Put on your purple gloves. The ones I bought you. They were nice and warm."

The purple gloves! *It had to be Jorge!* No one else knew about them. She'd hated them, and tossed them in the fireplace.

"Jorge!" she cried out. "If it's not you buried next to that alabaster angel, then who in the hell is?" A hollow sound echoed

5

from the phone. "Jorge?" She heard a click. Disconnected? Either he'd hung up on her, or something had cut them off. She slowly put the cell phone down on the entry hall table, then closed her eyes and shook her head. She did not need this! Damn him! Her life had finally stopped spiraling out of control. She did not have the horrific dreams about his death any more. She couldn't let anyone send her life out of control again. Not even resurrected Jorge!

She rubbed at her numbed legs to get their feeling back, and then walked into the living room of her condo and stood looking out the bay window, pressing back heated tears. What on earth was going on? In addition, what was dead Jorge doing working at a hotel, when he has a doctorate in bioengineering? What kind of mess has he gotten himself into? Damn it! This couldn't be happening! She swiped at the hot tears that had escaped and were sliding down her cheeks.

In the distance, she heard a rumbling. Thunder? Thunderstorms were rare in Southern California. Wind gusts rattled the eaves of the condo. As she watched, they blew the sky gray, creating ashen clouds which stretched themselves across the horizon, hanging there like dirty waterlogged curtains.

How dare Jorge ask her to go out in this weather? She wasn't going to risk driving the mountain roads without a GPS, even if she did have four-wheel drive on her Jeep. She pushed the thought of it out of her mind. He shaky legs were slowly getting better. She marched out of the living room, trying to shove some resolve into her small body.

She walked to the kitchen, pulled out a can of soup from the cupboard, opened it, poured it into a bowl, and then stuck it into the microwave. She located a packet of soda crackers, then rummaged through the refrigerator and found a bright red apple. She hadn't eaten breakfast, and only snacked on a small piece of leftover pizza for lunch. Her stomach growled its complaint. She looked at her watch which read five: thirty. Too early to eat dinner, but nevertheless she was hungry.

It took her only minutes to finish eating. The shock and anger over Jorge being alive diminished some. In its place, unusual sensations began to grow. Hope maybe? Curiosity? She didn't know exactly, but she realized it had been years since she had felt such sensations.

A divorce had been the last thing she wanted. For a long time she felt certain their marriage was good. Nevertheless, somewhere, somehow things went wrong. Jorge went from being quiet and withdrawn, to growling and shouting for no real reasons. He was away from home more and more, staying in Japan working for a bioengineering company for long stretches. He missed birthdays, anniversaries, even holidays. She had finally felt so alone she asked him if he wanted a separation, some time to sort out what he really wanted in their relationship. He quickly agreed. Only he used the word *divorce*.

Soon after, he left on an extended trip to Japan, to the parent company he worked for, and was due back in a week. Then the devastating call came. The call saying Jorge had been in a fatal accident. A sixteen-wheeler had crashed into his company-owned car. According to the call, a blazing ball of fire had consumed the car, and Jorge.

Two weeks later his ashes arrived by special delivery. All six-foot two, 198 pounds of Jorge were packed into a polished cherry-wood box with a matching carved lid and a shiny brass lock, all of which measured only 18 inches by 18 inches. She took it to the Brighter Day Memorial Park for interment.

With no siblings, and both her parents deceased, Jorge had been her world. When and why had all of their happiness dissolved like Misty trails of fog? It just happened, sneakily, slowly, and with little warning about the devastating outcome. The thought of all this gave her a throbbing headache.

Forcing the flood of memories from her mind, Isabel washed up the soup bowl, muttering to herself, "There is no way I'm going to do what Jorge asked." She dried her hands and made her way into the bedroom, still muttering. "It's a dangerous road. Not safe even in good weather."

7

In a mechanical manner, she began searching through her closet. She saw a grey wool jacket hanging in the back of her closet. She'd never worn it because it was too warm to wear most days in Southern California. She carried the jacket to the bed and sat down. Then, realization hit her. "Holy God!" she said aloud, her voice shaking. "What am I doing? I cannot go running up the mountain in the dark with a storm on the way just because Jorge called. Just because Jorge isn't dead after all."

She went into the small bathroom and grabbed a bottle of Aspirin from the medicine cabinet. She poured out two of the white tablets, and swallowed them without water. She looked at her pale face in the mirror. Even her freckles were pale. She ruffled her short lightly curled hair with her fingers, then finished off with a spritz of her favorite Estee Lauder cologne, and went back into the bedroom. "That's better," she said in a voice touched with a bit of bravado.

Feeling like a marionette with strings controlled by someone else, she reached under the bed, pulled out her overnight bag, and began stuffing it with several sweaters, some makeup, and her folding umbrella with the ivory handle. It's just in case, she told herself. In case she could actually find the hotel where Jorge said to meet him. In case the bad weather kept her from coming back later.

She'd heard the name of the old hotel before, in passing, but had never known exactly where it was, or that it was open again. Rumor had it that an odd little hunchbacked man had it built, a man who still haunted the place. Isabel didn't believe in ghosts. Nevertheless, Jorge had been dead for four years, and just a short while ago he had called her. Maybe it was Jorge's ghost that had called her. She wished that was true. Then she wouldn't have to contend with the live man who had faked his death for so long.

She shook her head, gave a garbled little laugh, and grabbed her car keys off the dresser. She pulled on the wool jacket, gathered her overnight bag and a small blanket, picked up her cell phone from the dresser, and headed for the garage. For a short moment, she came close to changing her mind about doing something so foolish. Instead, she took in a long deep breath, and climbed into her car.

The Gray Green Underground

As she backed the Jeep Cherokee out of the garage, a flash of lightening blinded her for a second. Thunder rumbled, rattling the windows of the car. It began to rain, and the wind blew it into undulating strands of liquid silver.

She stopped the car and took in a deep breath, fighting the urge to run back to the house, curl up on the sofa, and watch a movie on TV. She checked her watch. Six p.m. What was she thinking, racing out in the dark and the rain? More important, she should stay home and start working on grading her student's test papers. It was Friday and her students would be back from the Christmas holidays shortly after the first of the New Year. She squeezed her eyes closed so tight, her head hurt worse. What the hell was it that Jorge told her? Take the Angeles Crest Highway past Red Box, then to the Jump-off-Jimmy-Creek cutoff, and then it's about five miles on a gravel road to the Hotel Grande.

"Okay," she said. "I have actually lost my frigging mind!" Then she calmed herself. She knew the only reason she decided to go was to see if Jorge was actually alive, not just a tricky invention of her imagination. She wanted to get one last look at him so she didn't ever again think of him as powdery ashes inside a cherry wood box. More important, it would give her a chance to say a final goodbye. Something he'd deprived her of because of his sudden bogus death. He owed her that much, at least.

She checked her purse to make sure she had some cash as well as her credit cards. She hoped the hotel wasn't too expensive in case she had to stay overnight. She backed the car onto the street, put it into gear, and began driving. As she drove, long veins of dark-silver rain blurred the asphalt road ahead of her, painting it with a myriad of ominous night shadows.

Chapter Two

Isabel leaned forward in the Jeep, her eyes squinting through the rain-distorted windshield. There were no streetlights on the mountain road, so she could barely see what was ahead of her. It felt as if she'd been driving for hours, and hadn't found any sign of the turn off yet.

Thankfully, the Aspirin had finally chased away her throbbing headache. If she didn't find the turn-off before long she promised herself she would turn back, head for home, and snuggle into a warm bed. How on earth could anyone who wanted to stay at the Hotel Grande cope with the dozens of vicious twists and turns on the mountain road?

She expected that at any minute, the rain would turn to ice, and then snow would start to fall. Or would it? Having lived in Southern California all her life she had no idea what made it snow. She'd only been in the San Gabriel Mountains during summer months, and had only enjoyed the sight of their snowcapped peaks during the winter, from a long distance.

The jeep headlights suddenly caught something at the edge of the road. A pale reflection. She slowed the car, put it into reverse, and backed up so she could see whatever it was. "Thank God!" she almost shouted. "I found it!"

At the edge of a narrow cross-road stood a faded wooden sign with an arrow pointing to the left. It read:

JUMP-OFF-JIMMY CREEK 2 MI
HOTEL GRANDE 4 MI.

She breathed a sigh of relief and carefully drove the Jeep onto the narrow cut-off road, gritting her teeth as she heard the tires crunching on the pea gravel mixed with mud. Thank heaven it wasn't too far, or she might end up having to buy new tires. The road went downhill and even with gravel it turned slippery. She put the Jeep in four-wheel drive and felt the traction improve.

No lights of any kind showed anywhere around her. All she

could see were the two yellow-white orbs of her headlights reflecting off the rough wet road. She couldn't imagine how terrifying the black night would be if she didn't have the headlights. She hadn't even thought to bring a flashlight. A sense of anxiety began to crawl over her like insects with tiny feet. She shook herself, trying to dislodge the uncomfortable sensation.

As she drove, thick stands of rain-soaked pines began crowding close along each side of the road. It gave her the sensation of driving through a dark tunnel. No wonder the damn hotel had been closed for so long. Why on earth would anyone want to make this trip, even in the daylight?

Suddenly a soft glow of light in the rearview mirror caught her attention. Two pale spots a long way behind her. Another car's headlights? Was it Jorge's car on his way to meet her? Or was there someone else as crazy as she was driving this road at night, in the rain? That thought quickly increased her anxiety. What if her car broke down? What if her cell phone didn't work in this remote area? What if it hadn't been Jorge on the phone, but some serial killer convincing her to meet him in the wilderness? She sucked in her breath, forced down the rising panic, and concentrated on driving.

The rain began to ebb somewhat, but it felt like forever before she came to what she thought must be the Jump-off-Jimmy Creek. To her surprise the creek flowed out of the darkness and crossed the road like a wide black river. She thought there would at least be a little bridge crossing it. How stupid to make a road that went right through a creek! Slowing the car, she wondered how deep the water was. Would the Jeep make it across without shorting out? She stopped the car and sat there seriously questioning if she should turn back.

Damn it, she finally told herself. You've come this far, do not back out now. She slowly moved ahead, silently praying the car would reach the other side without stalling. The Jeep moved downward on a slope, edging into the water. Looking out the side window, she saw the dark water rising higher and higher against the side of the car. Any minute she expected water to begin surging into

11

the car. Then, with a crunch, she felt the tires grab hold of gravel once more, and the Jeep moved upward out of the water. "Ohhh, thank God!" she said aloud, startled to hear her own voice.

"Only two more miles," she told herself. She desperately wanted to turn on the radio, to hear some voices, or listen to music. However, she didn't want to take a chance with her battery since it had given her some trouble lately. Stupid, stupid woman, she told herself. Driving all this way alone, at night, in the dark, and with a winter storm raging like crazy. Plus an edgy car to boot!

All the loneliness in the world seemed to fill the inside of the car. She swallowed back the unpleasant taste of fear. She had come this far, she couldn't let it beat her now. She checked the rearview mirror again but the car lights behind her had vanished. Obviously, it hadn't been Jorge's car.

As she wheeled slowly around a narrow curve in the road she spotted a small sign stuck at an odd angle on the side of the road. The print on it was too small and her windshield too wet for her to read it. She stopped the Jeep, and put on the parking brake. Opening the car door, she looked nervously around, and then stepped out, her feet feeling the sharp bite of the wet gravel through the thin soles of her shoes. Rain pelted down against her face. Like many people living in SoCal, she didn't even own rain boots or a raincoat. She leaned back in the car and picked up her umbrella with the pearl handle. At least she did have an umbrella. Her dreadful anxiety eased some. As she stepped out of the car and opened her umbrella, the spicy scent of wet pines seemed to seep into her cheeks. She wiped them with the sleeve of her jacket. It only took a few steps to get close enough to the sign so she could read it. She expected it to say Hotel Grande. It didn't. Instead, in bold letters it read:

Private Property. No Trespassing
Bertrand Corp.

Isabel gulped in a breath of the icy wet air, then let it out slowly.

Her breath made a little white cloud of steam. Had there been some other turn off? One she missed? No, she was certain there wasn't. Then where was the hotel? She scrambled back to the Jeep, closed her umbrella, climbed in and quickly closed the door. A curl of icy damp air followed her in.

There was no gate across the road and she didn't see any chain or barbed wire so after a few moments she decided to move ahead. Perhaps the hotel was nearby and she'd find it before she actually reached the private property to which the sign referred. She might as well go ahead. What was the worst that could happen? Someone could stop her and send her back, nothing more. She moved the car ahead slowly.

It was only a few minutes before she saw it. In the middle of a narrow canyon, surrounded by an army of dark pine trees, stood a gigantic stone-stacked edifice, looking greatly like a castle out of sixteenth century England. Complete with belfries, turrets, and parapet walks. All it lacked was a moat. Despite its imposing nature, a sense of relief washed over her. This had to be the old stone hotel Jorge had talked about.

Thankfully, the gravel road turned into an asphalt parking area where several parked cars sat dripping with rainwater. Barely lighting the area were two small lamps, both made up of small opaque globes atop two white posts. She strained through the dim light trying to locate the hotel name on the building. All she could see were the walls of stacked stones which stood two stories high. Expansive stone steps led to a wide stone porch entrance. More stones arched across a gargantuan carved wood door.

She parked the car and sat looking around. "Great ghosts!" she whispered in a hoarse voice. "This place gives me the heebie-jeebies." The wind gave a wail. Where in the hell was the Bertrand Company whose name she's seen on the sign? The road dead-ended at the parking lot. Nothing beyond but a tight tangle of dark trees. Could this giant stone monstrosity be the Hotel Grande Jorge had mentioned?

She cautiously opened the car door and looked around to see if

Jorge was anywhere about. The parking lot was vacant except for the few cars. The rain was fairly light, but she picked up her purse, grabbed her umbrella, opened it and quickly made her way to the bottom of the stone steps. "Jorge!" she called out. All she heard in return was the wind snarling through the pines. Then she looked up at the stones over the top of the porch and to her relief she saw a warped piece of wood, about three feet long, hanging there. In faded letters it read: HOTEL GRANDE. "Well, thank God!" she said aloud. At least Jorge's instructions had gotten her to their meeting place.

She quickly walked up the steps and stood on the lengthy covered porch. "Jorge! Where the hell are you?" she yelled out. The icy wind wrapped itself around her. The zesty smell of wet pines saturated her nose. You son of a bitch, Jorge, she said to herself, you had better be waiting for me inside. Otherwise, I'll head back to the car, and get the hell out of here. On the humungous wooden door she spotted a brass latch, and took hold of it. It felt as if it were made of ice. She twisted the latch and then gave the door a push. It opened much easier than she expected. It seemed to fling itself wide open in a sort of welcoming gesture. Startled, it took her a moment before she found herself capable of moving. She peered through the open doorway. The sight of what looked like an English hooded fireplace glowing with flames eating away at several massive logs sent a warm surge of comfort through her. This might not be so bad after all, she told herself.

She closed the umbrella and set it to one side of the door, then moved inside and quietly pushed the door shut behind her. The soles of her shoes felt squishy wet, so she slipped them off, but left her socks on. The gigantic room smelled of ancient dust, like something one would expect when opening a pharaohs' tomb. She looked down at her watch. The time surprised her. It was almost nine! The trip had taken her much longer than she'd expected with all its twists and turns, and the bad weather. Her eyes scanned the room searching for Jorge, but she finally accepted the fact that she was the only person in the large room.

The Gray Green Underground

Several portraits of stern faced men hung on the heavily paneled walls. Hanging Tiffany style lamps, fringed with long strands of crystal beads, cast a soft amber light in strange patterns onto the shadowy wood-planked flooring. Only in front of the fireplace did she see a small richly patterned Persian carpet soften the expanse of dark floor.

Carrying her shoes in one hand, her purse in the other, she moved slowly through the long room trying to locate the desk where she could arrange for a room for the night. She certainly didn't want to make the rough trip back until daylight. Her search of the large entry, however, did not turn up a registration desk of any kind which she thought odd.

The one comfort in the room was the giant fireplace. She found the warmth of it extremely seductive. Two long burgundy leather sofas flanked the front and one side of the fireplace. If Jorge didn't show up soon, she would remove her jacket, plop down on one of the sofas, and rid herself of the damp chill. At the far end of the room was a giant stone archway which obviously led to other parts of the hotel. She took a few strides around the room, and then peered through the archway, spotting a daunting staircase that seemed to reach up to heaven itself. She shook her head in disbelief that she had actually come all this way to this strange place, a place that made her stomach feel like jelly. What on earth was wrong with her?

"Jorge!" she called out. "Jorge!" this time louder. Not surprisingly, her voice echoed back from the dark wood paneled walls. "Damn it, Jorge! Where the hell are you?"

"I beg your pardon," someone said suddenly, in a tight-throated female voice.

She turned around to see a tall, pinched woman wearing what appeared to be a white cotton blouse laundered to almost transparency, along with white wool trousers. Her only addition to her attire was a small strand of creamy white pearls she kept rubbing with her thumb and forefinger. Pink patches stained the woman's narrow cheeks, but her lips were as pale as the cotton blouse. Bloodless, thought Isabel. Her flax-colored hair had been cut oddly

15

short and somewhat resembled a wheat field.

"Oh, I'm sorry," Isabel said, trying to remember what name Jorge had said he'd taken. "I just came in and was looking for . . . ahh . . . yes, well . . .for Joe . . . um, Joe Watson. I'm supposed to meet him here. I was told he worked here."

"Your name is?" the woman asked in a demanding voice.

"Isabel Warren," she answered.

The woman gave her a vacant look, as if nobody was home behind her eyes. "I thought you were calling for someone named George." She frowned again. "At this ridiculous hour! What were you thinking?" The woman gave her a dark look. "Besides, we have no idea where Joe is. We do not expect him. Therefore, you have to head back down the mountain. Immediately!"

"Yes, well . . . I mean, the road is awful, with all this rain," Isabel told her. "I'm really afraid to head back when it's so dark." She thought the woman had a rather odd, clipped manner of speech which made her sound quite stiff and unfriendly.

The woman pursed her lips together for a moment and then said, "What is it that you are you supposed to see Joe about?" She gave Isabel a narrow frown.

Isabel hesitated. Jorge had told her not to talk with anyone except him. Nevertheless, since he wasn't there as he said he would be, she wasn't going to be forced to make the trip home in the dark and the rain. She looked around the room again, examining the sparse furnishings. The two long burgundy leather sofas around the fireplace were terribly inviting. A shroud of fatigue settled over her and she shook her head and took in a deep breath.

"Well, you see . . . um," Isabel said hesitantly, not used to telling lies. Although it was sort of true, in a way. "Joe is a . . . well, a longtime friend I hadn't seen in years. He called earlier today and said he needed me to help him with something. I had no idea he worked here now, or what he does here, but he's a topnotch biologist so I really don't understand what he's doing here."

"I see. So then, are you a biologist also?"

"Well, in a way, yes." Isabel decided to not give this woman too

16

many details. There was something oddly uncomfortable about her.

"Unfortunately," the woman said in a tense voice. "Joe is not welcome here anymore, so I doubt he'll show." She lifted her arm and looked at a thin silver watch on her wrist. "It is not that late, so you will please get back to your car."

Disturbed by the words "not welcome" Isabel decided to be firm with the woman. "Yes, I see. Well then I would like to check in and get a room for the night. This *is* the Hotel Grande, isn't it?"

The woman's eyebrows pressed sharply together in the middle of her forehead giving her entire face an even more pinched appearance. Her narrow checks flushed a deeper pink and her eyes blinked in an odd rhythm. She continued to rub the pearls on her necklace in a steady repetitive manner. "Miss whatever your name is, this is not a hotel anymore!" the woman said. "Has not been for years. It is now a part of the Bertrand Corporation. I am sure you should not be here. We do not allow people to just drop by without notice. Even if they know one of our former workers."

"You mean Joe works . . . or worked here for the . . . Bertrand Company?

"That is correct. Until a few weeks ago. We are fairly certain he will not be returning."

"This is really strange since Joe definitely said I should meet him here. Just a few hours ago. He called it the Hotel Grande, and promised to meet me in the parking lot. But there was no sign of him outside, and it is raining still." she explained in a hurried voice.

"Now that I think about it though, maybe he's late because of the storm," Isabel said trying to remain calm, despite the somewhat hostile woman standing in front of her. After all, it could have been Jorge's car lights she saw behind her. If it was, maybe he had car trouble. Damn it Jorge, she said silently, if you don't show up soon, I am going to kill you, and this time you will stay dead!

The woman looked at her for a long moment, as if scrutinizing her carefully. Her narrow face appeared as if it might implode at any moment. Then she slowly appeared to relax slightly, and motioned to one of the leather sofas. "Take a seat. I will see what I can do."

She turned sharply, her flat leather shoes tapping against the wood floor with perfect cadence as she marched away, and disappeared through the archway at the far end of the room.

Isabel stood there for a moment, craving to sit down, but also wanting to inspect the room further. Instead of sitting, she first moved to the front of the fireplace for a few moments, sucking up the warmth of the crackling fire. It smelled of sweet pine and helped camouflage the ancient dusty smell of the massive stone and wood-paneled room around her.

Looking up she admired the heavy cast iron English hood on the fireplace. Above the hood, a great arched plaque of slightly rusty metal hung slightly lopsided on the stone wall above the hood. Stamped into the metal it read:

WELCOME TO POOLE'S
GRAY-GREEN UNDERGROUND

"Very odd," she said aloud, wondering what a gray-green underground might be. A wine cellar, perhaps? When she turned away from the fireplace she jumped and her heart skip a beat. A tall, sturdy, dark haired man stood several feet away from her. A few yards behind him under the archway stood the woman in white that she'd met first.

"Oh, my!" Isabel said, her voice low and hoarse. "I didn't hear you come in."

The man gave a rough laugh. "Our staff members are always accusing my beat-up old Reeboks of making my feet as quiet as a cat," the man said, smiling. "Sorry, I didn't mean to sneak up on you."

He took several steps toward her and extended his hand. "I'm Charles McGraw. I understand you are looking for Joe Watson."

Isabel fumbled with her purse and shoes, and finally reached for his hand and shook it, firmly. Never give a limp handshake, she had been told. A sign of weakness, the last impression she wanted to give. "Sorry for lack of shoes," she said, swallowing down a slightly hysterical laugh. "But they were wet so I thought it best not to track the rain in on these nice wood floors."

He smiled and said "That was thoughtful of you."

"I'm Isabel Warren and yes I have come at ah . . . Joe . . . Watson's beck and call. He promised he would meet me here. But obviously, he doesn't seem to be handy, does he?"

The man gave a frown, looked down at the floor, and then his eyes rose to meet hers. They were green eyes, the color of damp moss, ringed by thick dark lashes. He was just shy of being terribly handsome, with black wavy hair, which needed a trim. He had a strong nose, slightly full lips, and a dark sparsely whiskered five o'clock shadow which looked as if it would be the same no matter how many times a day he shaved. He had to be over six-feet tall. A giant, compared to her.

"I'm afraid, Miss Warren, that Joe probably won't show up," he said.

She looked him over and thought how at ease he looked in his high-necked tan sweater under a toasty brown, but well-worn jacket, and a pair of very ragged jeans. He had a pleasant relaxed look about him. The sight of him helped her feel calmer.

"We weren't aware that he was planning on coming here. I haven't seen him in several weeks." Charles frowned again. "How is it you know him? Darla, one of our staff members, said you were a biologist?"

Isabel flushed, her cheeks feeling uncomfortably hot. "I'm actually not much of a biologist. I just . . . well, I teach biology basics. High School level. I hadn't seen Joe in years, when he called. But . . . I knew him pretty well at one time." Her voice trailed off like a ragged ribbon, to a soft whisper.

"I see." His eyes narrowed for a moment but then he grinned at her. "I see."

"Charles, I brought my umbrella so the lady can get back to her car," Darla said in an insisting tone, still standing a few yards away. Then she marched up beside Charles, and pushed the umbrella

19

against Isabel, touching her hand with it.

"Ah, no, I have my own," Isabel protested. "On the porch."

"Darla! That won't be needed." Charles firmly motioned her away.

Darla gave a scowl. "But Charles, visitors at this time of night. Unheard of!"

"I'll take care of it Darla. Please go get yourself to bed."

Isabel felt her pulse thumping in her ears as she listened to their conversation.

Darla gave a strange little moan, then turned and marched her way out of the room, her shoes again smacking against the smooth floor.

"Don't let Darla bother you. She's harmless. She told me you had planned to stay the night. I don't know if she explained to you, this place isn't a hotel any longer. However, part of our staff lives here year round, and we do have a few rooms made up for company people who sometimes stay. It would be foolish for you to drive back on our God-awful mud and gravel road in this weather." He reached into the pocket of his toasty brown jacket and pulled out a large brass ring with a number of keys attached.

"I would appreciate that," she said, feeling her anxiety ebb some. "I'm awfully tired. But if Joe shows up in the morning, can someone let me know right away?"

"Of course. Now, let me see, which room would be good." He looked at her with a puzzling glance, as if trying to decide. The keys jangled loudly as he looked them over. He held one up. "Yes, this one I think. It's the only decently made up room here on the first floor. It's for corporate VIPs. Our regular staff members live upstairs where there are a dozen smaller bedrooms. This one's large, has a nice bath." He jangled the keys in his hand for a moment then walked to the front door and used one of them to lock it. "We don't need any more late night visitors," he said returning to where she stood by the fire.

"I do apologize. I had no idea—" she started to say.

He held up his hand. "No need. It's just like Joe to pull

something like this," he said, shaking his head.

"But what if he shows up later tonight?" she asked.

"He'll have to sleep in his car, I'm afraid. He surrendered his key when he left. So I can't imagine why Joe told you to meet him here. Of all the places." He motioned for her to follow him as he headed toward a hallway at the far end of the room.

"Well, I can't imagine why either," she growled, trying to keep up with him.

Charles guided her through the archway and led her down a dim hallway. He stopped at the first door and held up his keys. "This is it. It's close to the front door just in case you need to go to your car for anything. You can open the front door to go out without a key. However, leave the door open if you do go out, since you can't get back in without a key."

The metal key gave a screech as Charles unlocked the bedroom door. "Ah, good," he said. "A lot of these keys are so old they hardly work anymore."

The room was filled with murky shadows. She gave a nervous laugh.

"I know," he said in a soft tone. "This can be a spooky place until you get to know it. But contrary to the many rumors, it is not haunted." He strode ahead of her and turned on a small lamp beside the bed.

The soft glow of it helped, even though oddly shaped shadows still lay around the edges of the large room like large discarded puzzle pieces.

"It's safe to open the windows," Charles assured her. "There is no one around here for miles."

She gave him a weak smile, and watched as he walked across the room and pushed one of the large leaded windows open just a little. No crank and no latch. She felt a whirl of icy wet air wrap around her. Outside, the storm was making growling sounds.

"The rooms smell a little musty when closed up so much," Charles said. "This will help." A flash of lightning ignited the darkness outside the room with silvery incandescence and then

21

disappeared as quickly as it came. "It was a dark and stormy night," Charles said in a slightly dramatic voice, then gave a little laugh. He left the window slightly open and then turned to her. "A stone overhang should keep the rain out of the room. He turned and pointed toward a door near her. "The bath's there," he said. "There should be clean towels. Soap, whatever." He turned to leave.

"Ah . . . Mr. McGraw," she ventured. "I was wondering—"

"It's Charles, please," he insisted, turning back.

"Charles, I was wondering . . . ." She paused.

"About what?"

"Well, over the fireplace mantle there's a metal plaque."

"Ah, yes. Old man Poole's inscription. Do you know anything about the guy who built this place?"

"Not really. I was just wondering about the words "The gray-green underground.""

For a moment Charles stared at her, and his eyes seemed to turn a darker shade of green. He licked his lips slightly before speaking. "Joe didn't tell you anything at all, about this place, did he?"

"He just said to go to the hotel Grande. Except this place obviously isn't a hotel. He said he worked here which I thought a little odd, considering he has a doctorate in bio-engineering."

"But he asked you to meet him here because you are a . . . what did you say? A biology teacher?"

Slightly embarrassed, she said, "Yes. However, I have no idea what he wants." Charles looked away from her, gazing around at various objects in the room, giving off an air of fatigue. He sighed and then sat down on the end of the bed, and motioned for her to sit also. "I'll explain quickly," he said.

She hesitated, since there was no other place to sit in the room, except for a very small vanity chair against the far wall, and because she was so exhausted, she allowed herself to sit down on the bed, a few feet away from him.

"Good. Now I'll try to clarify. Underneath this old stone castle there are countless ragged caverns. It seems old man Poole had a thing for creating huge underground rooms. Only God knows why.

It's almost a maze down there. People say he was looking for silver since that was how he made his fortune. Of course, there isn't any here, but he must have thought there was. As for the plaque on the fireplace, I understand it refers to the ancient stone walls down-under. Every stone in this place was brought here from Scotland on sailing ships, well over a hundred years ago. Since then, each of the walls down-under has grown a thick coating of squishy gray-green fungus."

"Sounds kind of . . . creepy." She looked around the room for a moment then said "Then again, this whole place seems rather creepy."

"Right, but it's an extremely useful place. For several years, the Bertrand Corporation searched for a location to fill their special needs. Initially they wanted a large old mine. But they got much more when they found this place, at a remarkably low price." Charles gave a rather tight smile. "No one else wanted it! This structure certainly doesn't conform to modern day building codes. However, Bertrand has made a lot of renovations."

"But what kind of work can you do in a huge old place like this?" she asked. "It's rather like a medieval castle."

"What we have here is one of the few locations in the U.S. where various crops are being grown underground."

"Crops? Are you kidding me?" Isabel said in a breathless voice. "Underground? I mean, I've read some about it. But I had no idea it was being done anywhere around here."

"It's no secret. Science journals have written a few feature articles about us. We're small however, because it's mostly experimental work, not commercial. We have several crops here that are not modified, as well as some extremely advanced altered crops."

"I had no idea!"

"I'm wondering why Joe didn't tell you about this." He paused and looked at her with his deep green eyes narrowing with a look of concern. "Listen, you look totally bushed. And I sure am! We can talk more about it in the morning. Get some sleep." He gave her a reassuring smile, got up from the bed and made his way through the

23

doorway, tugging the door shut behind him with a loud thump.

Isabel suddenly felt terribly alone. She looked around at the heavy cranberry drapes which festooned the cane-leaded windows. Tarnished tin sconces lined an expanse of gold-flecked wallpaper on the wall behind a huge four-poster bed. Each of them held what looked like a hand dipped candle. There was only one little chair, but her eyes went to a long chest of some kind of polished wood which gleamed golden in the candlelight. She got up and walked over to it and carefully lifted the lid but found nothing there except a few folded white towels. It was just like the chest her mother had called a "Hope Chest" saying that it had been a long tradition for young women to save things in the chest for the day they married. She gently closed it thinking what a nice tradition that was. She wished she'd had a chest like that she could have shared with Jorge after they were married.

Looking up at the high ceiling, what she saw gave her a start. Glaring down at her were bizarre, almost grotesque faces deeply carved into planks of dark wood. The storm outside gave a howl, and a shiver rippled over her. What in the hell had she gotten herself into? What was she doing in this strange place, with no sign of Jorge, and with crops of some sort growing right underneath her! That was possible, she knew. Marijuana growers often used powerful grow lights underground. However, right then she couldn't make sense of any of it. Fatigue was about to shut down her brain. Thunder grumbled in the distance and another shiver hit her.

Suddenly she realized Charles had not given her a key to the bedroom door. It was a very old style door that had to be locked sing a key, inside or out. She walked to the door and opened it slightly. She heard several voices which were quite loud and sounded angry.

"Charles, we have no business having a stranger here, especially someone who knows Joe," said another man's voice. It certainly did not make her feel welcome. Fear, mixed with frustration caused her to quickly close the door. She then took her shoes and jacket into the little bathroom, hoping they would dry before morning.

Back in the bedroom, a frightening exhaustion overwhelmed her.

The Gray Green Underground

It was all she could do to walk to the bed. She tugged back the cranberry bedspread, crawled under it and curled up still wearing her Levis and sweater. She reached over intending to turn off the small bedside lamp, but instead she pulled her hand back. The room would be too dark, too threatening if it was completely dark. She looked up at the carved faces on the ceiling. Why, she wondered, would anyone want to have those things staring down at you while you slept? She snugged the cranberry bedspread up around her neck and closed her eyes, still feeling the strange eyes on the ceiling staring at her.

A terrible wailing sound abruptly opened her eyes again. What in the hell was that? she asked herself. The sound came again, this time a piercing animal scream. It was coming from outside the window, loud enough to be heard over the storm. Forest animals? Night birds? She pulled the spread up around her ears, trying to plug out the sound. She had the urge to get up and close the window, but couldn't force herself to do it. Whatever it was out there, she didn't want to see it. She pulled the bedspread even tighter around her, as if it were a safety net that would keep her safe.

She was on the edge of sleep when she heard an odd sound outside in the hallway. She opened her eyes and saw a faint light from the doorway. Someone had opened it! She tried to make out who it was. Then she realized it was that Darla woman she'd first met. Her instinct was to sit up and give a loud yell. Then again, maybe she should wait and see what she was up to. She closed her eyes to slits so she could still see somewhat, but hoped she looked as if she were asleep. The woman stood in the doorway for a moment, and then slowly walked across the room to the open window. She looked out and around, then reached out and pulled the window partially shut. With that, she turned and made her way out of the room, silently.

Well, she thought, thank God the woman hadn't tried to attack her. After all, she'd been against Charles allowing her stay. Feeling her muscles stiffen, Isabel tried to force her body to relax. At least the man, Charles, had been kind and protective. She forced herself to think about other things. About what she would be teaching her

25

students after the holidays. Of where she would go for next summer's break. Despite her anxiety and fear, it only took a few minutes before she slipped down into a deep, bottomless sleep.

Chapter Three

Charles McGraw took a sip of strong dark coffee from his cup which had the words "BOSS" decaled on the side. He looked up at the huge clock on kitchen wall. Eighth a.m. He yawned. Mornings were difficult for him, especially this morning after the unexpected visitor's arrival last night. Warning signals kept ringing in his head. He hoped it didn't mean trouble. Caution would be his word of the day.

He looked around at the two men and one woman seated with him at the huge oak kitchen table. One of them, Danny Chambers, sat staring down at his plate of pancakes as if wondering which of them to eat first. He gave out little frustrated snorts of breath. A short rotund little man, Danny had a saggy sad face and pale creampuff hands with shiny pink fingernails. The Chinos he had on appeared sleep-wrinkled as usual. He no doubt slept in them most nights. Next to him sat Travis Emerson, a dry stick of a man in his seventies with scrunched eyes, gull gray hair, and wearing his usual ill-fitting clothes. His gold-rimmed glasses were constantly sliding down his narrow nose, and he had a habit of fiddling with the hearing-aid tucked into one gnarled ear. Despite their appearance, Charles knew both men were extremely brilliant in their fields.

In addition, of course, there was poor pushed-together Darla Dodson who was way too tall for a woman, and whose thin facial features gave her the look of a Pincher dog. This morning she sat there stuffing syrup-dripping pancakes into her mouth, but not as fast as usual. In the past, she always devoured breakfast, eating up all the leftovers. Nevertheless, lately she had begun to fill out her pencil thin body with a little more weight. It was much more becoming, he thought. Darla's science specialty was extremely narrow but she was unbelievably good at it. He wondered how old she was. Mid-thirties he guessed. Never married, except to her work. He was certain she was somewhat autistic, Aspergers perhaps. However, it didn't matter since she was brilliant. After all, a lot of brilliant people had signs of Aspergers. Mozart, Einstein, Marie Curie, and Thomas Jefferson, among them. Darla was certainly a little off beat when it came to her social skills. Although he had to admit, she did try to fit in. Although when she did, it seemed quite an effort for her.

Charles took another drink of his coffee, enjoying the bitter taste. He began to feel human again. Fighting his early morning drowsiness was always tough. He often worked in the underground much later than he'd planned, crumpling into bed at closer to morning than night. Coming into the enormous kitchen with its warm copper and brick walls, stretches of granite counter tops, and two restaurant-sized stoves, helped retrieve him. The Bertrand Company had done a tremendous job of restoring it. This morning it had been Darla's turn to make breakfast. Piles of hot pancakes, real Maple syrup, and pitchers of orange juice had greeted him. However, the large metal coffee pot filled with coffee as black as a licorice, helped the most. He loved the kitchen more than any other place in the strange stone edifice. It was a shame he couldn't spend more time right there in the welcoming warmth and cheerfulness of the kitchen.

He looked around at the group seated at the table, knowing he had to tell them about their late night visitor. He cleared his throat and said, "Listen up gang. Something kinda unusual happened late last night. We had an unexpected visitor." He saw Darla look up, her eyebrows pinching tightly together as they often did.

Wiping syrup from her mouth, she nodded her head at him and said briskly, "She is still here in fact," she said, emphasizing the world *still*.

"Yes, she slept in the VIP bedroom. She was terribly tired from the drive here. I thought it best to just let her get some sleep."

Darla looked at the last pancake on her plate, made a strange face, and pushed the plate away "She was under the mistaken impression that this was still a hotel," she said. "You should have sent her home, Charles!"

"Late at night and in this weather? Don't be foolish, Darla."

Darla looked away, her eyes blinking rapidly. "Foolish is as

28

foolish does," she said, using a napkin to wipe some leftover syrup from the edge of her pale lips. Then her fingers went to her strand of pearls which she began rubbing slowly, as if trying to soothe them.

Danny Chambers looked up from his plate. "What does this lady want, Charles? Was she assigned here? I thought the place was considered locked down until things were straightened out with Joe."

Charles shook his head. "Actually, she was looking for Joe. Said she was supposed to meet him here. She sounded as if she and Joe had some sort of relationship."

Darla let out a little syrupy gasp. Charles saw the usual cherry color in her narrow cheeks fade, as if being sucked away. She started to say something, but stopped and went back to twisting her pearls.

What the hell was up between Joe and Darla, he wondered. He had discovered Joe in Darla's room on several occasions, when she wasn't there. Then later, when he told Darla about it, she would claim that she had given him permission. Several times he had seen the two of them sitting together having forceful discussions and what sounded like serious disagreements. However, at other times Darla became unsettled when Joe left for a day or two now and then. It concerned Charles because Joe's major biological delight came from messing up genetic codes. He was afraid Joe might be attempting to hijack some of Darla's genetic splicing techniques and use them as his own.

He reported his concerns to Bertrand, who had hired him as an overseer. However they didn't seem too interested in his report. However, they did ask him to investigate and see what was going on, and let them know if anything more problematic came up. So far, he hadn't discovered much else. Nevertheless, what little he did find caused him some apprehension. Especially after Joe left and he'd had a chance to inspect his lab. It held some unusual equipment, and he wondered if it was Joe's own stuff, or if Bertrand had paid for it. Expensive stuff, but he had no idea yet what most of it was used for.

Oddly, Darla hadn't seemed at all disturbed when Joe left on bad terms. But then Darla didn't react to a lot of things the average person does. He hoped Joe had enough sense to stay away. If he was involved in a project not approved by Bertrand, he would have to do it somewhere else from now on.

Travis turned to Charles, his mouth narrowed and his eyes scrunched tighter. "She was looking for whom?" he asked, sharply tapping his hearing aid as if trying to wake it up.

"For *Joe!* She came here looking for Joe, Travis," Charles said in a loud tone.

Travis gave a startled look. "He plans to meet her here? After what happened! What the devil is he up to?"

Darla lifted her fork, and then dropped it with a clang on her plate. She shook her head as if disapproving of the conversation.

"I don't know." Charles answered, "She claims Joe called her and asked her to meet him here tonight, but she has no idea why." He took the last swallow of his coffee. "Hard to believe."

"If it's true, do you suppose he will actually show up?" Travis asked. "Would he dare?"

Charles frowned. "I wouldn't think so, but you never know. He's a pretty gutsy guy."

"I just don't understand why he would ask this woman to meet him *here?*" Danny said.

holding his pancake filled fork a few inches from his mouth. "And at night, in this dreadful weather."

"Absurd!" Darla chimed in. "Ridiculous. I do not believe her for a second!"

"Well," Charles said leaning back in his chair, "I suppose we'll find out before long." He paused and gave each of them a stern look. "Okay, enough about the lady and Joe. Tell me, has the night crew gone home?"

"At the crack of dawn," Darla said. "Scooter is still here, although it's his day off. He was going to spend a cozy, rainy day in town with his girlfriend. However, the computer didn't adjust the carbon dioxide in Unit C close enough for his comfort. He stayed to make sure it was okay."

"Did all the night crew follow security when they left?"

Darla gave him a withering look.

30

The Gray Green Underground

"Sorry Darla, I wasn't questioning you. I know everyone's careful," he said. "But we can't afford even a small mistake, and let something escape by accident."

"Don't underestimate us, Charles," Danny said. "Besides, you know the chance of anything dangerous escaping from here is extremely small. Moreover, I'm certain there's only one person who can't be trusted, and he's no longer with us."

"Yes, but if he's meeting this what's her-name person, here," Travis said. "What unmitigated gall!"

"We'll manage," Charles said. "If he shows up."

"As long as he can't get into his lab," Danny stated. "I don't know what he's been up to in there. Not sure I really want to know."

"Not to worry, it's locked up tight," said Charles. At that point, he wasn't about to tell any of them about the unusual equipment he'd found in Joe's Lab. "Okay then, we should get to work. By the way, breakfast was great, Darla. Thanks."

"Pancakes are easy." Darla didn't look up at him as she picked up her plate and carried it to the sink. "But you are welcome," she said in a flat voice.

Charles got up from the table. It was time to check on their visitor. He actually found her quite attractive. Very petite, but nicely put together. He especially liked the rusty color of her hair, and the faint sprinkling of freckles on her cheeks.

He wondered what in the world Joe was thinking about having her drive here at night, by herself. Especially considering that he left here on the worst of terms a few weeks ago. After seeing the unusual equipment in his lab, Charles had developed an unsettled feeling. He hoped he was wrong. He'd tried to shake off the prickly sense of anxiety claiming him. With little success.

He rubbed a hand over one cheek and realized he hadn't yet shaved. He looked ragged enough even when he did shave. It was easy, living here for such long stretches of time, to get lazy. He headed for the winding stairway leading to the second floor and his small but comfortable bedroom. He wished the company had agreed to include an elevator for the second floor. The stone stairs were

31

daunting. He couldn't imagine how the small hunchbacked Poole, who'd designed them in the first place, could have managed them.

As he climbed the stairs, he realized how anxious he was to wake the woman and see if he could find out anything more about her strange situation as well as her relationship to Joe. Since every move connected to Joe was suspect, he needed to be on guard with her. With all the new equipment in his lab, he hoped to God Joe hadn't been working on some rogue genetic technique. That thought gave him a bone chilling ache.

Isabel awoke to the sound of pine trees stirring. The rain was light, but the wind seemed to be picking up. Despite the weather, she wanted to get out of this strange place as soon as possible, unless Jorge had shown up. She opened her eyes, but purposely avoided a look at the disturbing carved faces on the ceiling. However, as Charles said she would, she had slept peacefully, which was surprising after she heard that argument by some men in the hallway outside her room, then the screeching animal cries outside her window, and after all that the Darla women had the nerve to invade her room.

She pushed back the cranberry spread and sat up. The room seemed smaller and friendlier than it had the night before. She took a quick look around the room, examining how starkly the white and gold French style furniture contrasted with the dark wood of the poster bed.

Then she saw him! *Sitting on a small vanity chair in the corner of the room was her dead husband!* A strong jolt of adrenalin hit her, causing her heart to thump wildly against her ribs. "Oh, my God! Jorge! Where the hell did you come from? When did you get here?" Her heartbeat slowed, but the sudden sight of her not dead husband made her whole body go limp. He didn't look exactly the way she remembered him. Older maybe, and tired, his face tight and a little ragged around the edges. He had on a dark wool sweater and matching pants. His hair had a little touch of gray here and there, and it was longer than she'd ever seen him wear it. However, it **was** Jorge! He was undeniably alive!

A rush of anger replaced the fear she'd experienced on first seeing him. She tried to fight it off. No matter what, he had to explain what the hell had been so bad in his life he had to fake his death. She could not think of anything to justify someone doing such a thing.

Jorge gave her a rather crooked smile, the kind he always did when he was under pressure. "I've been watching you sleep." He got up and walked over to her.

"How dare you come sneaking in like this and watch me sleep?" she demanded.

"You're beautiful Isabel, when you are asleep. I couldn't resist."

"Bull shit!" She said scowling at him. "So Charles told you where I was," she said, swinging her legs over the side of the bed. Then she realized she was still wearing her clothes from the night before. "Damn!" she complained, looking down at her rather crumpled Levis. "I slept in my jeans!"

Jorge shook his head. "No. Charles doesn't know I'm here. Nevertheless, I knew where you would be. Company always sleeps in this room. And please, keep your voice down. I do not want anyone to know I'm here."

Isabel frowned at him. "Well why not, for heaven's sake! I thought you worked here! Or at least you did until recently, according to Charles."

Jorge sat down beside her on the edge of the bed. "I've used one of Bertrand's labs for the past four years. Recently a serious problem came up. So I need your help." He tried to put his arm around her but she pulled back, not at all ready to forgive or forget.

Isabel gave a shiver. His arm was the arm of a dead man, was all she could think about. "I don't understand any of this. It's all so . . . screwy. I don't know what to think. You said you needed help. Why did you send me to this ridiculous place? Charles told me they grow some kind of crops. Underground! I mean, we could have met at Denny's down the street from my condo, for God's sake!"

33

"No, I needed you to be here. But I do owe you an explanation." Jorge got up and began pacing the floor, not looking at her. "It all started in Japan, Issy. At Kawari. The project I've been working on there . . . something entirely new!"

"Yes, I know it's your specialty. I know by cutting and splicing DNA, sort of like doing surgery, you can transfer genes specific to one type of organism into any other organism on the earth. Sounds like science fiction, but I know it's not."

"Right," Jorge continued. "It's not hard to do. The great thing about it is you can actually change the world with it."

"Yes, well, didn't I always tell you I was proud of the work you were doing?"

He stopped pacing and turned to look at her for a moment, his eyes dark and unreadable, and then turned away. "Believe it or not, Issy, what I have managed to do is something everyone said could never be done. In the end, even I didn't realize what I was on to." He stopped and looked around the room with blind eyes. Obviously, he was picturing something other than what was in the room. Then it appeared he made a concerted effort to shake off the images. "I'm sorry I didn't share much of it with you when I first started, but I couldn't. I had signed a non-disclosure contract with Kawari. All of the work I did there belonged to them. I was bound by my contract . . . until . . . ."

Isabel felt her face go pale. "Until you . . . died!"

"It was terrifying, what happened," he said, his eyes finally looking back at her. "Kawari asked me to take my newest work and personally deliver the specs to their U.S.A. unit. I took a company car and headed for the airport. One of their company men recently laid off said he needed to get to the airport also. So he bummed a lift from me. On the way there, he asked if I would stop and get him some heartburn meds. I parked to get them for him along with a few things for me to take on the plane." He shook his head and let out a sigh that was more of a moan. "How irresponsible that was!"

"So what the hell finally happened?" Isabel asked. "Did the guy in the car try to rob you of all your precious genetic information?"

"You got it! I'd left the car keys in the ignition, and that fuckin guy started the car and took off. I should never have left my stuff in the car with him. I know! I was so damn careless!" He paused for a moment, chewing nervously at his bottom lip. Then with a resigned shrug, he went on. "So, there was that fucker zipping up the street in the company car, like a bolt of lightning. As I watched, a giant gasoline truck came out of nowhere, and smashed into him. Everything burst into bright blue flames. The briefcase with all my work, the guy, and almost the entire car turned into crispy critters. I didn't know if Kawari planted the guy so he could steal my stuff. Or if the guy did it on his own." He paused; his eyes darted around as if visualizing the horrifying scene again. "Maybe the truck crash was an accident, or maybe it was intentional. After all, I was supposed to be the person in the car."

"So, you played dead." Isabel took in a long breath and slowly let it out. She noticed a small prickle of sweat breaking out across Jorge's forehead even though the room was cold. He was still scared, she realized. She'd never before seen him this way. "All that, for creating a better type of corn." She shook her head. "Unbelievable."

"No! Something better than my corn, Issy. Much better," he said with a tight expression. His cheeks looked like taut little knots. "Thank God I had my wallet and my passport with me when it happened. Being so terrified after the accident, I just continued to let everyone think it was me in the car." He paused for a minute, looking at her intently. Then he went on. "Fortunately, I'd sent duplicates of all my work to my U.S. post office mailbox because I was worried something might happen to them when I traveled." He began pacing again. "I got back to the U.S. ASAP! I wanted the entire hullabaloo about my death to be over with. After a month or so, I went to my mailbox and picked up my work. No one noticed. Then I changed my name. I've been Joe Watson ever since."

Isabel gave him a suspicious look. "But it's been four years! Four damn long years, Jorge. So what have you done in the meantime?"

Jorge's eyes looked about nervously as if wanting some sort of answer. He cleared his throat finally and said, "Kawari never filed for a patent on my work because I washed the computer files before I left, and obviously they didn't have duplicates of it. I had everything. I felt it was safe for me to continue working on it, using a different name. That's when I started using one of Bertrand's underground labs. And now I need to get a patent. But Bertrand won't let me take my technique specs out of here."

"Don't they know what you're working on? Are you saying it's not corn? You've always worked with corn."

"Yes, well altering things is basically the same, no matter what the thing is. So that isn't an important factor. My technique for genetic splicing was always quite good. But since I came here I've improved the technique so much that it's . . . well, it's pure genius, that's what it is. And I really need your help." Jorge looked at her. "Issy, it was the hardest thing I have ever done, leaving you. But I had no choice." He sat down heavily on the bed next to her. He reached out and put both his arms around her. She thought that after so much time she would want to sink into his still familiar arms, to hold him again, to feel his warm touch, but she didn't. She pulled away. She wasn't ready. She might never be. First, she had to find out what he wanted from her. She got up from the bed and walked away from him toward the door, intending to call for Charles.

Jorge shrugged, and his mouth pinched forward. "Issy, I know I don't have a right to ask. But it's unbelievably important," he said, as if reading her mind. "I'm sorry to have been so secretive about it." He looked toward the door. "Is the door locked?"

"No, Charles left with the key. But he needs to know you're here!"

"Damn it! Just hear me out first. Since I've worked at Bertrand, I haven't had a non-disclosure contract like I did in Japan. I'm a free agent here, just using the facilities."

"So why on earth do you need me?"

"What I've developed is . . . ." He hesitated for a moment, as if trying to gather his thoughts. Then he continued. "It's something extremely complicated. I don't want to bore you with the details."

The tone of Jorge's voice sounded strained, as if he was scrambling to think of what to tell her.

Frowning, Jorge got up and went to her. "When I told them I planned to leave here with everything, they said no! Something about Corporate having to sign off on it. They needed to see and inspect everything and wouldn't agree to let me take it until they did that. I made an attempt to leave anyway, but they stopped me and confiscated everything. Now I can't even use the facilities here. I'm locked out, damn it!" Jorge suddenly gave a wry smile, looking quite smug. "What they didn't realize was that the stuff they took away from me was fake. I hid the real stuff here in the underground because I anticipated what would happen when I needed to leave. Unfortunately, there is no way now that I can get to it. So that is where you come in."

"Oh, come on Jorge!" Isabel tilted her head to look up at him so she could see his eyes. "I can't possibly get your work out of here. I would have no idea what I was looking for. Besides, when I leave here, they would probably check me out too. Besides, even if it is your stuff, Bertrand might be afraid that you've been working on something dangerous."

"It's just a big corporation hold up!" Jorge growled. "I may be a little guy, but it's *my* work. There is nothing in my contract about my using their facilities and then having to have their permission before I can remove my specimens and methods. And yes, they do have a very tight security protocol here. But you can get around it. I can't. I crunched the specs on a flash drive which is safely hidden in the underground. You can easily hide it on yourself before you leave here."

"And you really want *me* to try and get them out of here?"

"Yes! After all, they belong to me! To us! With the money from this new work, I can make up for what all I've put you through, Issy."

"So, what is the danger you said that I might be in because of something you've done?"

"Just get me back my stuff, and I'll fill you in on everything."

"Is it just an idle threat Jorge? To get me to steal something for you?"

"Issy, I would do it myself if there was a way! Besides, it is not stealing! It is *my* work!"

"So, you don't have a key to this place?

"No."

"Then how did you get in here this morning? Without their knowing you were here."

"Through the window." He pointed to the window Charles had opened the night before. Obviously, the Darla lady hadn't closed it completely. But then it didn't have a latch or anything.

She reached out and felt Jorge's jacket. It was quite damp. "Damn it, Jorge, what the hell's going on? If you can get in through the window, why can't you go cautiously and get the stuff yourself and go back out the window?"

Jorge's eyes narrowed. "Issy, you don't understand. This whole place is bugged. I managed to snafu the alarm on the window. But if I go anywhere else in here, the sensors will light up like the fourth of July. If I open the bedroom door and go out into the hall, all hell will break loose. Take my word for it!"

"Then why didn't it go off when *I* walked in the front door?"

"It's only for me. The walls have eyes, and they can send a shot of me to the computer which has been told to sound the alarm if I'm spotted."

"Is it worth it, Jorge? Your new corn or whatever the heck it is? Can it be that valuable and worth all the deception?

Jorge gave a small but angry twist to his mouth. "Issy, you can't begin to understand how valuable my process will be. A ton of the green stuff! For the two of us."

Isabel looked at him, his eyes suddenly bright now. Too bright. His work really was his whole life and it was the reason why their marriage hadn't worked. Why it would never work.

"I'm at the point where I need a patent, Issy. As fast as possible," Jorge said with excitement. "I need to get to trials with it."

The brightness in his eyes increased as he talked. It didn't look

38

natural to her. She felt torn between doing one last thing for a man she still thought of as dead or saying no because of how much he had hurt her. Besides, she wasn't good at subterfuge. Even so, maybe she could at least give it a try. Heaven help her if she ended up in jail. "Okay Jorge," she finally said. "If I agree, how would I get whatever it is, out of here? Charles knows you sent me here. He'll be suspicious! He's bound to be."

"I'm sure you can think of a cover story. Tell him we were good friends. Make him think I wanted to renew my relationship with you. Impress you. Show you my work here. You can do it."

"Pretty flimsy, Jorge. Damn it anyway! You should have thought this through better."

A sudden knock on the door made both of them jump. Isabel felt a sickening contraction of her stomach muscles. She called out "Who is it?"

"Charles. May I come in?"

"Oh, well give me a minute please." She turned to Jorge.

Jorge leaned down and whispered in her ear. "The flash drive is on the unfinished level below the labs. You can only get there via the old stone stairs. The first open space you come to on your left is a small cavern, all rough stone. Step inside and about five feet in on the right side of the interior, you'll find a part of one of the stones is loose. It is two stones up from the stone floor. Slide the stone out. The drive is in there."

"Okay, but how do I find those stone stairs?"

"They're at the end of a long hallway. Just get a chance to explore the place a little."

"Yeah, sure I'm going to wander around. Make people suspicious." Isabel shook her head.

He straightened up and said, "You can do it Issy, I know you can." He touched the side of her face with chilly fingers then turned away. "Get it as soon as you can. And watch out for Charles. He's charming, and likeable on the surface, but take my word for it, he's not to be trusted. Be extremely careful!"

"You'd better go!" she said getting up. "Out the window!" She walked toward the bedroom door, and put her hand on the doorknob. "Wait a minute Jorge," she whispered. "If I manage to get your things, what should I do with them?" A muffled knock on the door came again. "Yes! I'll be right there," she called out to Charles.

She turned back to ask Jorge again how she could get his specimens to him but to her dismay, Jorge had vanished! The window was left wide open and the pine-scented breeze was blowing in rather fierce. "Oh, God!" she said, her voice shaky. "I can't believe this!"

With her mind a complete clutter, she opened the door. Charles stood there, a grin on his face and a plate of pancakes streaming with melted butter and syrup in one hand, and two yellow coffee mugs in the other.

"Breakfast," he said. "It's almost nine."

"Oh, sorry. The awful drive here really got to me."

"With my hands full I had to knock with my foot. Are you okay?" he asked, scrutinizing her face. "You look awfully pale woman. Not sick are you?"

"No. I just woke up. I'm afraid I slept in my clothes," she said apologetically.

"Well, breakfast will help. The staff has already finished eating. So I brought you some *hot cakes*, and some coffee in that pot on the floor. So please give me a hand will you?"

Isabel looked from him to the coffee cups and pot, to the pancakes, and then to his face. There was something strong and dependable about him. His smile sent a note of cheer through her. She wondered what he would do if he had any idea why Jorge had sent her here. And why was it that Jorge distrusted him? Was it just because he wouldn't let him remove his research materials? Or was it something else?

"Of course," she said, picking up the coffee pot. "Come in. And thanks for thinking of me."

"No problem. These are leftovers I'm afraid." He set the plate and two coffee cups on the end table by the bed. Isabel handed him the pot of coffee. He poured some coffee into both mugs. Then he walked to the open window and peered out, looking around for a minute. The breeze blew his large curls of dark hair about, leaving them quite disheveled. Isabel sucked in her breath and prayed Jorge was out of sight.

"The storm has refreshed itself, I'm afraid." Charles pulled the widow closed, moved the vanity chair in the corner of the room over beside the bed, and sat on it. He motioned for her to sit on the bed and eat, and then he picked up one of the coffee mugs and took a long sip.

As she watched, a hard dark look slowly took hold of his eyes and erased his smile.

"Okay, it's time" he said, his voice deep and throaty. "You and I have some very important things to discuss."

Chapter Four

Despite a sharp jolt of nerves, Isabel managed to pick up a fork and begin eating the pancakes Charles brought her. Light and fluffy, she thought. Why can't I make light and fluffy pancakes? Damn! Scattered thoughts. She had to get it together.

She washed down the pancakes with strong hot coffee. When she was finished, she looked up at Charles for the first time since she'd begun eating. Could she go through with this? Or should she just tell him goodbye, and get the hell away from this place. His eyes were still dark and hard. They didn't help her case of nerves. Jorge's warning about him still rang in her ears.

"Okay then," she said, "what did you want to talk about? Have you heard from, ah . . . Joe?" She wondered if he could hear the quiver in her voice.

"He emailed a short while ago. Frankly, I'm surprised he did. We had an incident when he left here a few weeks ago. Not a good one." His eyes held hers so steadily she could almost feel them. "Did he tell you about it?"

Isabel blanched. "No," she lied, feeling a hot flush all over body. "He called me out of the blue yesterday. Before that, I hadn't heard from him in about . . . um . . . four years, or so. We didn't talk long, he just asked me to meet him here. He never said why. Said he'd fill me in when we met."

Charles leaned forward toward her. "Okay, so tell me why you were so willing to jump in the car and race out here in the dark. He must have been a very good friend."

Isabel put down her plate and coffee mug on the bedside table. She stood up and moved around the bed to the window. She pushed it open slightly and saw that rain was again pelting down. The cold bite of the air felt good. The sky was covered with thick bundles of dark clouds knitting themselves across the sky. She took in another deep breath and let it out slowly. "Yes, we were very good friends.

We were together off and on for a while." She pulled the window closed again.

"A lover?"

She turned back sharply and said, "That, Mr. McGraw is none of your damn business!"

Charles got up from the chair and raised one of his hands. "You are right. It's not. I'm sorry. Nevertheless, you must admit it does seem kind of odd. Having him meet you out here in the middle of nowhere."

Isabel frantically searched her mind for some idea to explain things and finally said, "Yes, it was kind of odd, but I got the feeling that . . . well, maybe he wanted us to get together again." She let out a little sigh. "Then again, maybe he just thought this place was something I could share with my biology students. What with all the underground crops growing here, I'm sure it would be." She found it a strain to try and sound convincing. She didn't like the way it made her feel.

"Yes, but meeting you all the way up here at night, in this weather? Didn't you think that was kind of odd?"

Isabel looked at him, a little taken aback for a minute. "Well, yes and no. Jor . . . Joe was always impetuous. He never did what you expected him to do. He would show up one time, not the next. And, he was out of the country a lot."

"Doing what?"

She took another swallow of coffee, giving her a moment to think before answering. "Yes, well, he worked for a Japanese firm. Doing his gene splicing stuff. So, our relationship never really got off the ground.

"Well, it's no secret, what we do here," Charles said. "And it's fine if you want to tell your students. So, how about I show you what this place is all about." He motioned for her to follow him. "Come on and I'll take you through the whole place. I think you'll find it quite interesting."

"I would love it," Isabel said, relieved to change the subject. "But I should clean up first. I left some of my things in the Jeep."

43

"Give me your car keys and I'll get them for you. It's miserable outside. The storm is getting stronger by the minute. You can shower and change, and meet me in the entry room by the fireplace where we met last night. Okay?"

"Yes. Just bring in whatever is there." She picked up the car keys on the bedside table and handed them to him. "Thanks."

"No problem."

"Charles . . . when Joe emailed you this morning did he say anything at all to you about when he'd be meeting me here?"

"Yes. He said he was delayed, but for you to wait. He didn't say how long he'll be."

Isabel felt a sense of relief. If Jorge was really coming back, she would feel much easier about this whole thing. If she somehow managed to get Jorge's flash drive, she would hand it over to him the minute he arrived.. Maybe Charles would turn off the alarm system and let him in without any trouble.

"I'm sorry, Isabel," Charles said in a pensive tone. "About my rude remark. I don't even know if you're married. But I guess you're not if Joe wants to get back together with you."

Isabel felt her cheeks flush slightly. She started to say no, I'm not married. Then with a sudden shock, she remembered she *was* married! Jorge was alive! However, she had his death certificate so . . . damn, where the hell did it leave her? She wasn't at all sure.

With a tight little frown she finally said, "I'm a widow. Have been for some time now." She saw Charles eyes soften when he looked at her.

"I'm so sorry," he said gently. "I'll go get your things from the car." His gaze on her lingered a minute, then he turned and left the room.

Isabel stood looking after him. It was hard to figure out this guy, she realized. His expressions went from hard to soft and somewhere in-between. She had no idea if he was on to her or not. If things got too risky, she'd bow out and go home. She suddenly remembered what Jorge had told her on the phone yesterday. That he was in some kind of serious danger. Yet this morning he had not mentioned it at

44

all. He just sounded indignant because they hadn't allowed him to remove his work from this place. Was Charles part of the danger? Or was there any danger at all? Did he just say it to get her to help him? "Damn it!." she said aloud, feeling confused and frustrated.

After Charles brought her the things from the car, she took a shower and changed her sweater. She only had her Levis so they would have to do. She took her blow dryer out of her suitcase and used it to get her shoes dry. She went to the window and saw the rain was even heavier than before. She shivered, and pulled the window closed.

Charles was standing in front of the fireplace when she came into the huge entry room. Someone had added new logs to the fireplace which were burning with long amber flames. The flicker of flames made the room seem more alive.

"Ready?" Charles asked. "For the tour? If you teach biology, you'll enjoy our underground area. Not many people get to see crops growing this way."

"I've only read a little about it. Sounds remarkable though."

"It is, really. However, we don't grow crops here to market. They do that in Japan, by the way. There's a large underground rice and vegetable farm called Pasona 02 underneath Tokyo which had its first harvest in 2005. I guess you could call it a new age method of farming. Computer-controlled temperature, lack of insects, and LED lights make for huge healthy crops. That's part of what we are trying to do here."

"I had no idea! Is this Pasona farm a large place?"

"About a square kilometer I think. They say it started out in an old underground bank vault."

"So Bertrand started this one under an old stone castle," she said, giving a little laugh.

He smiled and motioned to her. "Come on, it takes quite a while to see everything. We have an elevator, thank heaven! We'll go to Unit A and B to begin with. One level down." He reached out and took her hand, urging her to move. It was a rather personal thing to do, but he had such an eager little boy look, as if wanting to share his treasures, she didn't object.

She hated to leave the warmth of the fireplace, but walked obediently with him across the room and through the archway. He made a sharp turn to the left and into a dimly lit hallway. Only a few steps more and she saw the elevator. Charles took out a plastic card from his pocket and swiped it across a small box on the side of the elevator. The elevator doors whispered open and they stepped inside.

Once the elevator doors closed, Isabel had a moment of panic. She felt her heart give a sharp leap and she had trouble taking in a breath. She was actually going under the ground! Underneath this huge stone dwelling that had to weigh tons. Not at all like the basement of some department store.

She'd never been claustrophobic but was suddenly afraid she was going to be. An awful sensation gripped her, sweaty and paralyzing. She wanted Charles to open the elevator doors and let her out.

Charles put his hand on her shoulder. "Easy. Everyone feels the same way the first time going underground. It will pass."

"How did you know?" The paralyzing sensation began to ebb with his words.

"It happens a lot with people who get into this little box and go underground for the first time. But I assure you, there is plenty of air down below. The plants and the humans both need it. It's a steady temperature in all of the labs depending on the crops. Below the labs, I'm not sure about the temperature. It should be about 72 degrees year-round underground. However, our Darla, who you met, has ventured below the labs via the old stone steps, and she claims it's extremely cold down there. In fact, she claims there is a tunnel leading up to the surface from below the lab areas. It could be the reason why it's so cold down there. She says stray cats find their way into the underground through it."

"Really?'

"She's kind of an eccentric woman, sometimes. But then, who knows?"

The elevator came to a slow hissing stop and the doors opened into a large room with a sign over the opening which read UNIT A.

Isabel sucked in a deep breath and stepped out of the elevator with Charles, and looked around. It wasn't your usual large room. All of the walls were made entirely of brightly polished metal, with large inset lamps. The lamps flooded the room with brilliant light which reflected almost blindingly off the metal walls. The sight of large hardwood tubs lined up in long rows greeted her. To her amazement, fruit-loaded grape vines were burgeoning from every tub.

"Wow!" she remarked. "Bright!" She shaded her eyes with the back of her hand.

"Those are LED lights. Light emitting diodes. A lot more light for the buck, or actually for the electricity. Diodes are devices which only allow electricity to flow through in one direction. None of it is lost."

"Aren't they sort of like the new style light bulbs we've been urged to use?"

"You're probably thinking of mercury vapor light bulbs," he said. "As for me, I'd prefer to stick with LEDs. I don't like the idea of fooling around with mercury."

"Interesting."

He chuckled. "Not to worry, I don't completely understand electrical stuff either. But LEDs do make it more practical for growing crops like this. Power is expensive and hard to come by. Especially in a wilderness like where we are. It also helps us use far less power since the metal walls reflect the light back and forth"

"Come along," he said and began leading her down one of the narrow paths between the grapes vines.

"So, what do you think?" he asked, as they walked.

"For some reason, I expected to see the gray-green stone walls you mentioned. Not all of this!" she said.

"There's no way we could do our highly controlled work in here if we kept the stone walls as they were. They are still here of course, but covered with these reflecting panels. If you go three levels down past all the labs, however, it's exactly the same way Hagan Poole, the man who built it, left it. Dark dungeons, creepy crawly things, and lots of gray-green stone walls."

47

"Sounds hostile!"

"Bertrand says they plan to create more labs down there one day. I kind of doubt it though. Extremely expensive. Other places grow much more marketable food stuff underground than we do. Tokyo grows tomatoes, lettuces, strawberries, and even has rice paddies underground. However here we are mostly into research and experimentation."

She followed him around another row of grapevines, amazed at the sight. Vines overwhelmed with perfectly shaped dark-purple grapes. Huge bunches of them. "So beautiful!" she said.

"Some of the finest wine grapes you'll ever see." He gave her a big grin. "And I'm proud to say these are my beauties. Grapes that will make remarkable wine."

"So then, you are a grape expert?" she asked as they reached the end of one of the long rows.

He gave a laugh. "Hardly. However, I'm learning. I rely on experts to advise me on the type of grapes to work with. My first attempt wasn't so wine-worthy, even though they tasted good. Everyone who works here ate most of them, and we had the rest made into raisins. All day long we chewed on grapes. We had purple lips, purple tongues, purple teeth!"

"How funny that must have looked!" She gave a laugh.

"You can't imagine."

"I hope you took photos" she said with a chuckle.

"I quickly realized I needed to know a lot more about which grapes were the best for winemaking. I've only been here a short while so I'm learning in a hurry."

Charles led her to another row of tubs. "One more row and then we'll get back to the elevator so you can meet Travis in Lab 2."

"So, are they going to make wine from this crop?" Isabel asked.

"Soon These are about to burst. I said we don't grow things for market, but I meant for the general food supply. These grapes are the exception however. The Bertrand Corp. plans to sell the wine from these grapes to help finance the underground work. After harvesting these, the next crop will start. We'll have an endless supply as long as we are vigilant in keeping the correct atmosphere in here, which is computer controlled. And since they are not bio-engineered in any way, there's no danger to the environment."

"Danger?" she asked.

"There's always a lot of controversy about the safety of genetically altered foods. Or genetically altered anything."

"But didn't you say that kind of thing is being done here also?"

Charles shrugged. "Yes. But not by me. We have Danny, and then of course your friend Joe who worked here." He hesitated then said, "Oh, and of course there's Darla. Travis and I are the two regular crop specialists. We give the crops the best environment possible. We don't perform genetic surgery. Actually, I have mixed feelings about altering. We don't yet know enough about the short and long-term ramifications. There can be serious hazards when we make those kinds of changes."

"Really? Like what kind of hazards? Jor . . . I mean Joe never mentioned any hazards to me."

Charles looked down at her and took a moment to answer. "Your friend Joe works in the gene altering field as an independent, but he's had permission to use our labs. Unfortunately, as I've told you, we had a serious disagreement the last time he was here. A safety issue. He refused to comply with our rules. Now, he needs permission from Corporate in order to work here again."

"Well, maybe it's the reason why he wanted me to meet him here. Maybe speak up on his behalf. But it's been a long time since I've seen him."

"I kind of doubt that's what he wanted. But I suppose you'll find out when he gets here."

She stopped walking and looked around at all of the lush green and purple plants growing out of the wooden tubs. "So tell me why it could be dangerous to genetically engineer various types of plants?"

"It seems there are two different opinions on the safety." Charles reached out, picked a fat purple grape, and held it out to her. "Taste the real thing the way God made it." He gave her a warm smile.

She took the grape and put it into her mouth, biting into the skin with her front teeth. It burst open, firm, sweet, and juicy. "This is so delicious," she told him, trying not to let any of the juice drool down her lip.

"Let me tell you, I'm not sure yet if the kind of work Danny, Darla, and your friend Joe do, is meant to be done. Nature has always balanced things. Changing this balance has caused some serious problems. The Toxic Potatoes for instance."

"The what?" Isabel asked in a puzzled voice.

"Awhile back some researchers fed groups of rats some engineered potatoes which apparently caused some of the rat's cells, the ones in their stomach and intestines, to overgrow, and others to fail to grow. The virus that's used to transfer foreign genetic material into the potatoes could have been the cause, or it could have been the transfer technique itself. There's still no agreement on what caused it. And I'm not too familiar with that kind of work."

"My God!" was all she could think of to say. She started walking again. "It does make you wonder, doesn't it?"

"It does. And Danny here works with altered food crops like corn, rice, and potatoes. Some people call the engineered crops Frankenfoods. One of the serious threats is the fact that by inserting virus genes into a vegetable's DNA it could possibly cause highly virulent *new* viruses to form. There is a possibility that modified or mutant viruses can destroy crops, cause famine, and or create human diseases. And stupid people are rushing out to get a patent on all sorts of things, before they even know if they are safe. And some of these patents they are trying to get are for . . . ." He closed his eyes for a moment and let out a sigh. "Well, for some things, I consider to be extremely dangerous. Things like creating new species of animals, or mixing altered animal genes with humans."

She gave him a questioning look. "I thought it was impossible to mix animals DNA with humans, or vice versa."

"Not at all impossible. They have already added the DNA of humans into pigs. They are also making insulin in a similar way. Danny keeps telling me it is still theoretically possible to do a heck of a lot more,

50

"So what do they use pigs for?"

"The heart valves from those pigs have human DNA and can sometimes be transferred to humans without being rejected. When it comes to emerging bio technologies a lot of researchers do not think they should have any limits as long as their work has the possibility to produce a large benefit. Which of course, will bring a large profit." He closed his eyes for a moment. When he opened them he said, "Anyway, enough of the ick factor."

Isabel found it difficult to grasp the enormous implications he was talking about. "I had no idea," she said, a little breathless. "Joe never mentioned—"

"Bertrand chose this place for improved food crops, as well as for crops that can make medications and other things." Charles explained. "If any of these crops have dangers not yet known, and if some of the altered seeds escaped they could migrate via insects, water, wind, or whatever. Therefore, we have strict security rules here in order to stop any accidental migration."

Isabel felt some color drain from her face. So that's why Jorge needed her to get his flash drive out of there. The information on it had not been checked to see if it was something illegal to fool around with. It was obvious it could be. After all, he never was a stickler for rules, any rules, even in college.

Almost as if he'd read her mind Charles said, "On this first level there are two Units with natural foods, mine and Travis' Natural crops. No danger."

"That sounds good."

"But then, when we get to one of the units on the next level down we'll need to change into lab gowns and then change out of them before we go back up. Not difficult at all," he assured her. "On that level we have three well equipped laboratories. One is a Unit for bio-engineered pharmaceuticals; one is for Danny's Frankenfoods, and the other is Joe's for his highly modified corn. That one is off limits for the time being."

Isabel tried to digest the huge amount of information Charles was giving her. No matter how safe Jorge might think his work was

51

Isabel wondered if she should do what he wanted. She looked away from Charles, afraid her fear would show on her face. Was it possible Jorge was creating a different kind of crop, with an inherent danger? She wanted to believe whatever it was, was safe, but the worry began to bite at her like sharp jagged teeth.

"So exactly what might happen if something from here accidentally did get outside?" She asked him.

Charles looked pensive for several moments and then he said, "Hopefully nothing. Nothing at all. Nevertheless, we don't yet know what some of these mutants could do. Worst case scenario?" He paused again. "If a dangerous genetic mutant got into the hands of the wrong people, who knows? Take my word for it! It could a weapon far worse than an atom bomb!"

For reasons she didn't understand, his words hit Isabel's legs which suddenly went out from under her and she found herself grabbing onto Charles to keep from falling.

Chapter Five

Charles felt Isabel grab him as she started to fall. He quickly took hold of her and held her up on her feet. "My God woman! Are you going to faint on me? Do women today still have the vapors?"

"No, no! I'm so sorry! What you were saying kind of hit me. Joe never mentioned them." She gave him an apologetic smile. "Even in College I hadn't heard much about the serious dangers of genetic engineering. I'm just a little unnerved by the call from Jor. . . ah, Joe after so many years, and the unsettling drive out here. Then, not finding him here, and having to spend the night. I feel as if I'm in some kind of peculiar dream!"

Charles couldn't help noticing the odd expressions crossing her pale face. It was difficult to read her. Something serious was bothering her, and he was sure it had to do with Joe. Was Joe just trying to resurrect their past relationship? Or was she really as perplexed by Joe's sending her here as he was? Then again, maybe she had her own agenda. He hoped not because he found himself attracted to her. It had been a long time since he had dated anyone, much less become serious about a woman. Not since his wife Nancy had died three years ago. At least he had something in common with Isabel. That is, if she was being honest with him. With everything going on with Joe, and with Bertrand, he knew he shouldn't get involved with anyone. Not yet. Maybe never.

"Look, I didn't mean to alarm you," he assured her. "Those are just possibilities. I automatically mention them when I'm talking about the subject. Your students should be aware of both points of view about genetic engineering." Charles studied her face again. He saw the color coming back and she seemed to be more relaxed. She probably did have an unsettling trip coming out here. He sensed something else also, but wasn't sure what it was. Some sort of tension seemed to have settled around her eyes.

He leaned down close to her. "Are you okay?" he asked. The

53

scent of some familiar perfume seemed to surround him. How long it had been since he'd smelled the honeyed scent of perfume wafting from a woman. He lingered there, inhaling the sweetness of it.

She gently pulled herself away from him. "I'm fine now," she assured him, straightening her shoulders. "I'd like to see the rest of this remarkable place."

He lamented the loss of her perfumed scent. "Are you sure? We don't have to. You can go topside and wait for Joe if you'd prefer."

"No, if he arrives, he can wait for me. I really would like to see everything."

"Okay then. Next stop, Travis' Unit B. A lot of corn. No mutants." he said, then breathed in, hoping for one last wisp of the perfume. "Because of the controlled climate," he continued. "plus the use of continual light, and no bugs, it grows like crazy. We harvest some of it for ourselves to eat all year round."

"So why do you grow it if you don't sell it?"

"Well, there really isn't a stable marketplace for it outside. Also, what with the hope some people have for Ethanol, farmers are planting more acres of corn than ever before. We can't begin to compete. So, we use all of the corn we grow right here."

"Then I guess you must eat a lot of corn!"

Charles laughed. "Actually, we have buttered ears of corn two or three times a week. Great stuff. But the rest of the corn goes into creating energy for this place."

Isabel gave a little frown, but then her face lit up. "Ahhh, I bet you make Ethanol, right?"

"Right, cellulosic Ethanol."

"I thought making ethanol from corn wasn't cost-effective."

He shook his head. "It isn't very, yet. But here we aren't paying inflated prices to farmers for the corn so it's economical in our case." He took her hand again and then realized he was being unusually familiar with her, a woman he had just met. Nevertheless, he enjoyed the warm delicate touch of her fingers, along with her subtle scent of perfume. Besides, she didn't object. In fact, she seemed to welcome it. In some ways, she appeared to be a strong woman, having ventured all the way here at the request of an old friend, and yet she had a vulnerability that made him want to protect her.

He walked her back to the elevator and used his card to open the doors again. Once inside with the doors closed he felt Isabel react again. He hoped it was just the usual nerves, and she wasn't actually claustrophobic. In what he knew would be a surprise to her, he didn't move the elevator, but just turned around and faced the back of the elevator. She looked puzzled, but turned around with him.

He gave her a grin. "Unit B is on this same level, and it opens from this side of the elevator." He leaned forward, used his card, and the door clicked and slowly began to open.

The two of them stepped out of the elevator and the door automatically closed behind them. In front of them was a wooden door painted blue with *Unit B* stenciled on it.

"Now, come and take a look at the largest crop of corn you've ever seen growing underground."

Isabel gave a little laugh. "I've never seen even a small crop of corn growing underground."

He reached out, opened the blue door, and led her into a room almost identical to his lab, except for the long rows of tall corn stalks growing there, instead of grape vines. The space was also brilliantly lit with polished metal walls and LED lights all around them.

"Well," Charles said. "You have now. These are Travis's babies."

"Holy shit!" Isabel blurted out at the astounding sight, and then clamped her hand over her mouth.

Charles found himself laughing heartily as he began to walk her around the mammoth space. For the moment, he really didn't care what her purpose was in being here. He was really enjoying her company.

Isabel couldn't believe what she was seeing. The corn-filled room was so huge she could barely see the far end of it. "My God! This is absolutely amazing!" Isabel said in awe, looking from one row of corn to another. She noticed in the various rows of corn some

55

were ready to harvest while others were at various stages of growth. This would no doubt give them a continuous supply.

Charles turned away from her. "Travis!" he shouted, "You in here?"

"Sure am!" The voice came from somewhere done the rows of corn.

"Come meet our visitor," Charles called in a booming voice.

"Sure thing," Travis called back.

As the man approached, Isabel was surprised to see he was older than she would expect for someone doing this type of work. A tall twiggy man with gray hair so thin his pink scalp showed through, and wearing a small hearing aid in one ear. He had on a pair of Chinos two sizes too large along with a billowing T-shirt with the words: *Bad President! No more Cookies!* printed on it. His gold-rimmed glasses glinted like flying sparks in the brilliant light of the room.

"Hi there," Travis said reaching out his hand. "How do you like our *pharm*? It's farm spelled with a ph."

"Impressive!" Isabel said, shaking his hand. "Very impressive. I can hardly believe all of this is . . . ah, well . . . growing *underground*. So this corn will be turned into Ethanol, right?"

Travis nodded. "Right. Of course, some of it we use for our meals here. I think I'm going to do some tomatoes and a few potatoes soon, for a more balanced diet.

"I have a question," Isabel said thoughtfully.

"A what?" Travis asked, his fingers adjusting his hearing aid. "Did you say you had a question?

Isabel took a minute to organize her thoughts. Then, in a louder voice she asked, "How the heck does Bertrand make any money on this endeavor? It seems as if the project money all goes back into keeping this place going."

Charles hesitated a moment before he spoke. Then he said "That's not quite accurate. First, backing experiments like those they do here is always expensive, with little payoff. However, when they create something that not only works well, but also helps to enhance

56

the world for everyone, that process is priceless. Most of these processes belong to Bertrand who will make good money with them, and once out in the marketplace the creator will get a percentage."

"Sounds good," Isabel said.

"Let's take a quick tour here, so we can get on to Unit C. It's Darla's and from what she says she's working on in there succeeds, it might make Bertrand a truck-load of money," Charles said.

"So what is it?" she asked, intrigued.

She is not telling us exactly . . . yet." Charles started walking down one of the rows of corn. Isabel followed with Travis behind her.

"Travis, let's harvest some corn for lunch today," Charles said. "I'm sure Isabel would enjoy it." He stopped and turned back to her. "You will be staying, won't you? At least until Joe shows up."

"Well, I guess so," Isabel said. "But if Joe doesn't show up right after lunch, then I'll leave. I don't want to make that trip in the dark again."

"Smart," Charles said."

"What about Joe's Unit?" Isabel asked.

"Off limits, I'm afraid. No one's been allowed in after he left."

"I'm expecting it to be genetically altered corn as he's always worked with. But at this point, I'm not sure."

"How much has he told you about his work?" Charles asked with an odd tight expression on his face, and then he began walking again.

"Ahhh, well, even when we first met, altered corn was on his mind." Isabel felt her heart race a little, as she tried not to sound nervous. Jorge was so damn vague about his project. Something better than corn. What the heck did that mean? Would getting his stuff be stealing if it belonged to him and he asked her to get it? Or did Bertrand have a legal right to detain it even for safety concerns? She had no idea.

"Charles," she asked as they reached the end of the corn row. "How did people get all the way below the ground areas before Bertrand put in the elevator?"

"They used the old stone steps," Charles said as he started down the next corn row toward the elevator. Isabel had a little trouble keeping up with his long strides. As if realizing it, he stopped to let her catch up.

"We still have miles and miles of giant steps. Tons and tons of huge old stones," Travis added. Some go to the bottom of this old place. Some go up to our bedrooms"

"I see. So they are still usable? The company didn't remove any of them when they put in the elevator?" Isabel hoped her questions didn't raise a red flag with Charles. She tried to sound just curious and interested.

"Yep, they kept them," Charles answered. "Just in case."

"In case of what?"

"In case the elevator decides to give up. Or the power just goes out. The backups don't do well with keeping the elevator going. So, for safety reasons, each lab still has a door that opens to the stone steps.

Isabel gave him a soft smile. "Well, I'd love to see them. Maybe take some photos with my smart phone."

Charles shrugged. "Nothing much to see except for huge stones, cobwebs, slimy gray-green fungus, and some little critters who love to live in the cracks between the stones."

Isabel shuddered. Charles was right. Not exactly what she wanted to see. But she at least should find out where the steps were located.

"I can't imagine that someone built this humungous place for just one person to live in," she told Charles. "My students would love to see this place."

"Maybe there are some old photos around here. I'll see if I can find them," Charles said. "I'll show you the steps later. They go way down below the labs so if anyone wants to get to the other vacant caverns down there, they can."

Travis fiddled with his hearing aid again and then said, "Such a waste of a life, if you ask me. That poor hunchbacked old guy building this place, then up and dying as soon as it was done." Travis pushed the gold-rimmed glasses higher on his nose. "By the way, have you seen Danny? I tried his lab a few minutes ago, but he's not there"

"Not since breakfast," Charles said.

"I've got to check the oxygen-carbon dioxide levels again." Travis said. "The night crew had a little problem. Nice to meet you, Isabel. I'll see you at lunch." He turned on his heels and disappeared into the rows of corn.

"Okay, my curious lady," Charles said to Isabel. "Are you ready to visit Unit C on the next level down?"

Isabel nodded solemnly. She felt a painful pinch of guilt and wondered if there was any possibility at all that she could attempt to do what Jorge asked of her. So why should she get herself involved in all this? She knew now that she and Jorge would never get back together. He was still dead to her.

Looking up she saw Charles had reached out to her, waiting to take her hand again. Why on earth, she asked herself, did Jorge distrust Charles? A little stirring of fear twisted its way through her body. Even so, she lifted her hand and let him take hold of it. She needed his strength if she was going to get through her involvement with all this insanity.

"Once more into the elevator, dear lady." Charles grinned at her and then gave her hand a tug. Inside the elevator the doors closed softly and it took only seconds for them to arrive at the next level down.

The white coat Charles gave Isabel was way too long for her. It almost touched the ground. Charles chuckled when he saw her. "Sorry about that. It's one of mine," he said.

"I feel like a two-year-old in a giant's nightgown," she laughed. "And you look like a doctor."

Charles led her out of the dressing room and down a short hallway to a large steel door which said *Unit C* on it. He swiped his ID card across a metal box fastened next to the door. She heard a soft sort of sigh and the door slowly slid open. The sighing turned into a whooshing sound. "What's the noise?" she asked, startled.

"Air, being sucked into the room,"

"Oh! Yes, of course! Reverse something or other. Is this a level 4 containment lab? I've heard about those!" Isabel felt herself automatically pull back from entering the room. "Don't tell me she's working on dangerous microorganisms or something in there?"

Charles shook his head. "Nope. No pathogens. We're not certified yet to deal with those kinds of things. No one-piece positive-pressure suits with life-support systems built-in. We're not a Hot Zone like the ones you see in the movies. However, we'll also need to do this in Danny's lab also since he's making Frankenfoods. Joe's lab is set up this same way, since we're not always sure what the heck he's doing in there. We just do our best to keep any part of the restructured vegetation from getting out of here and into the outside world." He held out his hand to her again.

Isabel hesitated taking it. "Well, okay then." She heard the whooshing sound increase which startled her again. "It's kind of creepy sounding though."

Charles didn't wait; he took her hand again. "We use what is called a volumetric air flow controller and a differential pressure controller. Come along, it's only air. Won't hurt a bit." He smiled and pulled her gently through the open door and into the lab. The door closed silently behind them and the whooshing sound stopped.

Isabel was surprised to find Unit C was the smallest of the underground labs she'd seen so far. She guessed it to be about thirty-feet wide by forty-feet long with one end filled with tubs of short pale green plants. The other end was what looked like a well-equipped laboratory. She identified a centrifuge, an electron microscope, and what appeared to be a tissue-slicing machine. Outside of those, she had no idea what all the other machines and tools were.

On one wall was a huge cupboard as tall as the ceiling and at least two feet deep and six feet wide. The cupboard was made of the same bright metal which covered all of the walls. The cupboard door had a bar across it, fastened on each end with heavy-duty combination locks. She wondered what on earth Darla kept in there. What would require so much security?

"Here's our visitor, Darla," Charles said. "I think you met last night. This is Isabel, a friend of Joes."

Darla turned to them. "A friend of Joes, yes." She said flicking her thin lips with a pale pink tongue. Then she turned back to whatever she was working on and in a tight voice she said, "You give her the tour, Charles. I am in the middle of checking tests I set up yesterday."

Charles gave Isabel a grimace. "Our Darla, always the over-achiever."

Darla turned slightly toward them and narrowed her eyes. "Someone has to be! Or the results would be . . . no results."

Isabel thought the woman's face looked even more pinched with her narrowed eyes and her mouth pursed toward her.

"Yes," Charles nodded. "She's right. Darla here is the one person who takes the work here more seriously than the others. Bertrand is depending on her work paying off for them. For Darla as well. From what I understand, she's attempting to create medicines from plants. I don't know a darn thing more about it."

"What kind of medicines?" Isabel asked Darla.

Darla turned around slowly, her eyes opened wider now than Isabel had seen them. They were an odd color for eyes. She hadn't noticed it when they first met. A furry gray surrounded by pale lashes. She couldn't remember having seen eyes that color before. Ghostly, was the only word she could think of to describe them?

"I cannot be specific yet," Darla said. "But if things keep going as they have been, I will have a solution for one of the world's worst problems."

Charles gave a chuckle. "She works with bugs and meds."

Darla shot him a dark look. "The conventional methods used to create medicines are hugely expensive," she said. "Pharmaceutical companies go after diseases that affect a large group of people. It creates a great need for their product. They make huge profits."

Isabel noted Darla spoke in an odd clipped tone, as if she'd given

61

this information number of times. "Yes of course." Isabel agreed.

"However," Darla continued, "What I am doing is growing genetically engineered plants. The plants contain a medical substance which can be isolated and obtained at a fraction of the cost of conventional methods. What it will do, is stop diseases from killing their hosts. If offered at a low cost it will make it possible to treat people in countries which have scourges such as AIDS, Africa for instance."

Impressed, Isabel said, "My God! Are you working on an AIDs vaccine?"

Darla shook her head and frowned. "No! AIDS is just an example. However, there is an HIV drug produced from tobacco plants called cyanovirin-N, which appears it might help stop the Aid's virus from entering cells. I believe it is a fusion inhibitor. They say it works in test animals and they are hopeful it will do the same in humans. Nevertheless, my work will make theirs unnecessary! It will make most all medicines unnecessary!"

Darla's words took Isabel aback. "I see, well then, it must be something really great. So what disease is it you are hoping to defeat?"

Darla ignored the question, turned away, and began working again. Isabel tried to peer around her to see what she was doing but backed away when Darla gave her an odd sideways glance.

"Sorry," Isabel said. But all of this is so interesting. I'll have some significant things to tell my students when my classes begin again the first of next year."

Darla stopped working and looked up at the wall in front of her. Isabel was afraid she'd stepped over the line with her. She hadn't meant to pry, or to upset her.

Darla nodded, still staring at the wall. "Not a lot of young people enter this field." Very slowly, she turned around. Her gray eyes darkened as she looked at Isabel. "Ask your students what they think is the worst disease in the world. One that hits every human being. See if they know the right answer."

"An interesting question. I will make a point of asking. So what is the answer?"

62

The Gray Green Underground

Darla just stood there looking at her. Anxious to keep Darla from staring at her with her ghostly gray eyes, Isabel pointed around at the tubs of plants on the other side of the room, and changed the subject. "So have all of these plants been . . . ah . . . engineered?" she asked.

"Yes." Darla gave her a pinched frown. "I thought you would have started back to your home by now."

"The storm is still pretty strong," Isabel said, feeling a little defensive.

Isabel turned and walked over to the first row of Darla's plants. Some had little pink flowers and others had what appeared to be small pods. They looked familiar but she couldn't think of what they were. It was hard to imagine these unimpressive looking plants were harboring a medicine or vaccine, and could save millions of lives. "I think I've seen these types of plants before," she said turning back toward Darla and Charles.

"Soybeans," Charles said. "Just plain old soybeans."

"Special pink-blossom soybeans," Darla said in a reprimanding tone. She turned back to them and gave Charles another pinched glance.

"Yes, of course, very special, Darla" Charles said.

Isabel turned to Darla. "Thank you for sharing, Darla. "Good luck with your project. I hope it's very successful!"

"Of course it will be!" Darla said in a very sharp tone. "It's right on track. Exactly where I want it."

A sudden bell sounded and Isabel jumped. Charles went to the wall next to the door and slid a phone from a niche in the wall. "What's up?" he said in a gruff tone. "What! When?" His voice started loud and then went to a raspy whisper. "Oh great, just what we need. I'll be right up. Don't do anything. Just hang loose, okay?" He slammed the phone back on its place and turned to Isabel, his face tight.

"Sorry, but there's a problem. We have to go top-side."

"Something serious?" Isabel asked.

"Could turn out to be. But not a catastrophic. Nothing for you to be alarmed about." Charles gave her a rather tight smile. "Sorry to

63

interrupt your tour. I know you wanted to see the old steps."

"It is always something around here," Darla said in an irritated tone. "What is the problem this time?"

"Have you seen Danny?" Charles asked.

Darla shook her head. "Should be snoozing and eating in his lab."

"Well, if you see him, tell him we have problem topside."

"I must continue working," Darla mumbled, going back to her work.

"Come on Isabel," Charles said. "Let's ditch these lab coats."

It only took minutes to get out of the coats and into the elevator. The more she thought about finding what Jorge wanted, the more aggravated she became. First, get it out of its hiding place, and then hide it somewhere on her person, then figure out how to get it back to him. What the hell was Jorge thinking about anyway? His pleading for her to help him brought back the painful images of their marriage and made her realize her marriage to Jorge had never really been much of a marriage.

Her stomach took a sudden twist as the elevator rushed them from the underground to the surface level at what felt like light speed. "Wow," she breathed softly. "Going up is fast!"

Charles put his hand on her shoulder. "You okay? No claustrophobia this time?"

"Actually, my mind was somewhere else. I didn't have time to panic. So far, I'm fascinated with everything we saw. Thank you so much for the tour."

"We can see the rest later, if you're up to it." Once again he took her hand and encouraged her out of the elevator. "I've got to do some trouble-shooting. You can come along, or you can go to the kitchen and wait for me. There is always hot coffee in the kitchen. Or maybe you can find some books in the entry room you might like to read. Unfortunately, our TV dish has probably been blown from here to Baja because of the storm." Charles forced smile dwindled as he spoke. The sharp little creases between his eyes told her he was greatly concerned about something.

"I'd prefer to stay with you, if you don't think I'll be in the way," she said.

"Okay then," he said, with a slight sigh. "It was one of our night guys who called while we were underground. His name is Scooter. We call him Scooter the trouble shooter. He had planned to leave this morning. However he ran into trouble on the road after he left here."

"What happened?" A touch of alarm hit her. She didn't like the idea of not being able to go home when she wanted to.

"The damn storm increased and circled back on us. The wind took out two large trees which have blocked the creek area of the road. Plus the creek's running extremely high. Right now, walking is the only way out of here. I've complained about our needing at least one all-terrain vehicle here, but Bertrand said we didn't need one"

As if to punctuate his words, a blue-white flash of lightning lit up the dark hallway around them, followed by a deafening clap of thunder. Isabel felt herself jump. "Oh, great!" she said, her words almost drowning in the noise?"

"Let's go. I'm meeting Scooter in the office so we can decide what to do." He started off at a fast pace. Isabel had trouble keeping up with him.

"Can it be fixed fairly fast?" she asked.

He looked back at her, and slowed a little. "We will probably have to wait until they can get some service guys up here with gas powered chain saws and some heavy-duty trucks. Something similar happened a few years back. Took us three days to clear up the mess."

"Oh," she said softly. She wondered if Jorge was stuck on the other side of the roadblock. Or, maybe he really hadn't intended to get back to her. If she actually got what he wanted out of here, he would probably just show up at her condo when she got home, and claim it. She felt her face flush with anger.

"Scooter can give us better details on what's happened," Charles said. He took her hand again, encouraging her to walk faster. "Not to worry, we have some food, plenty of water, and wood for the fireplaces. And we can always eat corn." He gave a little laugh. "And a few grapes maybe."

Isabel took in a deep breath and let it out slowly. The realization that she was trapped in this monstrous stone castle began to ignite another attack of claustrophobia. A burst of blue-white lightning flooded the dark hallway followed by the loudest boom of thunder she'd ever heard. The hairs on the back of her neck stood up like little electrical feelers.

"Here we are," Charles, said leading her into a small room furnished with a dark wood desk, teak paneled walls, and two burgundy leather sofas that matched the ones flanking the fireplace in the entry room. A warm, cozy room.

The look of it helped release the claustrophobic grip on her. Standing next to a polished teak desk she saw a man with a mop of thick black hair that, like Charles hair, badly needed a haircut. He turned to her and gave her a gentle smile, his unusual brindle colored eyes meeting hers, holding them for a moment. She guessed he stood well over six feet tall with the shoulders of a wrestler. Highly defined muscles in his thighs protruded from a pair of mushroom colored shorts. With icy rain outside, chilled wind, and rattling thunder, she felt herself shiver at the thought of anyone wearing shorts. She thought him rather good looking, probably late twenties or so. However, he didn't look like a Scooter. The name Attila or Bruno would have fit him better. She felt a giggle make its way into her throat. The result, she realized, of fear and her panic over the current situation.

"Scooter, this is Isabel Warren. She came looking for Joe but he hasn't shown up. Now, with the road closed, he won't be able to get here for some time. So she's our guest until things clear up around here."

Scooter gave Isabel a nod. "Might as well sit down, Sweetcheeks, and relax. This is not a bad place to be in a storm. Amazingly sturdy."

"Watch out for this guy, Isabel. A notorious womanizer," Charles said. "Besides that, Scooter is our prime tech guy here. Able to fix almost everything, including people, with some medical training. A man for all seasons. "By the way, Scooter, where's Danny?" Charles asked.

"He's probably in his lab. Haven't seen him since early this morning."

"Nope. He's not there. Travis checked on him a short while ago. Darla hasn't seen him either."

"We should check his room then. Maybe he's not feeling well." Scooter gave a concerned frown.

Isabel took Scooter's suggestion and sat down on one of the leather sofas. The soft yet supportive touch of the leather felt good. She turned around and looked out the windows behind the sofa. Rain was pelting down. Lightning flashed again, this time even closer as the thunder boomed at almost the same time as the lightning strike. It rumbled through the room vibrating everything not nailed down. Maybe, she tried to convince herself, it wouldn't be so bad. She had a room to herself, food and water, and some interesting people to talk to. It would give her some time to think about Jorge's request. It might be good to at least get a look at what it was he wanted her to get. After all, she didn't have to turn it over to him.

Just as she began to feel less trapped, an ear-cracking jolt struck the room. The jolt caused the old stone walls to screech like an animal in pain. Even though the windows were closed in the room, it came with an unbelievably strong metallic smell. Even the taste of it clung to the inside of her mouth.

"Fuck!" Scooter yelled. 'That's all we need."

"What happened?" Isabel said jumping to her feet.

"Could be something was hit by the lightning. Metal, from the smell of it," Scooter replied.

Charles frowned and looked out the window. "You really think so?"

As if to answer him, the lights in the room flickered and went off. "Ah, damn it!" Charles growled. "We'll all be playing poker by candlelight tonight. We'd better check on the auxiliary generator. We don't want the underground labs going dark. Isabel, you stay put," he said pointing at her. "There's enough light in here from the window, even though the storm is making it darker than usual. You'll find an oil lamp in the cupboard by the desk over there if you need it. And a number of flashlights. So don't panic, this has happened before so we're prepared. It should switch to auxiliary power automatically, but it goes to the labs first. We may not get it here. Scooter, grab us some flashlights."

Charles smiled at her, a little stiff but sincere. "Don't worry, Isabel, it shouldn't take us long."

Isabel nodded and sat back down leather of the sofa. She wasn't going to go anywhere, lights or no lights, until they got back. As Scooter and Charles disappeared through the doorway into the hall, she tried to make herself relax. The small room with its dark paneling still felt cozy in an odd way. She drew up her knees and rested her head on the padded back of the sofa. Lightning flashed now and then and thunder rumbled like an old man groaning in his sleep. Over the sound of the storm, Isabel heard a strange tapping sound. It seemed to be coming from outside the window. She squinted, trying to sharpen her sight. The sound grew louder. A small twinge of panic teased her stomach. What the hell was it? Then, to her relief, she saw little white pebbles bouncing off the windowpane.

"Oh, for heaven's sake," she said, calmed. "It's *hail!*" She hadn't seen hail for several years. It wasn't one of those things native to Southern California. The panic melted into a sense of relief and she gave a little laugh. The room slowly turned misty dim. She closed her eyes and let out a sigh.

It was then that she suddenly felt long icy fingers touch one of her hands.

Chapter Six

"Miss . . . Isabel? It is me, Darla." The woman's icy fingers lingered on Isabel a few seconds before she pulled them away. "The power is out in my lab. The backup generator has not activated yet. Makes me quite uncomfortable."

Isabel was relieved to have someone with her. Even Darla. Oh dear, your hands are like ice," she said. "Sit down and I'll help you rub them warm."

Darla sat down on the sofa next to her. Her hands were not only cold, but shaking. She allowed Isabel to rub them for only a few moments. Then she slipped them away and settled them in in her lap.

"Yes, better. Thank you." Her voice held a curious mixture of emotion and aloofness. "I am over anxious because the auxiliary power has not come on yet," she said, repeating herself. "My lab is totally black. It should have come on automatically. The elevator is not working. So I struggled in the dark to find the key to my lab door so I could get to the old stone steps." A tremor, a shivering, began in her voice. "There is a battery light system along the stairway. Like Christmas tree lights. I could see, but barely. It is bitter cold in the stairwell! Cold that bites into your skin! But everyone says I am crazy. They keep saying it is only about 45 degrees or so." She lifted her arms and shook her hands, her fingers swinging like long sticks from her thin wrists. "But you felt how cold my hands were." A passive expression crawled over Darla's face, despite her words.

"I think I read somewhere that it's different in various places, but is it usually in the 40's." Isabel asked.

"On the stairs and all the areas below the labs, it's supposed to.be But during the winter, it is a lot colder most of the time. I tell you, it eats the heat right out of a body."

"Do people use the old stone steps much anymore."

Darla fixed her odd gray eyes on Isabel and said, "There are occasions when it is necessary." Her paled cheeks finally began to

69

bloom a persimmon color, although her lips stayed as white as death.

To change the subject, Isabel said, "By the way, after the blackout, did you feel a blast of some kind. Like maybe lightning might have struck something?"

"I did not hear or feel anything. My lab just went black. That has not happened since I came here. I mean, it has happened before, but the auxiliary power always came on immediately."

"Charles and Scooter went to check it out," Isabel said. "I hope it's not serious considering the road is blocked. I was told no one will be able to get in or out. Some trees are down, and a high creek."

"What? The only frigging road is blocked? Damn it!! So that's why our Saturday tech crew isn't here. "

The small room was shadow carved, but even in the uneven light Isabel saw the woman's face narrow even more than usual. The persimmon bloom in her cheeks once again faded, leaving her face and lips milk-white. The changes on Darla's face began to disturb Isabel, since they were happening so often.

Darla was silent for a moment. "Oh great!" she finally growled. "Is not that just shit-spitting great? I told Charles he should have sent you home last night. Now the two of us are stuck here together for God knows how long."

The remark took Isabel off guard. Stuck here *together*! Was Darla resentful of her being here? She swallowed down her feelings and said, "I hope the guys can get things fixed fast. This place is going to be pretty eerie after dark, without any lights."

"They should have left the gas lamps here that old man Poole put in," Darla complained. "They would have helped. But then we probably don't have any gas connection here anymore."

"Charles said there was an oil lamp and flashlights in one of the cupboards if we needed it." Isabel squinted at her watch, trying to read it in the dim light. "It's darker than twilight. Already."

A flash of brilliant incandescence suddenly filled the little room. The whole place shook again. The razor sharp smell of metal filled the air again. The two of them looked at each other.

"Damn!" Isabel said, and took in a long shuttering breath.

70

Lightning? Or an explosion? She was not certain she wanted an answer.

Darla gave a resigned shrug. "I suppose we should try to put together some lunch. We can manage our way to the kitchen. We may need the oil lamp because there is only those high up bent-leaded-glass windows in there."

"Do you think we should?" Isabel asked. "The guys said I should stay right here while they're gone. I don't want to cause any problems." Isabel noticed that even though Charles had brought her a pancake breakfast and coffee, she was indeed hungry again.

"As long as we make enough lunch for them, they will not mind." Darla gave a knowing nod of her head. "I wonder if the other labs lost their power. I do not know if this whole place is on the same circuitry or not. With the elevator out, the climb up those stairs would be tough on Travis and Danny. They are not very young, you know."

"Are they really hard to manage? The stone stairs, I mean?" Isabel asked.

"The rise is way too high on every step. Just like the ones to our bedrooms upstairs," Darla got up and motioned to Isabel to do the same. "Come on. Grab the oil lamp from the cupboard."

Isabel got up and went to the cupboard where Charles said she'd find the oil lamp. It wasn't there. "Well, damn!" she sputtered. "No lamp. But there are two flashlights left, and several candles."

Darla was already at the door about to step out into the dark hallway. "Well then, bring them all." With a wave of her hand, she motioned for Isabel to follow. Darla kept a distance ahead of her with a spider-like scuttle. In Isabel's attempts to keep up with her, she fought to keep hold of the flashlights and candles.

Isabel's spirits grew when she found the kitchen warm and inviting. The huge wooden table surrounded by a bevy of mismatched chairs gave the place a homey feel. The room, faintly lit by the bent-glass windows overhead, was drummed loudly by the continuing rain. Darla took the candles from her and began setting them into small glasses in place of candle holders, then lit each of

71

them. Isabel set the flashlights down on one end of the countertop. She stood there listening to the storm, still going strong.

She looked at the huge clock on the wall. It was a little after twelve noon. "What can I do to help with lunch?" she asked, trying to keep her mind off the fact she was trapped in a huge stone castle with an odd assortment of people she hardly knew.

"Make a pot of coffee." Darla pointed to the large pot. "The guys always want coffee, day and night. It is a wonder they ever sleep." "Thank God, we have propane for the stove. The coffee beans are in the cupboard to your left. The grinder is right beside them."

Isabel gathered the needed things together and set them on the polished granite counter. "So, which of you live here? Do you have days off so you can go down the mountain if you need to?"

Darla washed her hands twice, then pulled a pile of things out of the huge refrigerator and began making sandwiches. "The night crew is only here to make sure the temperature and other stuff are running right," she finally answered. "They are not scientists. All on the day crew are, except that Neanderthal, Scooter. We live here full time, and have our own rooms upstairs. We take one or two days off a week if we want. The Neanderthal makes sure our labs are okay. Most of us do not leave unless we need to stock up on food, or get personal things. I do not know about the others, but this is the only place I live. I don't have an apartment or anything. You can't have any attachments if you do our kind of work.

"Attachments?"

"Wives, husbands."

"I see. It's obvious you love your work."

"We have a Dish on the roof here, at least we did before this storm hit. When it is working, we can get TV. Unfortunately, we do not have a hard line telephone and we cannot get a cell phone connection. The company should take care of that. However, we do have a short-wave battery radio we use to call out, in case of an emergency."

Isabel poured some coffee beans into the grinder and turned the switch. But nothing happened. "Oh damn! I forgot about the electricity! I can't grind the beans."

"Well of course not," Darla said as if Isabel should have known better. "Look on the back of the shelf. There should be a manual grinder."

Isabel located it, loaded the beans, and began grinding them. "Did my . . . ah, friend, Joe, live here most of the time?" She tried to sound casual but noticed her words had a tense edge.

"Joe? Good God yes!" Darla said. "Never went out. I shopped for him when I did my own. At least until two weeks ago." Sly little prickles of crystal sweat began to break out on Darla's forehead. She quickly whisked them away with the sleeve of her white blouse.

The kitchen felt toasty warm, but not warm enough to make someone sweat. Isabel wondered if Darla wasn't feeling well. On the other hand, maybe it was just the stress from worrying about her pink blossom soybeans.

"Nevertheless, Joe will be back," Darla continued. "He is one of those driven people. He needs us. He needs this place." She looked off into space for a moment, a preoccupied look on her face. Then she gave an odd little jerk of her body, and her attention turned back to the kitchen. She washed her hands again, and then began piling a stack of sandwiches onto a large tray. "Bologna and cheese. How the guys love their bologna and cheese with Miracle Whip. God awful combination."

Isabel filled the coffee pot with water. "Should I just dump in the ground beans? I can't find any insides to the pot."

"Makes rich unfiltered coffee. Strong as hell! Just what we need."

Isabel poured in the ground beans and Darla took the pot from her, lit the stove, and set the coffee on to boil.

"My poor soybean plants have *never* been without light." Darla said, finishing up the sandwiches. "They could die from the shock! Christ! Please! Not now when I am inches away from success."

"Yes, but even if you don't succeed at this point you can start over, can't you? You have all your notes, the specs on everything, I'm sure."

73

"I will succeed, and they will pay me millions for some shares of it." Darla blinked in a nervous, rapid manner, cleared her throat, and then began to restack the sandwiches. "Where the hell are the guys?" she said in an irritable tone.

Isabel looked at the huge stack of sandwiches as Darla set the overflowing tray in the middle of the table. Enough food for an Army!

"I will succeed!" Darla repeated. "I have already succeeded." Darla's face went tightly pinched as she said it. Then, her voice trailed off. "Nothing like a blackout is going to stop me!"

Isabel gave her a soft smile, but wondered about her agitation. "I'm sure the guys are on top of it. They know how much it means." She turned and walked toward the row of cupboards over the kitchen counter. "Should I put out some plates and mugs?"

"Yes. Then we sit." Darla said.

It took Isabel only a few minutes to get the table set. The water in the coffee pot filled with coffee beans, began to hiss and boil. Darla pulled it off the stove and set it on the table on a hot pad. The two of them sat down across from each other. The growing darkness and the sound of the storm outside made Isabel thankful for being close to someone, even though Darla wasn't the pleasantest person around. She would have felt a lot better if Charles had been with her. Darla had such a peculiar aloofness about her, as well as an uneven reaction to things. Isabel remembered Charles saying something about her being mildly autistic, or something. She'd heard some people with these types of syndromes did not interact too well with people.

Darla filled two of the mugs with coffee and offered one to Isabel. "There is always sugar on the table, but the cream is in the fridge."

"I prefer my coffee black," Isabel said. "Always have. My husband loved a ton of sugar and even more cream. Makes me cringe to think of it." She looked at Darla, startled to see the odd expression on her face. "Are you okay," she asked.

"What? Oh, yes. I just . . . ." Darla looked away from her and

74

took a swallow of her coffee. "I know someone who likes their coffee the exact same way. Rather unusual for a male."

"You're probably right."

"So then, you are married?"

Isabel took a moment to collect her thoughts. How much should she tell about her personal life? "I was married. But I was widowed four years ago."

"I am told that can be a most difficult thing."

An uncomfortable silence filled the space between the two of them, and then eased off. Isabel gave a sigh, relieved Darla hadn't questioned her on what had happened to her husband.

"Are you are a good friend of Joe's?" Darla asked. "How long have you known him?" She gave a little forced laugh which had no humor in it.

"Nothing much to tell. It's been a long time since we've seen each other. I'm not sure what his intentions are, especially his insisting we meet here. The fact is he might not even show up!"

Darla gave her a searching look, as if trying to read her mind. "So then you two are not involved."

"No . . . we really aren't."

Darla's narrow face became less pinched. "I see. Most interesting."

A sudden crackle of lightning and a burst of thunder made both of them jump. The sound of pelting rain, or maybe it was more hail, rattled around the kitchen. She heard the wind wailing over it. She could never have imagined being in such a strange situation as she was right then. It seemed to her things were, as Alice said, getting curiouser and curiouser. She swallowed a tight bunch of laughter in the back of her throat. Then she wrapped her arms as far around herself as she could in an effort to comfort herself.

It was well over an hour before Charles and Scooter came rushing into the kitchen, both of them wearing slate-gray rain slickers still dripping with water. Isabel felt a great sense of relief at the sight

75

of them. The more people around her, the better she felt. However, Charles had a shadowy look on his face she didn't like. She saw his lips twitch for a moment as if they wanted to talk, but couldn't.

Darla looked up at him, obviously disturbed. "Okay, Charles, what is it?" she barked nervously. "What has gone wrong?"

Charles slipped off his rain slicker and hung it on one of several metal pegs on the kitchen wall. He shook his head, spewing rainwater over the dark wood floor. "Some bad news, I'm afraid," he said. "We've been sabotaged! Someone blew our main generator into a thousand pieces!"

"The hell you say!" Darla almost shouted. "The labs! Oh my God!"

Charles put his hand on her shoulder to settle her down. "Don't panic. The labs are fine Darla. We've managed to get one backup generator humming like a beehive. Everything in the underground is okay."

Isabel saw Darla give a nod of relief and a rare smile. Her soybeans were safe. And yet, oddly enough, she didn't seem terrified by someone having done something as violent as trying to blow the place up. The possibility of the whole stone edifice coming down on top of them made Isabel's heart race.

Scooter plopped himself down next to Isabel, smelling like fresh rainwater. Charles sat down at the table on the other side of her and gave her a faint smile. She watched him as he turned away, leaned over, and ruffled his hair with his fingers. Silver beads of leftover rainwater scattered out over the dark floor. Darla jumped up and went to the little cupboard at the end of the kitchen. She came back with two raggedy towels and handed them to the two men.

"It is already too damp in here. So towel off before you drip more," Darla insisted.

"Thanks," Charles said, rubbing his head with the towel. "Good thing the kitchen is nice and warm. It's like an Artic tempest out there."

"Wow, lunch!" Scooter said. "Thanks, ladies. I'm starved." He dove into the tray of sandwiches and helped himself to two of them.

Isabel wondered how on earth Scooter could be so anxious for lunch, after all the things that were happening. Obviously, these types of things rolled right off him, like the rainwater.

"Okay, Charles, the lights are not on here. What is the problem?" Darla asked.

"Not to worry. As I said, the one backup generator is taking care of all the labs. We're not using the other backup because we don't want to run out of fuel before we are able to get some help in here. As a result, no lights topside, and of course, no elevator."

"What about the wind turbines?" Darla asked.

"Both are working, and adding to the backup generator's efforts."

Isabel watched as Charles helped himself to one of the sandwiches and poured some coffee into his cup. She then took half of a sandwich for herself and began to nibble on it. She was amazed at how good the baloney and cheese tasted after all the events of the day. Before she realized it, she had finished the sandwich and she timidly reached for another half.

"What about Travis and Danny?" Darla asked. "They have not come up yet. "Are you positive we cannot get the elevator working?"

"Positive. It's a big power drainer. We need all the power going to the labs. After I eat and change I'll go down and check on the two of them. They've both got cots down there. I'll bring them some sandwiches and a thermos of coffee."

"Good idea. They might not make it up those stone stairs," Darla said. "No one's sure if Danny is even down there."

"You said sabotaged. How was the generator blown up?" Isabel asked quietly.

Charles looked at her, his eyes tired and worried looking. "Some kind of homemade explosives, from the look of it. Plenty strong. Possibly remotely controlled, or very long fuses. I'm afraid it took out our TV Dish too. Can't really check everything out until this storm abates."

"Who would go to the trouble of blowing up your generator? And why?" Isabel asked.

"There are a lot of nuts out there who read about us and other experimental places in magazines and science journals. We've got a number of protest groups against the genetic altering of foods. However, as far as I know, they never blew up anything before. Here they just painted graffiti on the stone walls, dumped garbage on the porch, things like that." Charles took a bite of his sandwich, looking thoughtful as he chewed, and then said, "As soon as the roads clear, Bertrand will get us a new generator. They will have a police investigation, to see if the idiots left any evidence. So relax. This situation is fixable."

"We should have security cameras around the place," Darla grumbled. "Then we would know who did it."

"I tried to talk Bertrand into it but they didn't want to spend the money," Charles said with a shrug. "Besides, they would take more of our power."

Darla gave a dry laugh, and then said in a loud voice, "Yes, well now they have to replace an expensive generator someone blew! And without a camera image, we cannot get the fuckers put in jail!" She jumped up, went to the stove, and started making a fresh pot of coffee.

The look of Darla's cheeks made Isabel feel uncomfortable. The woman's blood was burning bright once again. Something was wrong with Darla. Not just autism. But she couldn't think of what it could be. A sudden blast of rain-filled wind echoed around all the stone bones of Hagan Poole's old Castillo Grande. Isabel picked up her coffee cup and since it had cooled enough, she sipped at the bitter brew. She tried to keep her mind functioning, not scattering. But at the moment, her brain felt bleached and was missing the ingredients necessary for comprehending her situation.

She turned her attention to Charles who had finished wolfing down three sandwiches and two cups of coffee. Isabel watched in amazement. Jorge had always been a picky eater, never appearing to enjoy food. It was as if he hated having to spend time chewing and swallowing food because it took time away from his damn gene splicing. She looked over at Scooter and saw he was devouring the better part of his third sandwich. She gave a little unexpected giggle. Everyone at the table looked at her.

She felt her face flush. "Oh, sorry," she said. I'm just so relieved to hear things are okay for now. I think I'm a little giddy. This has not been in any way, shape, or form, my usual day." To her relief, they smiled, nodded, and went back to chatting with each other. It gave her a pleasant sensation, a sort of cozy companionship. Something she had never had much of. Especially since Jorge had been in Japan most of the time during their marriage.

"Anyone want another sandwich?" Charles asked. No one spoke up, so he got up from his place at the table and began to wrap the remaining sandwiches.

Darla filled two thermoses with coffee, and then sat back down at the table. She looked idly around the kitchen, her eyes not seeming to stop and focus on anything.

"Okay then, I'll head underground," Charles said, "and make sure those two duffers are okay down there," He stashed the sandwiches and coffee into a large wicker basket with soft leather handles and hoisted them over his shoulder. "I'll bring back a ton of Travis' corn for dinner."

Scooter gave him a mock round of applause. Then Darla got up and walked over to Charles. "Thank you for saving my soy beans," she said patting him firmly on his cheek. "My, my, I see you forgot to shave again this morning?"

Charles blanched but smiled. "See you guys later. Take care of our visitor here."

Then he turned quickly and made his way out of the kitchen.

Isabel sat there wondering about the pat on the cheek Darla had given Charles. She didn't seem much like a pat-someone-on-the cheek kind of person. Maybe it was just her awkward way to thank him for getting a generator going. She guessed Darla was about the same age as Charles. However, she found it difficult to imagine a romance between them since Charles was just a shade shy of being extremely handsome, while Darla was just a shade shy of being homely. What a terrible thing to think about someone, she told

79

herself! Nevertheless, she couldn't help it. She gave her head a shake, and began helping Darla clear the table.

Darla wiped off the kitchen counter with a sponge, looked over at Isabel and said, "Listen, I am going to venture down to my lab again and check out everything. You will be fine with Scooter here."

"Are those little Christmas lights you mentioned, still on? The ones all along the stone steps?" Isabel asked.

"Yes, thank God. Otherwise, we would be pretty much trapped in our labs."

Isabel yawned and then said, "Would either of you mind if I went to my room and took a short nap? With all this stuff happening . . . well, I'm feeling really drained. You can get me up anytime if you need my help with something." She gave them a nervous smile, hoping they would buy her faked sleepiness.

Darla gave her a curt nod. "Yes. Good idea."

"Thanks." Isabel yawned again. "I really am sleepy."

"Happy dreams, Sweetcheeks." Scooter said. "Rain or shine, or no electricity, dinner is usually about six. Great corn tonight. With salt and butter." He looked back and forth at the two of them. "I guess I'm chef tonight then, aren't I?"

"Yes indeed," Darla said.

"Keep some candles handy," Scooter reminded Isabel. "In case it's sundown before you wake up."

Isabel blanched at the word Sweetcheeks, but realized it was just his way. She tried not to let it bother her. "I have some candles in my room," she said. "I'll only nap a short while."

"Good," Scooter said, grinning at her. "Too bad you don't have an oil lamp."

"The candles will work fine," Darla said as she walked to the refrigerator. She opened it and took out the remaining few pieces of bologna. "You go take your nap. Scooter will hold down the kitchen."

"Are you taking a little snack with you?" Isabel asked, referring to the bologna slices.

"No, no. My stray kitties usually stay in the underground during bad weather. I try to feed them now and then, when they cannot be outside hunting for food. Since I have to use the old stairs anyway, it is a good time to do it. Then I will check out my lab." She gave Isabel a rigid little Queen's wave of her hand, and quickly made her way out of the kitchen.

Isabel got up and walked to the kitchen doorway and watched which way Darla had turned. If she was careful, maybe she could find where the old steps were located. Jorge said they were down a long hallway. But there were so many long hallways, and she didn't want to just guess which one. Following Darla seemed her best bet.

"Okay then, I'm off for a little nap," she told Scooter as she made her way out the door, and then turned in the direction she'd seen Darla go. She made her way, staying in the shadows and found herself at the top of the steep stone Steps. She saw a faint image of Darla far below, then a moment later, she disappeared. At least now, she knew how to find the stairs. She wondered if she could make her way down right then, and possibly locate Jorge's stuff, and get it over with. But what if she ran into Charles or Darla when they were heading back up? Then again, if she was careful, and fast, maybe it would work. It might be her only opportunity. Yes, she decided, and then turned on her heels, and quickly felt her way in the darkness to her bedroom in order to get her jacket since Darla complained about the cold in the stone stairway.

The bedroom was almost twilight dark because of the storm. She went to the window which was slightly open, but no rain appeared to be blowing in. The air felt fresh and smelled pine sweet. How long, she wondered, would it be before she could get out of this strange place and home to her cozy condo? A disturbing thought hit her. Was Jorge planning to get back inside through her window? In this storm? If so, when? And where was he now? She shook the thoughts away.

Looking at the bed she saw the cranberry coverlet was still pulled back from when she had gotten up that morning. It looked so dang inviting. Concerned with the thought of getting caught on the stairs, she told herself she should wait for a better time. If it didn't come, then she'd forget about it. She owed Jorge nothing. In fact, it was

81

Dorothy McMillan

Jorge who owed her. Big time! Not the least of which was for making her struggle with his bogus death for the past four years.

She looked at the bed again, then slipped off her shoes, took off her jeans, pulled back the covers on the bed, and slid in. The luxurious feel of the sheets, all silky and soothing, calmed her. She didn't even mind the grotesque carved faces peering down at her from the ceiling. She risked their wrath by sticking out her tongue at them.

For a few minutes, she tried to think about where on earth Jorge might have gone. As angry as she was with him, she hoped he wasn't out in the storm, or sitting in his car alongside the road where the trees went down. Once the road was open, all she wanted to do was get in her car and drive back to her condo. The holidays would soon be over and it would be back to teaching. That was all she needed in her life. Her students. Nothing more. Nothing less. Especially, not Jorge!

With these thoughts tumbling around in her head, sleep finally overtook her, whisking her off to a sweet dry place with the scent of antique roses, and where she was certain she could hear the sound of the surf somewhere close by.

82

Chapter Seven

Charles felt the muscles in his legs begin to burn as he climbed back up the old stone steps carrying a heavy gunnysack of corn. "Damn that hunchback Poole!" he growled. As if the leg burning wasn't bad enough, his mind was a storm of apprehension. Danny had not been in his lab when he'd arrived with the sandwiches and coffee. Where the hell did he disappear to? He hadn't been with Travis in his lab, and Joe's lab was double padlocked. There was nothing below Joe's unit but unfinished basements and hollow cavern areas. Darla had checked her lab for him earlier. Could Danny have come topside without anyone having seen him? He was one to take a nap most every day. However, he almost always used the cot in his lab.

Charles groaned as he finally made it up the last of the stone steps, ready to ream Danny out once he found him. He should go to Danny's bedroom upstairs first; however his legs were too tired to attempt it now. He hoped there would be some coffee left in the kitchen. A rest and some caffeine would help. He'd become a caffeine fiend since he'd been working in the big old castle.

An empty kitchen greeted him, but the coffee pot was still hot and full. He dumped the gunnysack of corn he'd gathered from his lab on the sink. He grabbed a mug and filled it with coffee, then sat down at the table. "Damn it Danny!" he growled aloud, hearing his words crawl around the walls of the large kitchen.

"What about damn Danny?" Darla said appearing in the kitchen doorway.

Charles looked up. "So, how did you make out in your lab, Darla,"

"Oh, yes, well . . . I started to go down . . . but changed my mind. Those damn steps. And I am a little off my feed today," she said hesitantly. "So what did Danny say to piss you off?"

"It's what he didn't say!" Charles said. "He wasn't in his lab!"

He took a long sip of his coffee. "Travis, however, was busy working, grateful to have the lights on. He appreciated the food and coffee."

Darla frowned, her eyebrows seriously together. "Danny is not topside as far as I know."

Charles let out a long sigh. "I'll go up and check his room. Everything was working okay in his lab."

"You would think if he came up right after the lights went out, he would have tried to find one of us."

"You'd think so, wouldn't you?" Charles agreed. Looking over, he noticed an unusual expression on Darla's face.

"What is it, Darla?" he asked.

"What?"

"Something is bugging you. I can always tell. What's up?"

Darla sat quiet for a few moments then she said, "It is the Isabel woman."

Charles was puzzled. "What about her?"

Darla's frown got tighter. "I do not know exactly. She is rather genial, but there is something else, something . . . ."

Charles nodded. "Something she's hiding maybe?"

"Ah yes, that may be it. Why would she come here in this storm just to meet an old friend? She is not a daring type of person. If anything, she is uneasy about being here."

"And, the person who sent her here happens to be our troublesome Joe," Charles added. "According to Isabel, they did have a short relationship at one time."

Darla leaned her chair back, her eyes squinting as if she was trying to decide something. "I cannot match her and Joe together. After all, she just teaches high school. Joe has a doctorate. A true genius you know. It is not a match."

Charles got up from the table and looked at Darla. She was blinking her eyes rapidly, and her mouth was thrust forward, almost a pout. Something more was certainly bothering her, but he decided not to ask again. There were too many other things to worry about. Charles turned and made his way toward the kitchen door. Then he turned back, puzzled. "Where the heck is Isabel? And Scooter?"

"Scooter went out to check on the road block again. Isabel went to take a nap. She seemed . . . tense." Darla pursed her lips and frowned. "Too tense for my taste."

Charles nodded. "Okay. Keep an eye on her. I'm going to go upstairs and see if Danny is in his bedroom. He may have taken a nap there. But he should have been down some time ago. It's late, and it's so damn dark outside because of the storm, it seems almost like late night." He quickly left the room and went to the stone stairs that led to the second floor.

"Damn you, Poole, for making these steps so fucking steep," he grumbled. "How the hell did you ever manage them? It's probably what killed you so soon after you moved in."

He made his way up the elongated steps to the second floor, his legs still burning fiercely from climbing up from the underground. As he climbed, he ran over all the events of the day as well as those of last night. His mind tried to make sense out of everything, but it couldn't. The only thing he knew was he had to be extremely careful. Fighting a leaden sensation in the pit of his stomach, he prayed that it wasn't already too late for him to uncover the problem for which Bertrand was depending on him to do.

Isabel woke from her nap with a sudden start wondering where on earth she was. Then her memory came back, slowly like a bank of fog allowing the sun to shine through it. She heard a few creaking sounds and wondered if someone was in her room. She lay still and moved her eyes, searching as much of the room as possible. Not a sign of anyone there. She gave a small sigh. The tail end of a dream, she reasoned. Or else it was the castle flexing its ancient bones a little. The room was darker than she thought it would be when she woke up. Looking up she saw the grotesque carved faces leering down at her. She stuck out her tongue at them again, all of a sudden feeling rebellious and feisty.

"I mock you," she called up at the faces. "Do your worst!"

Dorothy McMillan

She sat up in bed and thought about her situation. Then she looked at her watch. It was five p.m. so there was still a little time before dinner to try going down the stone stairs to see if there was any possible way she locate Jorge's flash drive. She wanted to get it over with. It was huge relief to her, that she felt nothing for him. No love left. He had sucked away all the love she'd once felt. He might be alive, but at this point, he still seemed dead to her.

She climbed out of the bed, went to the bathroom, splashed water on her face, ran her fingers through her short hair, and then made her way out into the hallway. Right now was as good as any time to give the stone steps a try. If she hurried, she could get back before dinner was ready. She just prayed she would not meet anyone coming up the old stairs. If that should happen, she would just say she was exploring the place. She pulled on her jacket and made her way to where she'd seen Darla go earlier. She quickly found the stairs again. There they were yawning right in front of her, at least ten feet wide, like a giant mouth. Tiny pale white bulbs, strung all along the stone walls, provided barely enough light. She remembered someone mentioning to her that they were battery powered. It was then she realized she probably should have taken one of the flashlights from the kitchen, or at least a candle.

"Shoot!" she hissed, furious at herself. Well then, the bulbs on the stone walls would have to do. She took one step down the stairs, surprised at how deep the rise was. The landing behind her almost reached the back of her knees. "Holy moley!" she said aloud. Her voice echoed off the granite walls despite their coating of gray-green fungus. She had to be quiet. She began to understand why everyone complained about the stairs. She took another step and reluctantly put her hand on the wall to her left, in order to balance herself. When she removed it some of the fungus clung to her fingers. She wiped it off on her jacket.

She counted each step. When she reached nineteen, she began to have doubts about what she was doing. Still, the strong part of her rebelled at stopping. This might be the only way she could get rid of Jorge, and go back to her comfortable and safe life. A slight rush of

86

adrenaline urged her on. In several places, she reached a narrow landing flanked on one side with steel doors set into the huge stone walls. Each was marked with the letter of the lab it led to. She remembered that when the elevator wasn't working, these doors were the only way in or out of each lab.

When she came to the door marked Lab D, Jorge's lab, she found a metal bar across it, held tightly in place by two steel padlocks. It was like one she'd seen on the cupboard doors in Darla's Unit. Someone was sure anxious to keep people out of there.

No matter, she would give Jorge's request one chance and if she couldn't locate his flash drive, she would stop there, and to heck with him. She sat down on one of the steps to rest for a few minute. Jorge's lab was the last one. She knew she would now have to look a little further down for the little cavern where he said he'd hidden his flash drive. It was hard enough climbing down, but she couldn't imagine how difficult it would be going back up. If she didn't come to the small cavern he'd described quickly, she would give the whole damn thing up.

After a few minutes she got to her feet again, groaning, and continued with her descent. Her legs began to ache fiercely. She wished she had done more physical exercising the past few years. She spent most of her free time reading and grading her students work. She put both hands on the wall to steady herself. The wall felt slimy and damp and she heard strange little scurrying sounds all around her. It gave her tiny goose bumps down her back. She was glad the light wasn't any brighter because she didn't want to see what was scurrying so close around her. A dozen more steps, she told herself, and if she didn't see an opening then she was going to turn back. Nothing in the world was worth doing this!

Exhaustion hit her, and just as she was about to turn and start back, her hand suddenly found an open area. It appeared to be an opening of about eight or nine feet wide. She couldn't tell how deep it was. She could only see into it about three feet. Past that, it was dead black. The dim light from the little bulbs along the stairs didn't reach any further. Hopefully, this was the cavern Jorge had told her about.

"Dummy," she said to herself. "Why did I have to forget a candle or flashlight?" It took her several minutes before she was able to get up enough courage to force herself to step inside the opening. Finally, when she had inched only several feet inside, total blackness swallowed her.

Charles lumbered into the kitchen, thankful Darla was still there, along with Scooter, both of them sitting at the large table drinking more coffee. "Have you seen him?" he roared. "He's not upstairs."

"You mean Danny?" Scooter said.

"Of course I mean Danny."

"Neither of us has seen him," Darla said shaking her head. "And I checked for Isabel, and she is not in her room."

Charles sat down heavily on one of the kitchen chairs. "Great! We're playing hide and seek now. Damn it!"

"Well, I told you to send her home!" Darla gave him a sour look.

"Yes, I know it, Darla, so knock it off! Please," Charles said.

"The road is still heavily blocked, so neither of them has gotten out of here," Scooter said. "The rain's slowed a little, which is good."

Darla shrugged and gave him one of her pinched frowns. "Well, I certainly cannot imagine where either of them might be."

"At least I got the short-wave radio up and running on a battery," Scooter said, getting up from his place at the table and taking his coffee mug to the sink. He looked over at Charles. "Travis was able to contact Bertrand so they know our situation. I let authorities in Red Box know, and also touched bases with the Los Angeles police and the sheriffs. Now that the rain has slowed a little they are getting a crew ready to help clear the road. Hopefully by early morning".

"Good going," Charles said. "Now if you can just find Danny and Isabel, I'll be less panicked."

"They are here somewhere," Darla said in a clipped voice.

"We also know someone else is here, or was here," Charles reminded them.

"Who?" Darla said looking startled. "Who else!" Her voice was sharp edged.

"You mean the idiot, or idiots who blew up our main generator," Scooter said as he came back and sat down at the table. "Listen, I did something else, Charles. With the short-wave setup, I got some information I don't think you'll like."

Charles gave him a puzzled look. "Great, something more I don't like!"

"I radioed a friend and asked him to get information for me. He ran a background check on our Isabel Warren. And guess what I found out."

Charles didn't answer. He just gave Scooter a more puzzled look.

"Isabel Warren is the widow of Jorge Allen Warren."

It took a minute for Charles to realize Scooter was talking about a well-known genetic biologist. He remembered hearing the news a few years ago, about the man's terrible accident in Japan. A great loss, everyone said. Charles had never met him, or even seen a photo of him, but all the science digests had featured his feats in genetically altering a variety of crops. He wasn't a fan of the guy's work however, as he felt his ambition far surpassed his caution.

"This is for certain?" Charles asked.

"Yes Charles, it's for certain," Scooter said, nodding.

"I knew there was something about Isabel that bothered me," Darla snapped.

Charles was silent for a few moments. Isabel *had* told him she was a widow. Moreover, it was possible she'd hooked up with Joe, a former friend, because he was a genetic biologist so she felt comfortable with him. He had mixed feelings. It could all be a coincidence. Or maybe there was some connection to it and his search for the worrisome problems that Bertrand wanted him to ferret out. He had no idea, and thinking about it he found himself growing more and more frustrated.

"We have to find Isabel and see what she has to say for herself," Darla suddenly remarked.

Charles slammed his hand down on the table. "Darla, please go and check out every nook and cranny on this floor. Scooter, you look around upstairs, and for God's sake find the two of them! They have to be here someplace. They wouldn't have walked out in this weather."

"Not in any weather," Darla said with bit of an animal snarl.

All three of them got up from the table.

"I'll go to the underground again and check my own lab," Charles said. "Maybe Danny's there. I loaned him a key once. Can't remember why. When he didn't find me there, maybe he took over my cot." Charles let out a groan, still feeling the burn in his legs from all the stair climbing.

Scooter gave a longing look at the stove. "Couldn't we cook the corn first? I'm starving."

Charles gave him a grumpy look. "My God! You sound like Danny! We'll eat as soon as we find Danny and Isabel."

Scooter shoved his hands into the pockets of his short pants and started toward the kitchen door.

"I will put some food together for dinner as soon as I get this floor checked out again for Danny and Isabel," said Darla. "Even though today is Scooter's day to do it."

Scooter smiled back at her over his shoulder. "Thanks, darlyn. We can always count on you."

Darla scowled at him. Shook her head, and left the room.

After both Scooter and Darla had left, Charles paced back and forth across the tiled kitchen floor. The last thing he wanted to do was to head underground again and then have to climb back up. If only the elevator was working. It had never been connected to the backup generator. Suddenly a thought hit him. What if Danny was trapped in the elevator? What if he decided to come topside in the elevator, and then the power went out? Christ! Why had no one thought about such a possibility? With the thought burning in his head, he moved out of the kitchen and raced toward the elevator as fast as he could. What a relief it would be if he found Danny napping on the elevator floor. A sudden thought caused him to stop. Without electricity, would his card open the elevator door? If not, would he be able to force it open? Damn! He wasn't sure. However, no matter what, he had to find Danny!

90

The Gray Green Underground

It had taken Isabel several minutes before she forced herself to step inside the cavern she'd found. The awful green fungus covered all the walls near the entrance. Did Jorge say the loose stone was on the right wall, or the left? It was supposed to be about three feet up from the stone floor. The dim light from the little bulbs by the steps reached three feet into the cavern. Beyond that, the cavern was death black.

Her hands trembling, she blindly began to feel her way along the left side wall, moving further into the cavern darkness. Each time she touched the wall, some of the fungus squeezed itself between her fingers like icy toothpaste. The underground area should have been dry, not so damp. Darla may have been right about the tunnel to the outside. Something was not right.

As she moved further into the cavern, she felt dozens of slimy little critters begin to wriggle over her hands when she touched the stone wall. What the hell were those? It was too dark to see, but the feel of them crawling all over the skin of her hands gave her a shudder so hard it caused her to bite her tongue.

"Ouch!" she yelled. Her mouth tasted salty and she spit out what she knew had to be blood. "Oh, great!" she growled, seriously regretting her decision to be there. With great effort, she moved on despite the creepy sensation of the fungus, and the scuttling of unseen critters. Please God, don't let them bite me, she said silently. They were, she reasoned, probably more afraid of her than she was of them. After all, it was possible they had never encountered a human before. Of course, she had never experienced having slimy little crawly things exploring her hands.

She continued to keep her fingers over the lower part of the wall, hoping to find a loose stone. She made her way all around the interior of the cavern, stopping now and then to shake the fungus and the crawly things off her hands. As she came to where she was certain she was near the entrance of the cavern she feared that what she was searching for was not there after all. Maybe Jorge had given

91

her the wrong directions. Or maybe she was in the wrong cavern.

She fought the urge to quit and get back to her room as fast as the stone steps would allow her. But as discouraged as she was, she was not yet willing to give up. The thick fungus still clung to her skin, and some of it was on her clothing as well. She hoped to heaven she could clean it off quickly when she got topside so no one would notice where she'd been.

She ran her hands over the last foot of the wall. At about three feet from the stone floor, the fingers of her right hand suddenly touched a stone that wobbled slightly. She used both hands to explore the area, and there it was! Finally! A loose stone! "Thank you, God," she whispered, praying she had actually found it.

The area was so close to the opening of the cavern the small stair lights helped her to see what she was doing. She wiggled and tugged at the loose stone and finally managed to pull it out, and then carefully set it down on the stone floor. With apprehension, she slowly slid her hand inside the small opening. Her fingers touched something which she slowly loosened from its hiding place. Once she had it in her hand, she found it was a small rectangular piece made of plastic and metal, a little over two inches long. She reached back into the hole but found nothing else.

She sat back on her heels and closed her eyes and let herself relax slightly. Opening them again she looked at the object in her hand. She had managed to find the flash drive that should hold Jorge's specs for God knows what. For improved corn, or some other vegetables? If not, then what the hell was he up to with all his secretiveness? She leaned down and picked up the loose stone and slid it back into the hole, and gave a sigh of relief.

Stepping out of the cavern, she sat down on a stone step, under one of the little lights on the stone wall. She set the small item on her lap. Did it simply hold the information on the making of Jorge's improved corn, or was it as Charles feared, something much more dangerous, or maybe illegal?

Why would Jorge be working on something hazardous? She had very little knowledge about what his work entailed. The only thing left for her was to hide the flash drive until the road opened, and then get the hell out of there. Hopefully Jorge would get to her and pick it up. Then she could wash her hands of the whole damn thing!

She stood up and realized she had not even thought about how she was going to hide the drive once she found it. She decided the only place it could go was into one of her pants pockets. She tried to scrape off as much of the fungus from her hands and the flash drive as possible, along with a few errant critters. Then slowly and carefully she slid it into a front pocket a far down as she could, hoping it didn't make any bulge. She looked up at the daunting stairs she had to climb in order to get back to the top. They seemed to reach miles above her. "One step at a time," she told herself. "Just take it one step at a time."

As she was about to take the first step, she heard a loud grating sound behind her. She turned to see what it was. As she did something heavy hit her head with a brutal, painful blow and left her reeling. A sickening dizziness rushed over her, and she felt herself falling, tumbling, spiraling, to where she did not know. She tried to reach out and grasp something to gain her balance. Her arms flailed about but were unable to find anything solid. She let out a scream that danced crazily around her. Then her mind went numb, and a suffocating darkness wrapped around her, choking the air from her lungs.

Isabel had no idea how long it had been since she fell. She tried to move but pain spread across her like a spiked metal blanket. Where was she? She blinked her eyes, trying to rid herself of the licorice blackness surrounding her. She took in a trembling breath; the air was icy and raw. She tried to move again and realized she was lying on something rough and bumpy. She ran her fingers over it and felt certain it was a stone floor inside one of the underground caverns. She had apparently hit her head on something, probably the stone wall, and had taken a terrible fall. Her head throbbed. Her hand went to her head and she found a lump the size of a plum under her hair on the left side.

"Ouch!" she yelped. "Damn it!"

She felt several places on her body which were extremely painful to the touch. She tried to sit up to see where the stairs were, but no light was visible anywhere. Maybe the bump and the fall had done something to her eyesight. That thought ran a thunderbolt of alarm through her.

She could not spot any glow from the little white bulbs lining the wall next to the stairs. An endless stretch of nothingness surrounded her. She finally managed to sit up, pain gnawing at her. With her hands, she checked her legs. Nothing felt broken. However, what she did find was one leg of her pants torn open at the knee, and the skin there was raw. One of her shoes was off, and the foot without it felt swollen. "Dear God," she said in a whisper. "I really messed myself up!" How the hell could she find her way out of there? If she was inside one of the caverns, then the first thing she needed to do was to find the stone steps.

When Charles arrived back in the kitchen he found Darla was absent, but she had lit candles against the growing dark, put a bottle of beer at each place on the table, shucked some corn, and had a pot of water on the stove. However, even with a very low flame, almost all of the water had boiled away so he turned off the flame and refilled the pot before adding the corn, and put it back on the stove.

"Oh, you are back!" Darla said as she rushed into the room. "I put some beer out for everyone," she said, slightly breathless. "It has been a hell of day. I believe we need to un-tense ourselves."

"I noticed," Charles said. "By the way, I refilled the pot. Not much water left. Were you distracted by something? "

"Oh, Sorry," she said. "I had a rather urgent call from Mother Nature. Did you find Danny?"

"Nope. I thought maybe he was trapped in the elevator. But, like an idiot, I forgot that it might have been on a different level when the power went out, which it was. I pried the doors open a few inches and hollered down the shaft, which echoed all over the place. If

Danny was anywhere in the elevator area, he didn't holler back.

"Such a nuisance," Darla grumbled.

"So I decided to try his lab again. "Did you locate Isabel?" Charles asked. "And where's Scooter?"

"Her room's empty. Danny's too. Scooter went to shower and change clothes." Darla motioned for him to sit down.

Charles plopped down wearily at the table and opened a beer. "Ah, *Dos Equis* dark. Good! I'm in great need." He looked up at the kitchen windows where rain was pelting them again. "To top things off, the storm seems to be getting worse again."

"Don't we have any meat to go with the corn?" he asked.

"You had it at lunch. The last of the baloney," Darla growled, and turned the flame down on the stove and let the corn boil gently. "So, Charles, what was it that took you so long?"

"After the elevator check, I started to go on down to Joe's unit, wanting to take a look at it. Bertrand is concerned about all of Joe's unauthorized equipment. But I changed my mind not far down. Those damn god-awful stone stairs. I'll head back down after I eat and rest."

"I just do not see why they should be concerned about any of Joe's equipment." Darla said frowning.

Charles shrugged. He knew better than to go too far with his mention of a problem. But he did want to get some reactions from those he mentioned a few things to. "Just safety concerns, as far as I know."

Darla pursed her lips for a few moments, then relaxed and asked, "So where do you think little miss curious has disappeared to?" Darla asked.

"Miss Curious?"

"She has asked a lot of questions about this place, would you not agree?"

Charles sighed, took a long swallow of his cold beer, loving the slight bite of it, and shook his head. "I'll be darned if I know where she went. She should have known better than to wander around here. The place is so huge we could have several dozen people here and

95

not be able to find any of them."

"Well, you remember what Scooter discovered about her." Darla sat down across from Charles.

"It wasn't exactly a secret. She told me right off she was a widow."

"But she forgot to mention her husband was a well-known scientist."

"Maybe she didn't think it was important. She didn't work with him at all. Probably knew very little about what he was working on."

Darla was silent, her face reflecting the fact her mind was suddenly racing at top speed, apparently trying to understand the situation. Charles had seen that look on her face a number of occasions during the time he'd worked with her. A curious, unpredictable personality. Whenever things got stressful, she would often take off at times and go jogging through the pines for an hour or so. Always came back looking bedraggled, but more relaxed. He sized her up as one of those brilliant scientists who were willing to go bonkers trying to win a Nobel Prize.

Charles wanted to know exactly what her pharmaceutical project was, but even he was not privy to it. Darla had not visited her lab he realized, even though the lights were on in there. She had seemed oddly calm and thoughtful until they talked about Isabel. A little strange. Then again, the entire day had been a little strange. He shrugged off the thought and watched Darla load a large platter with steaming corn. "Do we have to wait for Scooter before we eat?" he asked.

Darla gave him a pinched smile. "Dig in. You brought up plenty." She set the platter of corn down on the table. "Be careful, it's boiling hot!"

Charles reached for an ear of corn, fumbled with it for a few moments because it burned his fingers, and then finally settled it on his plate. "Ouch!" He gave Darla a pained look.

"Men never listen, do you not know." Darla jabbed an ear of corn with a fork, and quickly dropped it on her plate. "Travis will probably show up in a few minutes. So, do you have any more ideas where to look for our other two people?"

Charles shook his head. "Christ! I don't know. The two of them have to be around here somewhere. I'm certain they wouldn't take off outside and try to get through the roadblock." He picked up his corn by the ends and began blowing on it, trying to cool it. The corn grown underground certainly had a much better, sweeter taste than any type of corn grown topside. Travis had done well with it. He felt a moment of pride about his own work. His grapes were premium because he let them grow in the right environment. No bad weather, no bugs. 24 hours of light. Plus good seeds and soil. The moment was spoiled by the fact that he was not a very qualified scientist, and was basically assigned to just uncover something Bertrand was extremely concerned about. They gave him no clues as to what it might be. The grapes were not the important thing. The orders were to look, listen, and discover if anything was going on that shouldn't be.

"It is damn dark outside," Darla said, looking up at the windows. "The storm eased earlier. But listen to it now. It is coming down like a band of drummers. This means we have no idea how long until we get out of here."

"I'm sure Bertrand will get it done ASAP once the storm blows over. They've got too much to lose if we run out of fuel for the one working generator. Two wind turbines alone are not reliable enough keep the labs going."

"What about Joe's engineered corn? Does Bertrand know anything about it?"

Charles frowned at her. "No. Neither do I. That's why we made Joe leave his specs for it here. To give Bertrand a chance to see how successful it is. After all, Bertrand owns a part of any profit Joe may make with it, for providing Joe with everything he needed to engineer it.

"Damn big business! They encourage people like Joe, and then they grab a ton of money from every successful project. Big money for them, but not as much for the person who's genius is responsible for their making the money. Plus they get all the credit!" Darla's face tightened and her narrow cheeks flushed their persimmon color.

Charles gave her a sharp look. "Listen Darla, you and I both know Joe was working on something else . . . something more than just his corn."

"Joe was corn. Just corn." Darla said in a flat tone. "I have no idea what you are talking about,"

"Sure you do. All the equipment he has hidden away. What the hell is he using all that crap for?"

"You did not have the right to go through his lab after he left."

Charles let out a quiet sigh. "Legally, maybe not. Nevertheless, Bertrand no doubt got the bill for the equipment so technically it belongs to them, unless Joe pays them for it."

Darla gave him a scowl. "So he needed some new stuff. So maybe he is going a different way with the corn."

"You know as well as I do that the new equipment has nothing to do with altering corn. You checked it out the same time I did."

"But there was nothing unusual there from what I could see," Darla assured him.

"Okay, okay, okay!" Charles said, grabbing another ear of corn. "Let's forget it for now, and figure out where the heck Danny and Isabel have disappeared to. Danny would never miss a meal unless he was unable to get to it!"

Chapter Eight

Isabel managed to get to her feet. Her knee wasn't so painful now, but her foot gave her a throbbing pain every time she stepped on it. There was still nothing but blackness around her. She moved carefully, feeling ahead with her hands and her good foot until she found a wall.

A sudden thought caused her to take a sharp breath. After her tumble, did she still have Jorge's drive? She forced her hands into the narrow pocket of her pants. Relieved, she found it still there. The feel of it against her fingers suddenly made her realize she could well be stealing from the Bertrand Company. What if it really didn't belong to Jorge like he claimed? What if he was just using her to steal it from Bertrand? If this was what was happening, there was no way she should be a part of it. She would have to give it to Charles, no matter what Jorge said about not trusting him. She didn't trust Jorge either, after the horrible thing he'd done to her by hiding the fact he was still alive.

She began moving in the darkness again, slowly and carefully along the wall. She would find the steps if she just kept following the wall to the opening. Her foot suddenly hit something unexpected on the stone floor and she almost stumbled. She used both hands against the wall in order to steady herself. "What on earth is that!" she cried. She gingerly touched whatever it was with her toe. It didn't move, and it wasn't soft but it wasn't hard either. Could it be one of Darla's cats? She knelt down and reached out a shaking hand, afraid to discover what it was. Would it move when she touched it again? Her fingers shook as she cautiously let them touch it. This time, what she felt was wet wrinkled fabric of some kind. It didn't move. She pressed at it a little, feeling the form underneath the fabric. It was only then she realized what it was that she was touching. It was *a person!*

She froze for a moment wishing she could get up and run, but found herself unable to move. It took her a moment to accept her situation, to accept the fact she was kneeling beside a person lying on the stone floor. Was she or he alive? "Oh my God!" she yelled. "This isn't happening!" Her words came out in a peculiar voice she hardly recognized as being her own.

The body lying on the stone floor didn't say anything. She couldn't hear any breathing. She had to get out of this miserable underground hell, and tell someone. She reached out both hands, which were now trembling violently, and found what felt like an arm. The arm was dead cold even though it had a shirt sleeve around it. She followed the arm with her fingers hoping to find a hand, not a head. She sure as hell didn't want to touch the face of a dead person. She didn't want to touch a hand either, but she finally managed it. It was a man's hand. A hand that felt as if it had been stored in a freezer.

She fumbled trying to find a pulse. When she finally touched the wrist firmly, there was no sign of a pulse. She tried to flex the hand which gave her some resistance. Was it beginning to go into rigor mortis? She choked back a scream, and found it impossible to force herself to reach up and feel the face. She did not want to know what it might look like. She tried getting to her feet, but found it too painful. Instead, she began to crawl, cautiously making her way past the body lying on the stone floor. She moved her hands out in front of her to feel what was ahead. The crawling caused the scraped area of her knee to pulse with pain. Nevertheless, she wasn't ready to stand up.

A few minutes later an odd sensation hit her. She stopped crawling. Something near her was moving. She felt a small wave of cold air. Whatever was moving began to make a peculiar snuffling sound. The sound moved closer to her. If only she could see! In seconds, she sensed its presence was only inches away. Waves of fear washed over her as she began to hear it breathing. Whatever it was blew its warm breath on her which felt like a thick noxious fog. As the dank smell of it invaded her nose, the hairs on the back of her neck stood up like tiny antennae. Wasn't finding a dead body enough, she asked, close to hysteria.

She wanted to scramble backward but suppressed the urge. If it was some kind of animal she was afraid if she moved it might attack. Whatever it was began making strange muffled humming sound. Then something wet licked across her left cheek. A rough hot tongue! Her hand automatically reached out and touched the animal. She wanted to both laugh and cry at the same time. It was a cat, like Darla said sometimes lived in the underground! At least its face felt like a cat, with the exception of two long walrus teeth, and the lack of stand-up pointy ears. She didn't like the long teeth. Their tips felt as sharp as the tip of a metal dart. Praying it wouldn't attack her, she slowly moved her hand over it. It didn't move away but sat almost motionless. Yes, a cat, but a very strange feeling cat. Its flesh was hairless and wrinkled; it felt like cold dead meat to the touch. Maybe it was one of those strange looking Sphinx cats. Darla had mentioned several times that she had some kitties which she fed in the underground. She claimed they came and went through a tunnel that went up to ground level, outside. Certainly, this had to be one of those cats. She wondered if it could be the cat she'd heard screeching outside her window when she had gone to bed the night before. She petted it gently, and it didn't move away. It made a faint rumbling sound coming from its throat, not exactly a purring sound, but similar.

"Sorry, little Kitty. I have to keep moving," she said in a whisper... Cautiously she crawled her way around the cat wondering if it would follow her. Cat or no cat, she had to find the stone stairs, and get herself out of the abysmal darkness. She swallowed hard, and then sucked in some of the icy air surrounding her. She fumbled for several minutes, trying to locate the wall she had been using to find her away around the cavern. She moved slowly, and then with a great sense of relief her outstretched hands found the stone wall. She then began moving as fast as her aching body would allow her. When she reached the end of the wall, she found herself at what had to be the open end of the cavern.

None of the small white lights were lit. Darkness still surrounded her so dense it made her feel as if there was no air, only the blackness. She struggled to breathe for a moment, and then told herself to be sensible. There was plenty of air. Icy air as Darla had insisted she felt on the stairs. The distance she'd crawled made her realize with a surge of alarm she was in a very large cavern. She was positive it was a different cavern from the small one where Jorge had hidden his computer drive. The possibility of how she got there gave her stomach a sickening twist. Maybe she hadn't fallen. Maybe someone had struck her and knocked her out. She touched the large painful lump on her head. Maybe someone thought she was dead and had dumped her in the same cavern with the dead body she'd just found. All these thoughts began spinning around in her head. It was a terrible sensation, stirring up the some of the worst fear she'd ever felt. She pushed against it determined to get topside where everyone else was. She'd be safer there then down in the bowels of this damn stone citadel.

Keeping that thought in mind, she moved her good foot forward, investigating to see if the stairs were outside the cavern opening. Her heartbeat increased radically when her toe touched one edge of a step. A step to take her up, not further down in the underground. All she had to do now was to sit on each step, then hoist herself up one step at a time, backward. She'd never make it all the way up if she did it standing up. Not with the painful foot, and a dozen other places on her body throbbing.

The darkness was so thick she couldn't even see her hands right in front of her. Nothing but endless blackness. Slowly she hoisted herself up one step, and sat on it. She took in a long deep breath and felt her heart rate slow. She struggled to push the thought of the dead man out of her mind as well the possibility of someone having tried to kill her. She concentrated solely on getting topside. She struggled to ignore the pain her body felt. She wondered how many steps there were to the top. She began to count them one by one as she painfully and slowly hoisted herself upward.

The Gray Green Underground

Sitting at the kitchen table, Charles felt a sudden chill. He looked at his watch. It was after six, and dark outside. Rain continued to pelt down making pounding sounds on the stained glass ceiling. Because of the storm, the kitchen seemed clammier than usual. No matter how thick the stone walls were, right then the damp seemed to be seeping through them. It had been hours since he'd seen Danny or Isabel. Both their cars were still parked out front. So where in the hell were they? He fought off a surge of anger. He couldn't think of any reason why the two of them would purposely cause everyone else to worry about their absence.

His anxiety level began to rise as he thought about what could be at stake if things went wrong. The thought of Isabel arriving out of nowhere, then claiming Joe had sent her here, increased his anxiety. He'd been so sure he had everything under control, and that his investigation for Bertrand was going along slowly, but as expected. However, the storm was unexpected, Isabel's arrival was unexpected, and his increasing suspicion that Joe was somehow involved in an unknown project, was unexpected, Now, to top it off, two people had disappeared unexpectedly. The whole situation was like a maze that twisted and turned and he wondered if he would ever find his way out.

A flood of fatigue hit him. All the caffeine he'd had since morning was no longer having any effect on him. The beer had probably slowed him down. Maybe it was a good thing. He needed to feel less agitated about the two missing people. He would check the underground again. Maybe he'd missed something. Danny could have passed out somewhere in his mass of corn. It would be difficult to see him, and he had not gone down every row. He'd just checked the cot in each of the labs to see if Danny was on one of them. He was responsible for the people who worked for Bertrand, as well as visitors. Not formally, but if it wasn't his job, then whose was it?

Once the storm let up, and Bertrand and the police got there, it would be an even bigger mess if Danny and Isabel were still missing. There was no way he was going to allow that to happen.

103

Isabel desperately wanted to rest. For just a few moments at least. However, she feared if she stopped, she would find herself unable to continue moving up the giant stone steps. A throbbing pain invaded her arms; arms she needed to move up each step. Choosing to sit on the steps and hoist herself up backwards made it difficult. Walking up the steps would have taken less energy, but her injured foot sent a pain from her toe to her mid-calf every time she stepped on it. Besides, she had a terrible fear of falling down into the black hole below. She stopped for a moment to feel her wounded knee with her fingertips. She was relieved to find, although she couldn't see it, it seemed to be oozing blood, but it was a slow bleed. At least she wouldn't bleed to death while getting herself out of this ridiculous situation she had managed to get herself into.

She hoisted herself up another step, then another. "Fifty one, fifty two," she said aloud, hearing her voice echo down the steps. Then jolted, she was certain she heard another sound. She stopped moving, hearing the sound coming from the stairs above her. Panic pounded at her heart. The realization she might not have fallen, that someone might have tried to kill her, washed over her again. After all, there was a dead body in a cavern below. Maybe someone was coming to see if she was finished for good. If so, there was nowhere for her to go. Not in the pitch-black darkness surrounding her. She heard the sound again, soft but definite. Were they footsteps? The stones seemed to cushion the sound of shoes. But even so, it did sound like footsteps.

She persuaded her exhausted arms to help lift her up one more step. She looked up behind her, and that's when she saw it! A small bright light! Someone was on the steps above her holding a flashlight! Its light focused on her. Her arms, exhausted of energy, began to tremble. Was she being saved? Or threatened?

No matter which it was she had never been so relieved to see a light. She let out a yell that ricochet off the dark stone walls. The footsteps hurried their movement sounding like a fat cat running across a roof.

"Isabel!" Charles voice came bellowing down to her, and then he was beside her, lifting her up in his arms. "For God's sake, woman! We've been trying to find you for God knows how long! What the hell are you doing down here?"

When he looked down at her she saw her pale face reflecting in his eyes.

"I . . . ," she started but her voice failed.

"Are you hurt?" Charles asked, trying to flash his light on her, which was near to impossible while holding her.

"Ah . . . a little I'm afraid . . . ."

"What are you doing on these damn stone stairs? They're bad enough when they're lit, but treacherous when there's no light anywhere."

Shakes from the deep chill of the underground where she'd been for what seemed forever, took hold of Isabel's body. Charles must have felt it because he held her tighter. He began to climb the stairs. His movements were slow.

"There . . . is ah . . . I mean, you have to know something." Her voice sounded weak to her. "Something terrible!"

"Save your strength!"

"Really terrible! And there was a cat," she said weakly, trying to get her thoughts in order. "A really weird cat with no fur. And . . . something else. There was a—"

"Never mind," he said softly. "We can talk about it later. I need to make sure you're okay."

In the dimness of the flashlight reflecting slightly off dark walls, Isabel looked at Charles face. The sight of it gave her a sense of relief combined with an uncomfortable aura of panic. The two of them combined created a maddening sensation! Maybe Charles shouldn't be trusted, as Jorge had warned her. Still, here he was rescuing her after she had accomplished her possibly illegal actions. She knew now she would have to tell him about what she had done. What she had found. Nevertheless, she wasn't ready to do it yet. First, she had to tell him about the body. The sudden memory of it jabbed an electric spark through her and her body increased its trembling.

105

Dorothy McMillan

"How did you know where I was?" she asked.

"I didn't. I searched everywhere numerous times. Then I wanted to try the labs again because Danny has gone missing too. Good God, you feel so damn cold!" he said. "The temperature on these stairs does feel a hell of a lot colder than it should, and so do you. I hope you are not going into shock," Charles said rather breathless from the climbing. "I'll find Scooter and we'll get you cleaned up and checked over, and then maybe some coffee and a touch of Brandy. Scooter is our medic, when he's not doing all our mechanical stuff. He keeps everything around here running smoothly." He paused. "Except when some idiot decides to blow up our generator." He said with a blaze of anger in his voice.

"Scooter is a . . . medic?" Isabel's body continued to shake.

"Yep. Put himself through college working as an EMT. Comes in handy having him here."

"What . . . is . . . an EMT?"

"Emergency Medical Technician. He even worked as a medic for the filming of several movies, not to mention saving a little girl who had a rattlesnake bite. Versatile guy."

They reached the top of the stairs and Charles quickly carried her down the hall and into the large entry room where as usual, there was a crackling fire in the huge hearth. It pretty much lit up the room, with the aid of a few candles here and there. He set her gently down on one of the leather sofas. Isabel suddenly felt so sleepy she could barely keep her eyes open.

"Isabel," Charles said in a demanding voice, "I do not want you to sleep yet. Did you hit your head?"

Isabel nodded and moved her head so she could show him the large bump. He reached over and felt it.

"Ah, for crying out loud!" he said shaking his head. "Did you pass out?"

Isabel thought about it for a moment. "Yes, I must have because I woke up in a different place than I had been when I fell. At least I think I fell . . . but—"

Charles shook his head again, and chewed on his lip for a

106

minute. She saw an odd look running through his eyes. For a second she was tempted to just reach into the pocket of her jeans and pull out the flash drive she'd gotten for Jorge, and hand it to him. Then maybe he'd let her sleep. However, even doing anything at all sounded like more than she could manage right then.

"I'll find Scooter. He can tell us if you are seriously injured or not and he'll know the best way to treat you. Okay?"

Isabel looked up at him, still struggling to keep her eyes open. She gave him a quick nod.

"I won't be gone long." He took one of her hands which she knew was still icy cold and rubbed it with his strong warm hands. "Gotta get you warmed up," he said. Then obviously seeing the rip in her jeans, he pulled the material away from the blood oozing contusion on her knee. "We need to clean this up. So damn much fungus underground. Scooter will have some meds."

Isabel gave him a pale smile. "Gotta put Humpty Dumpty together again," she mumbled. It took her a few moments before she could remember what it was she needed to tell them. "Oh, wait! Listen to me! There is something terrible down there . . . in the underground!"

Charles gave her a frown. "Well, I know how terrible falling down those steps can be. I did it once when I first started here. I tripped on a loose shoelace." He gave a mirthless chuckle. "But I did it just once, mind you! I learn fast. Now, stay put, stay awake, and get warm. I'll be back in a jiff. I promise."

Before Isabel could say another word, Charles disappeared from view. She was way too exhausted to try and sit up and see where he went. She listened to the crackle of the fire and began to enjoy the delicious warmth of it against her cold skin. She struggled to stay awake and as she did, she felt some sort of inner strength begin to grow. It had always been there, she knew, but she had never really needed it this much before. Well, actually it did come in handy when Jorge died. Or rather when he made her believe he had died. At least it got her through it.

Now she found herself resolute to get herself through whatever

Dorothy McMillan

was happening in this absurd place. It was her own dang fault she was there! She should never have trusted Jorge. She vowed to herself she would never be as stupid again. She would somehow get out of this mess and back to her safe little condo, to her students, and to her right mind. Her body stopped shaking. Good, she told herself. So much for my going into shock.

Isabel wasn't certain if she'd fallen asleep or if Charles had managed to get back to her really fast. It seemed like only seconds before he was standing over her again, this time with Scooter beside him.

"Let's move her to the bedroom," Scooter said. "It will be easier and more comfortable to check her over and make sure she's okay."

"Right," Charles said. "I remember seeing a number of candles in her room."

Scooter leaned down and gave her a smile. 'How you doing, Sweetcheeks?" he said.

"Better," Isabel answered in a quiet but firm voice. "Except there is something you have to know!" she insisted.

"As soon as we get you moved," Charles said, sounding a little too sympathetic.

Isabel sat up; not allowing herself to be distracted by the way her body ached. "No!" she said in a louder voice. "I need to tell you! Right now!"

She saw Charles eyes open wider than usual, as if he was surprised at her shrill insistence. "Yes, well okay then. If it's so damn important."

Scooter gave her a half grin. "I don't think you can be too badly injured, Sweetcheeks. You're right feisty. A good sign."

Isabel swallowed hard, cleared her throat, and then looked up at both of them. "There is a dead body down there!"

The silence lasted uncomfortably long. Both men looked at each other, a baffled expression on their faces, then back at her.

"Did you hear me?" Isabel said, raising her voice. "There's a dead body in the underground!"

"Are you positive?" Charles finally asked.

108

"Yes! After I came to, it was so damn dark! I thought I was still in the small cavern where I had been before I fell. I got to my feet and began feeling my way around the walls trying to find the opening, and I realized it was a different cavern than I'd been in before. It was much larger." She chewed at her lip for a moment, not wanting to hear the words aloud. "As I kept moving, I stumbled on something! A person!" she managed to say. "A dead person! No pulse. No breathing. He was as cold as polar ice, and beginning, I think, to go into rigor. His hand and fingers were pretty stiff."

A moment of silence rolled over the three of them. Isabel used the moment to push away the thought of how the dead body had felt when she touched it. For a fleeting moment she wondered if it was possible she had imagined the body. Maybe it was just some sort of hallucination caused by her banged up head. However, the idea withdrew itself fast. It *was* a dead body, not a hallucination, not a bad dream.

"Isabel, are you positive?" Charles asked.

"I told you! Absolutely!" The strength of her voice surprised her.

The two men exchanged a peculiar expression.

"When I moved away from the body, I almost stumbled on a . . . cat. At least I think it was a cat. A hairless cat!"

"Was it dead too? Scooter asked.

"No. It was making strange noises."

Charles shook his head. "Couldn't be. Nothing's alive below the labs."

"Except maybe the kitties Darla mentions sometimes," Scooter reminded him. "I'll get Isabel to her room" Scooter said firmly. "Then we'll go down below and see about the body. Ask Darla to bring some ice, Charles. And I need the large first aid kit. It's in the left hall cupboard next to the soap and towels."

Isabel looked up and noticed Scooter was wearing a leather bag over his shoulder. Charles nodded okay and took off jogging toward the hallway leading to the kitchen. Scooter reached down and effortlessly scooped her up. He carried her as if she weighed no more than a feather pillow. Several candles in sconces on the wall lighted

109

the hallway and partly into the bedroom when Scooter opened the door. Inside, he set her gently down on the bed, and propped some pillows behind her so she could sit up comfortably. He rummaged through the bedside chest and found two yellowed candles and quickly stuck them into two of the sconces on the wall behind the bed and lit them. The room took on a golden glow. The comfort of the soft bed welcomed her, bringing back at least a small amount of normalcy.

Scooter helped her out of her jacket, and then looked at all the gray-green fungus on her. He got up and made his way to the bathroom. She heard him run some water. He brought out a warm wet wash cloth and a towel. He sat down on the edge of the bed and gently washed off all of the fungus on her hands and arms. Then he picked up her hand and placed his fingers firmly on her wrist. "Ah, a nice normal pulse," he reported. "Pretty damn good for someone who's just gone through what you have. The shock must be wearing off. Good girl." He smiled and set her hand down.

"Yeah, well you should have checked it earlier," Isabel said closing her eyes for a moment, pushing away all the unwanted thoughts.

"I can imagine," he said in a sympathetic tone. He reached for the bag he carried and opened it. "Let's take a BP," he said. "Just to be safe. Your color is good." He wrapped her arm with the blood pressure cuff and pumped it up. "Nice. Perfect, in fact."

He took out a tiny flashlight and checked her eyes. "Equal and reactive," he said.

She gave him a puzzled frown.

"It means the lump on your head hasn't scrambled your brains . . . at least not too much." He gave a throaty laugh. "We'll ice the bump and it should be okay by tomorrow. I just want you to stay awake for a while so I can keep checking." He began feeling first one of her arms, and then another, gave her a shrug and a grin, and started on her right leg. "Don't worry, Isabel, I've had some medical training. I had planned on being a doctor. In fact, I was in medical school for some time. But . . . well, circumstances . . . mostly

110

money." He was silent for a few moments before saying, "I wasn't able to finish. So, I took a different direction."

Isabel thought it was a little odd Charles had mentioned Scooter's EMT training, but hadn't mentioned his desire to be a doctor.

"Anything really painful?" he asked her.

Isabel let out a little breath she didn't know she had been holding. "I'm kinda bruised all over, but my right foot really hurts, and my knee too. Feels like there's no skin left on it."

Scooter tugged away the torn material from the edges of her raw knee. He gave her a kindly faux wince. "Looks mighty uncomfortable. We'll clean it up, put on some antibacterial stuff, and bandage it as soon as Charles gets back with the first aid kit. I don't have much of those things in my medical bag." He moved down to the edge of the bed and checked her injured foot. "I'll wrap it and try to get your shoe back on to help minimize the swelling."

Isabel leaned forward a little and saw all of her toes and part of her one foot was swollen and stained purple mixed with swirls of magenta. Colorful, but a little horrifying. "Oh my God!" she said looking at it. "Is it broken?"

Scooter gave a shake of his head. "Can't tell for sure without an X-ray. But just being swollen doesn't mean bones are fractured. I'll put on a pressure wrap and your shoe, and give you some pain meds a little later."

"Why later?" she asked as he gently laid her foot back on the bed. "It hurts now!"

He laughed softly. "Okay then."

"Anything else hurting?" he asked. "Is your skin broken anywhere else? We don't want you to get an infection."

"Everything hurts, but I don't think there are any more wounds. My fingers are a little raw, but don't seem to be bleeding."

Scooter put his equipment back in his bag, took out a little white bottle, and poured out two small pills. "Well then, except for the ouches, you seem to be in pretty good shape. You've earned a couple of pain killers." He handed her the pills and then got up from the bed

111

and went to the bedroom door. He leaned out and yelled, "Charles! Where the hell is the first aid kit?"

Isabel heard Charles voice came echoing from the hallway. Hearing it she wondered if now was the time to tell him about what Jorge had asked her to do. Then she could hand him the flash drive, and apologize for having retrieved it. The idea of having to do it made her newfound courage retreat some. Maybe it wasn't the best time. First, they needed to go underground to find the dead body. Things were in such a jumble. If she waited a little, until things settled down, it might be better. She pushed her hand into the pocket of her jeans and felt the drive there. Safe, she told herself. Still safe! She would keep it there a little longer.

Charles came rushing into the room carrying a large box marked First Aid. Things were going to be okay, she said silently. She just had to be patient and not rock the boat.

"Haven't found Danny yet, but Darla's on her way," Charles said with a sound of frustration in his voice. "Says she's fixed some sort of surprise for us in the kitchen. As far as I'm concerned, we've had way too many surprises."

"I didn't tell Darla about the body yet," Charles said to Isabel. "Since we don't know who it is, please wait until we get back from checking it out. It could be Danny, or God knows who!" He turned away, and paced the room nervously.

Scooter opened the First Aid box and took out several articles. He moved to the bed and sat down beside her. "Let's clean up the knee, Sweetcheeks." It took him only a few minutes to clean and bandage the area. Then he wrapped her injured foot and ankle and snugged her shoe back on. "Don't walk around too much," he told her.

"My other shoe is in the underground," she said, suddenly remembering.

He reached for a small blanket folded up on the end of the bed, and covered her with it. "Stay warm."

"Okay, let's get going," Charles insisted. "We've got a dead body waiting for us.

"You don't suppose," Scooter said as he got up from the bed, "that it's Danny? He's been missing for-"

Scooter's words were cut off as Darla walked into the room with a coffee mug in her hand. Scooter gave her a tight smile, and then turned to Charles, "I'll put my med stuff away and meet you at the stairs in a minute. Then we'll go and look . . . for Danny." Then he swiftly made his way out of the room.

"Oh really, Isabel!" Darla scolded. "What were you thinking? Going down those steps by yourself? In the dark no less! What's wrong with you?" She went to the dressing table and pulled the vanity chair over beside the bed. "I brought you some hot coffee to help shake off the wilted way you must be feeling. She handed the mug to Isabel who took it, gladly, using the hot liquid to swallow the two pain pills Scooter had given her.

"Those little lights on the wall were on when I started," Isabel tried to explain. "I was just curious."

"Careless, is what it was." Darla said. "Did Scooter say you were okay?"

"I'll live," she said, hating all the attention she was getting. She wanted to forget her stupidity and just sleep for a while. "Doc Scooter has patched me up."

Darla's eyes narrowed and her lips pursed tightly as she said, "Why did you call him Doctor?"

Isabel wondered why she asked. "Well, he seems so expert for someone so young. How old is he anyway? In his mid-twenties?"

Darla eyes remained narrow as she said, "God no! He's in his thirties. He works out a lot. Has equipment in his room upstairs. Makes him look younger I suppose."

Isabel realized she'd been wondering how Scooter had managed to have not only EMT training, but work as an EMT and still get in some medical schooling,

"Whatever his age, he still acts like a teen-ager at times," Charles added as he walked over to the bed. "Darla can keep you company while we're gone. You just rest." He reached out and touched Isabel's cheek with one of his large warm hands. "I'm so damn sorry

113

you're gotten mixed up in all of this. As a rule this is a rather interesting place to visit."

Isabel gave him an irritated look. "Well, it's been far more than interesting."

"Isabel and I are going to stay right here," Darla said. "However, if you take too long, I will help her into the kitchen and we'll start eating the carrot cake I made." Darla gave an odd chopped-up kind of laugh. "Charles and I ate all the corn, so there's nothing left for dinner but carrot cake. So you better hurry it up."

Isabel wondered how Darla would react when Charles and Scooter came back and told her about finding the dead body. Of course, it would depend on whose body it was. Charles turned and quickly left the room and Isabel felt a sudden sensation of loss. She wasn't alone, but having both Charles and Scooter with her had given her a more comfortable sense of safety. She took another sip of the coffee Darla and brought, savoring its richly bitter taste. "Thank you, Darla, for the coffee" she said, enjoying the warmth of the blanket, and the comfort of the soft pillows behind her head.

"It is Nairobi," Darla replied and then walked to the window and pushed it open a little. "Storm is still bad," she said. "They can't get the road open until the damn thing blows itself out." She shook her head and sat down on the vanity chair she'd pulled over next to Isabel.

"I think I saw one of the cats you feed," Isabel said. "Well, I didn't actually see it because it was so dark, but I did feel it. Heard it purr. It was kind of an odd cat."

Darla folded her arms tightly, and sat silent with owl eyes open and staring.

"Are your kitties those hairless kind maybe? I hear they cost a fortune to own. Maybe someone lost them, and would like to know where they are."

Darla remained stone-like, as if not hearing, not responding. Sort of catatonic-like.

Isabel gave up talking to her.

Even though she tried to suppress them, her thoughts turned to

114

what had happened to her on the stone stairs. Was it just a weird accident, or did someone purposely cause her to fall? Otherwise, how had she gotten into a different cavern? Had it been their intention to kill her? Or did they just intend to derail her and maybe keep her from finding what Jorge had hidden? Then again, maybe it was the person who had blown up the generator! If so, it could be more than one person, which was a more frightening thought. She hated having so dang many scattered questions in her head. Most of all she didn't like the questions because her mind kept painfully injecting her with alarming answers.

Chapter Nine

Charles raised his flashlight. He could see Scooter about ten steps below him obviously trying not to get too far ahead. Charles seriously doubted his legs would make it back down the stone steps another time much less making it back up again. How many trips had he made today? It irritated him that Scooter, with his muscle bulging body, seemed to enjoy all the exercise. Envy, he told himself. He gave a little snort of a laugh which Scooter heard. "You okay, Chucky?" Scooter yelled up at him.

"No, my legs are killing me," he answered. "But call me Chucky one more time and I'll have enough energy to kill you!" It helped to banter, Charles knew. It kept the morbidity out of their situation.

"You and what army?" Scooter said. "Do you have any idea how far down Isabel was when she found the body?"

"She said a large cavern. But how large is large to her?"

"Well, we've already passed a fairly small one, with no sign of a body."

Charles tried to speed up his gait down the steps and had almost caught up with Scooter when he saw him flash his light into a wide opening in the stone wall.

"This might be it," Scooter shouted. "It's quite large."

Charles watched as he flashed the light around, praying it was the right place and they wouldn't have to go any deeper. Another few steps and he was beside Scooter.

"Yep, sure as hell looks like a body lying next to the back wall," Scooter said, flashing his light against the wall. "Damn, I had hoped it might have been a delusion Isabel had because of the bad bump on her head."

Charles squinted into the flashlight lit cavern. He wasn't sure he could force himself to go inside and look. "Can you tell . . . is it Danny? I don't remember what he was wearing this morning."

"Can't tell from here." Scooter walked into the cavern and made

116

his way toward the body which was curled up slightly. Reluctantly Charles followed him. He had never thought of himself as a coward, at least not until three years ago when Nancy died. This situation was testing him harshly. He forced himself to look away from the scene. He looked at the stone walls, at the odd-looking green fungus covering them, thinking that it probably had never seen much light before. He wondered if it could survive in a well-lit environment, while knowing full well that it could not. Sort of like some people he knew.

Scooter reached the body and looked down. "Oh my God!" he yelled in a hoarse voice. "Charles . . . you will not believe this!"

Charles reached his side and looked down at the body. His heart started to race. He let out a gasp. "Oh no! Christ *no!* What the hell are we going to do?" he cried.

"Looks like the cause of death is a blow to the head." Scooter said, squatting down to check the body. "His head is split open in front! He's in rigor which lasts a good twenty-four hours. I need a liver temp to know how long he's been gone."

"God help us!" Charles felt his heartbeat thumping painfully against his ribs. He closed his eyes, not wanting to see death up close again. He let out a long breath. "What do we do now?"

"We get topside. Send a message to the LA sheriffs with the short-wave radio." Scooter said. "Not much else we can do. At least until the road opens up. The weather's still too bad to get a chopper in here. It's gonna take some time I'm afraid. I'm thankful it's so frigging cold down here. Because of the body, that is."

"Time isn't the thing worrying me! Think about it. Did he take a bad fall, like Isabel might have? These are treacherous stairs, Scooter."

Scooter frowned, and was silent for a few moments. He finally said, "Not unless a dead man can get up and walk from the stairs to the back side of this cavern. This kind of a blow would probably kill him instantly."

"Jesus! Then maybe Isabel didn't fall either. Someone may have tried . . . ." Charles had trouble finishing the sentence.

117

Scooter gave him a disturbed look, his eyes dark and narrowed. "It means someone probably tried to kill her, but fucked it up. This means we have a killer on the loose around here!"

"God damn it Scooter! Let's get back. We have to keep everyone together until we can get some help in here."

Charles looked down at the body. "Wish we had something to cover him up with." The sight of his wife Nancy's body lying on the grass in the backyard of their little ranch home in San Fernando flashed across his mind. He'd covered her with his leather army style jacket thinking how cold she looked. A long QT heart problem had taken her. He had no idea she had the problem. He doubted she knew about it either.

"Could it have been one of our daytime techs?" Charles asked.

"I can't imagine any of them doing this. Besides, they were already out of here hours before someone hit on Isabel. None of their cars are still here," Scooter said looking down at the body. "I'll take him to Danny's lab and put him on the cot. There's a blanket there we can use to cover him. You go ahead topside and see about Isabel and the others."

Charles quickly turned around and headed out of the cavern. He looked up at the miles of steps ahead of them. He didn't hesitate. He didn't feel the fatigue or pain in his legs. They had gone totally numb. All he thought about as he bounded up the stairs was the safety of the others, as well as what the hell was he going to do about the situation. However, his mind refused to come up with any answer. This can't be happening, he said to himself! This just can't be happening!

Isabel finished the coffee Darla had brought her, and she began to feel considerably better. Whatever Scooter had put on her knee seemed to have numbed the pain there. It didn't hurt much now, nor did the bump on her head, thankfully. The swelling in her foot seemed to have gone down some. Her shoe that Scooter had laced up snug, didn't feel so tight, and she had very little pain. Then she remembered that Scooter had given her some pain pills. Bless them!"

Darla still sat on the vanity chair, stone-still, as if looking at something in another dimension. Isabel slowly got up from the bed and limped her way to the window. The storm still growled like an angry animal, spitting out rain, as well as hail now and then. The window, slightly open, let in a small amount of icy air. She drank it in like cold juice. It felt good now that she was warm.

She wondered where Jorge was. If he'd gone back down the mountain, he'd be unable to get back because of the blocked road. She was glad he hadn't come back because there was absolutely no way she was going to give him the flash0 drive in her pocket. He would be furious, but she didn't care. He had ruined any leftover feelings for him by his asking her to do what she did. The frightening thought of a dead body in the underground amplified those feelings.

She looked over at Darla who was suddenly looking around the room as if for some reason it displeased her. Her face looked hard and unhappy. "This room is twice the size of mine upstairs," she grumbled. "And you have no stairs to climb." She let out a sigh. "Sorry. I feel grumpy what with the storm, and the power being off. And why are the guys taking so long? I want to get back to the kitchen. I finally found an oil lamp which makes it nice and bright.

Rain began blowing in through the slightly open window with an obvious change of the wind so Isabel closed it. "Listen, Darla. I can make it to the kitchen if you want. I'll have to go slow, but it's not bad."

Darla's narrow face softened. "How helpful. Thank you. We could start eating carrot cake if you like. I lied about the corn. There's plenty."

Isabel gave a nervous laugh, thankful Darla had returned to the life of the living. "I can't believe with all this going on, you actually stopped to make a cake." Then she remembered they had not told Darla about the body in the underground. If it was Danny's body, she was certain Darla would be disturbed. After all, they had apparently worked together for a long time.

"The cake took me hours over a hot stove!" Darla gave an

uncharacteristic giggle. She had actually made a joke.

"Hours! My goodness," Isabel said, going along with Darla's unusual lightheartedness. Anything to keep the thought of the dead body out of her mind was welcome.

"Actually, it is just a frozen store bought cake," Darla said, her giggle retreating. "I found it in the back of the freezer. I just thawed it out. Do not tell the guys that."

"Never," Isabel said, trying to sound nonchalant. "I had sandwiches at lunch, so cake for dinner would be great!" she said. "At least I think I ate lunch. Since I got this bad bump on my head things are a bit hazy."

Darla gave her a startled look. "Oh, for lord's sake, I forgot to bring the ice for your head. I never forget things! What's wrong with me? We will take care of it in the kitchen, if there is any ice left with the power out. Do you have a headache?"

"No, the pain pills took care of it. The bump is tender to the touch, however." When she looked at Darla, she was certain the woman's hands quivered slightly. Obviously, all of this had really gotten to her. Her momentary playfulness was a cover up.

Darla got up from the chair, reached for one of the lit candles in a sconce on the wall behind the bed, and headed for the bedroom door. "You had better take a candle too," she said looking over her shoulder at Isabel. "There are a few candles around the hallways but it is still pretty dim. "I do not want you to fall . . . again. Can you make it on your own, or do you need my help?"

"I'm okay. You go ahead," Isabel said and grabbed the other lit candle. "It will take me awhile to get there. But I can make it." She reached the bedroom doorway behind Darla who gave a quirky little nod then whipped off down the hall like a Greyhound entering a race.

Isabel had almost reached the kitchen when she heard voices. The two men couldn't be back already. She hurried her speed a little, but the extra effort caused her foot to throb worse. When she finally reached the kitchen doorway and looked in, she saw Travis and Darla sitting at the table next to a chubby little owl of a man with a coffee mug in one of his creampuff hands. White curls of steam wriggled out of the cup. His pinkish fingernails gleamed in the light from an oil lamp in the center of the table.

"Hey there!" Danny said. "I hear you and I have been the objects of a Castle Grande search."

"Isabel," Darla said, waving her into the room. This is Danny, the lost Danny and now the found Danny."

"So what happened," Isabel asked. "I mean where did you disappear to? I hear everyone was looking for you."

"The bed in my room is an uncomfortable lumpy mess so I went into one of the empty rooms upstairs and took a nap. Most of the rooms here aren't locked. Metal's too rusty. That room had a much better bed then mine. Slept the sleep of the dead, I did."

The word dead jolted Isabel and she had to grab the edge of the doorway to keep her balance.

"And where was it *you* disappeared to, dear lady," Travis asked.

"I fell down the dang stone steps in the dang gray-green underground," Isabel answered sharply, not really wanting to discuss the subject.

Danny took a long swig of his coffee, then chuckled and said. "Well, I think my nap was a much better idea!"

Isabel moved on into the room and sat down heavily at the table, her foot throbbing miserably because of the long walk from the bedroom. She grimaced on purpose. Darla caught the look, got up, and went to the refrigerator.

"I will get that ice for the bump on your head, Isabel," she said, opening the refrigerator door.

"I think it might be better on my foot."

"Foot it is," Darla said pulling open a cupboard and taking out a large plastic baggy. "Still have some ice left in the fridge, thank goodness." She filled the bag with a bunch of cubes, twisted a plastic wire around the opening, and handed the bag to Isabel who set it on top of her injured foot. Even with her shoe on, it was uncomfortably cold, but probably a good idea.

To Isabel, it seemed like she had been sitting at the table for hours listening to Darla, Danny, and Travis discuss gene splicing, frankenfoods, and all sorts of things that sounded quite bizarre to Isabel. Her degree in biology wasn't the least bit of help to her so she just sipped some of Darla's licorice black coffee, tendered this time with a spoonful of sugar. She smiled and nodded her head now and then. She yawned repeatedly, and wished she could just close her eyes and put her head down on the table and sleep. The strong coffee didn't do a thing to dispel her wish. Scooter's pain pills were obviously taking their toll, even though her foot still hurt.

She wondered how long it had been since Charles and Scooter had left. It seemed like forever. The sooner Charles got back the sooner she could hand over Jorge's flash drive. She couldn't stop thinking about it. It felt like a giant chunk of lead in her pocket.

"Well holy damn, here he is!" It was Charles' voice. He pointed at Danny. "The lost scientist materializes."

Isabel realized she had actually closed her eyes and put her head down on the table but was not quite sleeping. She tried to lift her head to make sure it was Charles, but found it too heavy. She must look so foolish, she thought. Nevertheless, she'd been through a hell of a lot and deserved to snooze anywhere she wanted. The thought of doing it made her feel better.

"God, Danny! Where the hell have you been?" Scooter asked in a sharp voice

"Napping," Danny said. "In one of the vacant bedrooms. More comfortable. Sorry to have worried everyone."

Isabel made another effort to lift her head off the table. This time successfully. She opened her eyes and saw Charles standing a few feet away from her.

"Coffee, Charles?" Darla said. "A fresh pot."

"Yes, thanks Darla." Scooter grabbed a coffee mug off the sink and sat down at the table.

Isabel saw Charles glance around the room, his face paler than usual. She wondered when he was going to tell Danny, Darla, and Travis about the body in the underground. Since it wasn't Danny's, she wondered if it was the person who destroyed their main generator as Charles had suggested earlier. The explosion might have injured him, and he probably crawled inside the underground, out of the rain. Then, without help, he died there. Darla swore there was an opening to the surface. The cat she'd found appeared to prove it. At least the body wasn't one of the people she'd met here.

She removed the pack of ice Darla had put on her foot and with some effort got up from the table. She took her coffee mug to the sink, poured out the remains of the cold coffee, and helped herself to some fresh from the pot Darla had set on the table. Sitting back down she wondered how many workers usually gathered at this gigantic table. She counted the chairs. Ten of them. Her still sleepy mind was scattered, as usual, and she didn't realize for a minute that Charles was calling her name. He was standing behind her chair and trying to get her attention.

"Isabel, I need to talk to you," he said in a low, whispery voice. "Privately. In the entry room."

"Oh," she finally reacted. "I'm sorry. I'm half-asleep. I guess I should have taken a longer nap instead of exploring the old stone steps."

"Instead of getting hurt!" he said, a bit of agitation in his voice.

Was he angry with her for some reason? He hadn't sounded that way before he and Scooter went to the underground. Did he know about Jorge's hidden flash drive? Maybe he knew about it, then looked for it and realized she may have found it. He might have guessed it was the reason she had gone down the stone steps. Her brain refused to clearly sort out her thoughts. Then she realized it was time . . . time to give Charles what Jorge had her retrieve. If she did it when they were alone in the other room, no one else would know about it, unless Charles chose to tell them. He would realize she hadn't intended to do anything wrong. At least not after she'd had time to think about it. It would be difficult to explain why she hadn't come to him in the first place. Oh, what a mess she'd made of things! Her first and biggest mistake was agreeing to meet Jorge at this mid-evil fortress in the middle of nowhere, in the rain, and in the middle of the night.

In the large entry room, the fire was still burning and throwing

123

long wavering shadows across the floor. Charles motioned for her to sit on the leather sofa closest to the fireplace. The warmth of it soothed her jangled nerves. He sat down next to her, looking first at the fire, then at Isabel and then he just sat there with his eyes closed. Her main fear was he already knew about the specs that Jorge had faked in order to leave with the real thing hidden away in the stone castle.

Now! She told herself. Be brave and do it now! Charles opened his eyes and looked at hers as if trying to keep them from moving away from his. "Isabel, there is something I have to tell you."

"Wait," Isabel said in a voice way too high and nervous sounding, but she had no control over it. "First, I have to tell *you* something. I should have told you sooner but . . . I wasn't sure . . . about it."

Charles eyes narrowed, the frown lines between them deepening. "Okay then, what is it?"

Isabel slid her hand into the pocket of her jeans. Her fingers touched the coolness of the flash drive. She grasped it tightly and pulled it out, raising it for Charles to see. "You should have this. When Jorge, I mean Joe called me yesterday and asked me to meet him here I didn't know why until this morning. He had this hidden in the underground and wanted me to get it for him. It may have the specs for his new, remarkable type of corn, or it could be for something else. It's the reason why I fell on the stairs. I shouldn't have gone down there! I should have just told you about them and let you take it from there. I just wasn't sure what to do. I thought maybe I should help him. He seemed to believe that Bertrand was trying to steal them from him. But something about it felt wrong to me."

Charles reached out, took the flash drive, and sat looking at it, but not saying anything. Then he put it into his ragged Levi pockets. She wondered if he could feel the mental weight of it as she had ever since she'd retrieved it.

"He was a little vague about what's on it," she said, hearing her voice diminish to a husky whisper. "So I just assumed it was for better corn yield."

124

"When did he ask you to do this?"

"Actually, he called me last night but didn't say what he wanted me to do. Just said I should meet him here. Then this morning he asked me to get his flash drive out of the underground,"

"How the hell did he get to you here?"

She hesitated and then said, "Yes, well he ended up climbing in the window of my room this morning. He'd messed up the alarm there. That's when he asked me to do it. He must have followed me last night, and maybe slept in his car."

"Did you see him any other time today?"

"No."

She looked at the odd expression on his face. Something was obviously wrong with her situation. Something more than her having found the flash drive.

"Thank you for giving me the drive, Isabel. You have no idea how important it may be. I'll explain later. But right now there is something you need to know." He cleared his throat, twice, and seemed to be having trouble talking.

"Okay, what is it? What's wrong?" she asked.

"The body you found. Scooter and I saw it and . . . I'm so sorry, Isabel. It was your . . . friend Joe's body." He looked at her as if wanting to say more, but couldn't.

Isabel's hands began to shake. Charles reached out and took hold of them. "You mean . . . it was Joe's body I stumbled on?" she asked in a vague tone, not wanting to understand what he was saying. "Are you positive?"

"Yes."

"You can't mean it's really him. It can't be!" She began to shake all over.

"I am so sorry to have to tell you this. However, Joe wasn't really your friend, Isabel. What he did by asking you to help him wasn't the act of a friend. He wasn't a good guy, believe me!"

Unable to speak, she just shook her head frantically from side to side.

"Listen to me Isabel, you have to understand. Joe is not the

125

person you thought he was."

Isabel fought to get some air in her lungs so she could speak. After a struggle she managed to say, "No Charles! You don't understand. *Joe was my husband!!"*

Charles tilted his head to one side. "You're right, I don't understand! Charles gave her a strange look she couldn't read. "Isabel, I have to tell you, we did a background check on you. We know you were married to Jorge Allen Warren. A fairly well known scientist. And we know he died. So how could he and Joe possibly be the same person?"

"For the past four years I thought Jorge was dead. Until he called me yesterday, said his name now was Joe Wilson, and asked me to meet him here."

Charles slowly let go of her hands. He had a deeply puzzled look on his face "So, his death back then was . . . ."

"A cruel hoax," she said, fighting back tears. "Obviously he's been hiding out here, working under an assumed name."

"And you didn't know?"

"I had no idea. Not until he called me."

"This is so difficult to believe," Charles shook his head. "So how did he supposedly die? I mean, what exactly happened when you thought he'd died?"

"He was a biologist who worked for Kowari Biotech in Japan a great deal of the time. She bit her lip and found it difficult to talk. "It's complicated. And now he's dead *again*."

The shock of what he had told her about Jorge's death crackled like static electricity inside her head. How could it be Jorge? How did he get into the underground? How did he die? She couldn't piece anything together.

"Are you absolutely certain?" she asked in a pale voice. "That the body *is* Jorge's? I mean, is it actually Joe as you call him? He's . . . really dead?"

With a stricken look in his eyes, Charles said, "Yes. I am so sorry, Isabel!"

Isabel closed her eyes and fought back the tears trying to escape.

"I'm sorry I didn't tell you. But I promised Jorge. Does everyone else know who I was married to?"

"I'm afraid so.'

She gave out a rattling sigh, and then said, "Until yesterday, as far as I knew, he died four years ago. I even received his ashes. Yesterday was the first time I'd heard from him in the four years since his . . . death. The shock was . . . ." She couldn't get out any more words. She broke down and let herself sob. She felt Charles arms go around her and pull her close. Silently he let her cry.

Finally able to breathe, and after her tears had slowed, she looked up him. "How did he die? Was he ill or injured?"

"Badly injured."

"Do you think Joe was responsible for blowing up the generator? Could that be how he was injured?" she asked.

"We don't know for sure if he caused the explosion. But we did detect an odd odor about him, like burned metal. He may have had someone with him. However, like you, he had a blow to his head. Only it was much worse than what happened to you."

Startled, Isabel's mouth dropped open. "Oh God!"

"I don't believe you fell, Isabel. I think someone tried to do to you what they did to Joe. At this point, we all have to be extremely cautious until the road is open, or at least until a police chopper can in here. It could be one of us who is responsible, or there could be someone else here we don't know about. Maybe more than one person. This whole damn situation is treacherous and unbelievable!"

"But why? I mean why would anyone do all this? Why would they want to hurt *me*?"

"It might have something to do with the flash drive of Joe's you found."

"Could it be so valuable? So much so, that someone is willing to kill for it? After all, gene altered corn has been tried a lot, from what I've heard and read."

Charles gave her an unusual look. "Sounds like you know more about genetics than you led me to believe."

"No!" Isabel said angrily, thankful some anger had replaced the sorrow. "I've just heard things Jorge said to me from time to time, and looked at some of his books. He was always talking about it. However, my head really wasn't into it. So don't get any ideas that I had anything to do with this. After all, I turned the damn thing over to you."

"I'm sorry," he said in a kinder tone. "I'm just spooked by everything going on. I have some suspicions, but nothing concrete. I don't know who is involved. So for now, we need to all stick together."

Isabel used her sleeve to help damp off some of the tears that still clung to her cheeks. "Charles, I just can't believe it . . . that Jorge is actually dead. *Again!* I went through four years of grieving, and I do not want to go through it all over again." She bit her lip, hard, and the pain of it helped her focus her thoughts. "I will *not* go through it again! Especially knowing the reason why he let me know he was still alive. Just so he could use me." She licked her lip. It felt a little swollen from her fall. "So, what do we do now?" she asked him.

Charles gently took her face in his warm hands. "Isabel, please don't say anything about your Jorge and Joe being the same person. And about having you retrieve those things for him. Not yet. Can you do that for me?"

Isabel frowned. "I'm not sure. I'm feeling so many different emotions."

"I think it would be better for now. He might have told someone here who he actually was."

"Why would he do that? He told me he couldn't risk anyone here knowing his real name."

"There is something off kilter going on here. For quite some time. Something I can't get a handle on. Something very . . . well, a possible risky situation. It is the main reason why Bertrand has me here. Not for my grapes, but to see if I can discover what the hell is going on. So please don't say anything. At least until I get some answers." He slowly removed his hands from her face.

Isabel sucked in a long breath and let it out slowly. "Alright. I won't tell anyone anything. Not until you say it's okay. Or until we're rescued from this dreadful place."

"One more thing," Charles said. The CDC may need to have a look at what Joe gave you. Not sure yet if we'll need them in this situation, but better safe than sorry."

She looked up at Charles and nodded her understanding, but felt a surge of anxiety as she agreed. What was it that Charles feared Jorge was working on? She couldn't imagine.

"Okay good. Thank you. Now, I have to go and tell Darla about Joe's death. She's worked with him for a long time. I'm not sure how she's going to react." Charles got up and started to move away from her. He paused and leaned down. "Isabel, I really wish your visit to us had been so different," he said. "You may well have liked it here."

Isabel looked at him, at his close to handsome face, his strong mouth, and his mossy green eyes. She too wished her visit had been different. Charles was one of the few people who made her feel safe. Yet she could not forget Jorge's words about him, to not trust him because he wasn't what he seemed to be. Right then, it was difficult to believe that. All she could do was stay as strong as possible until the storm passed and then she could go home.

Chapter Ten

A late dinner of carrot cake and buttered corn had been quickly finished, and the kitchen was now uncomfortably quiet. Isabel sat across from Darla feeling a little unstrung by the fact that Darla was staring into space, as if no one else was in the room. Charles had been as gentle as possible when telling her they had found Joe's body in the underground and that his death wasn't from natural causes. At first, Darla had let out a few odd gasps but didn't say a word. Then she just made dreadfully strange noises. Those stopped and she appeared comatose except for her eyes. Her eyes darted around but never seemed to land on anything. The odd look chilled Isabel, even though the kitchen was quite warm.

She watched as Charles jumped up from his chair, rummaged through one of the pantry cupboards, and located an amber colored brandy bottle. It was a new bottle, never opened and he struggled with it for a moment before finally opening it. He poured Darla a small glassful but had difficulty getting her to drink some of it. Scooter took it from him and placed his free hand on Darla's cheek. "Come on darlyn," he said in a soft voice. "Just a little will make you feel better. This is Charles special one-hundred-year-old Brandy," Slowly Darla responded by opening her mouth and Scooter tipped a small amount of the Brandy into it. Darla promptly swallowed it and Isabel watched as her pale cheeks flushed to their usual persimmon color.

"Atta girl, luv," he said, smiling at her. "Better."

Charles took the glass from Scooter and finished off the remainder. He filled the glass half full again. "This is for Isabel."

"Sorry, no, Charles," Scooter said. "Not with the pain meds. Not a good idea."

Charles frowned but nodded his agreement, and put the bottle back into the cupboard. He drank down the small amount of Brandy in the glass, and then said, "I haven't had anything this good for years."

Looking over at Danny and Travis, Isabel thought they looked as if they too could use a drink. Nevertheless, Isabel assumed Scooter didn't want Darla or anyone to get drunk, which she supposed would be easy for some people to do under these conditions. Maybe the killer was sitting right there at the table with her. She looked around the kitchen, the only room in which she felt safe. No one in the room looked like what she thought a killer would look like.

Travis looked at his watch. "It's only eight, so there's a lot more hours before morning," he announced. "And this damn storm keeps on going. Worse one I've seen up here in years. It's going to be one hell of a long night."

"Do we have anything more to eat," Danny asked. "The carrot cake and one ear of corn didn't seem like enough for dinner." He looked at Darla who appeared to be getting better, her eyes not darting around so much now. Even so, she didn't respond. "But it was great, Darla," he said as a belated compliment. However, the compliment didn't penetrate Darla. She still hadn't said a word since Charles had told her Joe was dead.

"Cupboards have some stuff left," Scooter suggested. "Crackers, canned soup, cookies, some of those little weenies. Things like that."

"Vienna Sausages," Darla suddenly announced, startling everyone. "Every man for himself. I am not cooking. I am going to bed!" Acting more like herself, she pushed her chair back and started to get up.

"No, Darla, I think it would be better if you stayed here with the rest of us," Charles said.

"I am tired and I want my bed," she replied in an emotionless tone.

"Darla, someone killed Joe. Do you understand?" Charles asked. "We don't know who and we don't know if anyone else here is in danger. We need to stay together."

Scooter motioned to Darla to sit down. She hesitated for a little, looking around at everyone. With a deep sigh, she let herself back down in the chair. "Shit!" she said and laid her head down on the table, her arms alongside it. Then she made a fist of both her hands,

131

lifted them, and pounded them down on the table causing a vibrating boom. "Everything has gone to shit! You have no idea!"

Apparently, even the very small amount of Brandy Scooter had given her, affected Darla. It was obvious she wasn't used to it. Her whole life had probably been spent inside a specialized laboratory working on something to help make a better world. Now all of it could be pulled out from under her if she lost any of her research material, her plants, or whatever else she had in her lab. Isabel watched her eyes slowly close, her fists relaxed, and her breathing settle into a quiet rhythm. She had fallen asleep.

The small group was quiet for a while, with only a few words of conversation now and then. Danny looked in the cupboard, chose a can of soup, heated it, and sat down to eat. He finished it in seconds but still looked unsatisfied.

Charles suddenly put his hand on Isabel's shoulder. "Here's some fresh ice for that foot of yours.

"Oh, Charles, thank you."

"My pleasure," he said in a sympathetic voice. "He leaned down and removed the mostly melted bag of ice on her foot, and replaced it with the fresh one. "There you go. It looks like the swelling is pretty well down.

For the first time in hours, Isabel felt a tiny smile on her lips. She just couldn't imagine what Jorge had said about him was true. That he couldn't be trusted. So far, he'd been the most gentle and caring person she'd met in a long time.

Charles took a coke from the refrigerator, and sipped it slowly. He looked around at the little group. The problem before long would be the need for sleep. With enough coffee he could probably last another night, if need be. Nevertheless, he hoped the authorities would be able to get at least a few people here by midday tomorrow at the latest.

Charles decided they should start rotating people who needed some sleep. The same way Darla was sleeping. Nerves were no doubt threadbare and even a little sleep might help. Danny already had taken a long nap, but Travis should sleep for a couple of hours at least. And even though Isabel had taken a nap earlier, what with her injuries, she should sleep some too. He wasn't sure about Scooter. He was used to late hours. However he had stayed up last night in case something mechanical went wrong, so he didn't know if he'd gotten any sleep or not.

The main thing was not to let everyone in the kitchen sleep at the same time. He tried to convince himself that the killing had been done by someone outside. By the person or people who had blown up their generator. He didn't want to believe the killer was among the five of them sitting around the kitchen table. Nevertheless, it was possible. So, at least two people needed to be awake at all times. It wasn't a great plan, but he couldn't think of a better way.

"Isabel," he said quietly. "Would you like to nap for a little while now? The way Darla's doing. Even an hour or so would help."

He could tell Isabel wanted to say no, but being filled with the pain medicine, he was sure she wouldn't turn down the offer.

"Well . . . I guess so. But you know I did take a nap earlier." She said.

"You've been through a lot. A little more sleep will do you good. I'll wake you if I need you," he said. "Not to worry."

Isabel yawned, and he watched as she put a paper towel down on the table, and then laid her head down on it. Not exactly the most comfortable way to sleep, Charles knew. However, he didn't want her to go to her room and crawl into bed. Not with the chance of someone getting into the room through the window like Joe had done. She was doing remarkable well, considering all she'd been through since she'd arrived there last night. She had an unexpected strength about her, despite her diminutive size.

The next thing he needed was to decide what to do about the flash drive of Joe's he had in his pocket. He wanted to pull it out and look at it, but was afraid someone would wonder why he had it. He wondered if it was one that could contain mega gigabytes of information. *But for what?* Moreover, did he really want to have his

133

frightening suspicions confirmed? How could he get to a computer so he could at least get a quick look at the files? When the police finally arrived and begin investigating Joe's death, he really didn't want the flash drive found on him unless he knew what was on it. He needed to check it out before anyone else did. He was the only one who had a personal computer in his room. Since he kept the computer off most of the time, in order to save the battery, he hoped it had enough juice. He prayed to God the information on the flash drive was just procedures on how to make Joe's new corn. Unfortunately, he was almost sure it wasn't.

He leaned back in the kitchen chair and heard it give a little squeal as if its wooden legs were complaining. His main fear wouldn't leave his mind. In his pocket, it was possible he had a formula for creating something that he didn't even want to think about.

He got up from the table and went to the cupboard pretending to look for some crackers. He closed the cupboard, and went to the refrigerator and opened the freezer side. He took a quick look. There were two unopened packs of mixed vegetables, and a stack of spiced meat patties. He quietly closed the refrigerator door and casually walked to the table. A wave of fatigue washed over him. He fought it away. It wasn't unreasonable, but he couldn't let it take hold. Too many people were counting on him, and too much was at stake.

"Find anything more for us to eat?" Danny suddenly asked. "My stomach's grumbling like crazy."

Charles looked at Danny. "After you ate half the cake earlier?" He walked over to the table. "Maybe you can cook up the meat patties in the fridge."

"When all this mess is over we really need to stock up on a lot of food." Danny stretched a little and then looked at Travis next to him who, like Darla and Isabel, was sleeping, head and arms down on the table. "Doesn't snore, does he? I'm sure I do," Danny said.

Charles settled himself into a chair across the table from Danny. "So, tell me, how are things are going in your lab?" He knew Danny loved to talk about his work. Sure enough the man's face lit up, flooded with a little color, and he began to talk about what he'd accomplished the past week. As usual, Danny repeated most of the same details he always talked about when discussing his work. There were times when Charles wondered if Danny was actually making any progress. Maybe he just wanted to give the impression he was.

Listening to Danny chattering away as usual, Charles felt a twinge of relief for the first time in quite a while. He glanced over at Isabel who looked so peaceful with her eyes closed now, her arms stretched out on the table, with her rusty colored hair curled softly around her face. He had a sudden protective urge to go to her and put his arms around her. To hold her, to stroke her rusty colored hair, and even kiss her. It was the first time since Nancy had died that he had felt this way about a woman. If only they had met under different circumstance, perhaps they would have had a chance to develop a relationship. Regrettably, it appeared impossible now. He had to stay the course and make sure things went the way they had to. That was all that mattered.

Isabel awoke with a start, wondering why her arms felt so strange. She opened her eyes slightly and saw them stretched alongside her head which was lying with one cheek down on the table. Dang, she said to herself, where the hell am I? And what time is it? Then it came back, in a torrent. Everything! She sat upright, rubbed at her arms which had gone tingly. She looked around the table. Everyone else was awake. Even Darla. They were not paying any attention to her. She stretched, and took in a deep breath. Better.

"Well, welcome back," Scooter said to her as he got up from the table. "Is everything working okay?"

Isabel stretched again. "I think so. Is it morning?"

"I'm afraid not. So I'm glad you slept a little." Scooter picked up the coffee pot which was sitting on the stove, and then filled the pottery mug still sitting on the table in front of her. "Maybe this will help,"

"Thanks. Am I the only one who slept so long?" she asked him.

"You are the only one in combat yesterday. You needed the rest." He moved back to his chair and sat down.

Before drinking the coffee Isabel realized she needed to get to the bathroom. "She leaned over to Charles who was sitting in the chair next to her and whispered, "I have to use the bathroom. Should I go to my room?"

Charles shook his head. "No there's a little bathroom, just off the kitchen. Through the door at the far end, just past the fridge."

"Oh, thank heaven!"

"It's safe. No window, one door."

"Good." She tried squinting at her tiny wristwatch but her eyes were not yet in working order. "What time is it?"

Charles looked at his watch. "A little after midnight." Earlier, Travis showed me how to use the short-wave radio and they said we may get someone here to start clearing the road in about five or six hours. If the rain stays light and the winds don't come back they might get a chopper in sooner. Police mostly."

"So, have you told them about Jor . . . Joe?' she said softly.

"Yes."

"They'll investigate right away, won't they?" She looked down at the coffee in her cup as if she could find some answers in the dark liquid. "Then everyone will know about—"

"You and Joe." He said. "Yes, I'm afraid so."

Isabel leaned over close to him and said in a whisper. "How long before the people from the CDC will get here?"

He gave her a pinched frown, warning her not to let anyone hear her. "No idea. Besides, we may not need them. It will depend on what Joe . . . I mean what Jorge has been working on."

"You really don't think it's his corn, do you? All the controversy, his being banned from here, his try to get it out of here."

Charles gave a sigh. "We can get to all of it later." He leaned closer to her and whispered softly, "I have to get to my computer upstairs and checkout Joe's flash drive. I need to see exactly what we are dealing with here."

"I need to know too!"

136

The Gray Green Underground

"Yes, I understand," Charles said as if checking to see if anyone was paying attention to them. "The only one looking at him was Scooter who gave him a puzzled glance. Charles gave him a nonchalant smile and a shrug. "I think Scooter knows how serious this could be."

Isabel wasn't certain what kind of serious Charles meant. Of course Jorge's death was serious, and not knowing who or why someone killed him made it worse. Nevertheless, what really bothered her most was the fact she could sit there at the kitchen table acting calm and unaffected by Jorge's death. It wasn't because she was playacting for the others in the room, since they thought her relationship to their "Joe" was not very close. It was because she'd already mourned Jorge's death. She had lived with it for four years. Even hearing his voice on the phone, and seeing him for a few minutes didn't seem real to her. It was impossible to mourn a second time for the same person. The thought helped her forgive herself for not having more tears for Jorge.

She glanced at Charles and was startled by how tired his face looked; the little frown lines between his eyes were bunched together and his cheeks were darkly stubbled.

Was he extremely worried about the flash drive she had given him? Did he suspect Jorge, or maybe he thought one of the others was involved in something illegal. She remembered some of the things Charles had told her about what could go wrong with genetic splicing. Or was it possible that Jorge, or one of the others, had developed some kind of dangerous pathogen? The idea of being anywhere near anyone like that was unnerving. Could she and Charles have been exposed to it from handling the flash drive Jorge had her retrieve? She took in a long cleansing breath and let it out in an effort to rid herself of her rambling thoughts.

"Well," she finally said quietly, "if you think you should get to your computer and see what's on the flash drive, then you should do it0." She started to get up from the table but as she did, Charles pulled her down next to him, the pressure from his hand on her shoulder almost painfully tight.

"Yes," he said in a breathy whisper. "And I can manage doing that if you will help me. I need a distraction while I'm gone. *There are some meat patties in the fridge!*" He stopped talking suddenly and she realized that Darla was trying to get his attention. He removed his hand from Isabel's shoulder and began to carry on a conversation with Darla.

Isabel stood up, her eyes blinking almost as wildly as Darla's had earlier. What the hell was Charles talking about? She was afraid to look down at him, baffled by what he meant by *meat patties?* She rubbed her shoulder, still feeling his tight grip on it, and then woodenly she made her way to the tiny bathroom at the end of the kitchen. The thought of meat patties bounced rudely around in her head like two little rubber balls.

By the time she got back to the table she noticed her foot felt quite a bit better and the word meat patties had pretty much deserted her brain. At least there was something for which to be grateful. She sat down, picked up her mug, and took a sip of coffee, grateful for its bitter taste. She was more awake now. Maybe she'd imagined what Charles had said. She rubbed at her face, wondering if it had some imprints on it from the paper towel she'd slept on. There hadn't been a mirror in the tiny bathroom. It really didn't matter how she looked anyway, because everyone was busy chatting nervously and ignoring her. She leaned back in the chair, cup in hand, and tried to understand at least some of the things they were talking about. When she glanced up at the bent glass windows, she was glad to see the rain wasn't drumming so heavily.

If she could just get through until morning then hopefully everything would go back to normal. She'd get the hell out of this place the minute the road was open. Or maybe she could get a ride out in a police helicopter. What happened here would be up to Charles and Bertrand to take care of. After all, Jorge had worked for them . . . well actually; he had worked for himself, using their lab. Then she could go back to her normal world!

She stretched out a little in the hard wooden chair, trying to get more comfortable. She heard a slight moan coming from Darla.

When she looked at her, she realized there was something wrong. She was sitting up, her fingers clasping the table edge so hard her knuckles were colorless. Her cheeks were a bilious yellow, and she looked as if she was about to pass out.

"Charles!" she yelled. "Darla's ill!" She got up and went to where Darla was seated. "Darla! What is it? What's wrong?"

There was no response. Charles joined her and felt Darla's face.

"No fever. She's breathing okay. Darla! Are you sick?"

Scooter was suddenly beside her and said, "Move, please, and let me take a look. I don't like her color."

Isabel backed away and stood there in a state of deep fear. Could it have been the Brandy? Had someone put something into the hundred-year-old Brandy? If she remembered, Darla, Scooter and Charles were the only ones to drink it. Neither Scooter nor Charles was ill. However, it had been a full-unopened bottle and she had watched it being opened. No. she didn't think it could be the Brandy.

Scooter went to the far end of the table where he had left his backpack on one of the chairs. He rushed back holding a small box, opened it, and took out some things that looked like small pieces of hard candy. "It's ginger," Scooter said. "I probably shouldn't have given her the Brandy. She's never drinks."

"Stomach," Darla growled. "Sick."

Scooter set the ginger on the table, and then scooped her up, her thin legs waving about like two long pencils. "Bathroom!" he said and dashed her into the tiny room.

Isabel heard Darla throw up several times, and then Scooter turned on the water in the sink. She guessed he was washing her face. In sympathy, Isabel felt her stomach give a slightly nauseous twist.

Darla walked herself back to her chair and sat down. Scooter popped one of the ginger candies into her mouth. "This should help darlyn."

Scooter looked over at Isabel. "You okay Sweetcheeks?"

"I'm okay. I sometimes feel a little sick when someone else is sick."

"Here, try one of these. Ginger. Great for nausea," Scooter said in a firm voice.

Isabel took one and slipped it into her mouth. It tasted nice but was quite spicy. Her little sick feeling receded in just seconds. "Yes, better."

Charles leaned across the table and inspected Darla. "Are you sure you're okay?"

"Yes. Of course. Just one of those things." She answered.

"You've never been sick before, Darla. At least I was never aware you were," Charles said.

Darla gave him a dark look, and then looked at Scooter, and back at Charles. "I am not ill. Not at all. I *never* get ill. It will not happen again, so please do not worry about it." Her voice was clipped and sharp.

Charles exchanged glances with Scooter who just shrugged and went to pick up the coffee pot. He put the coffee pot on the stove without any flame under it. "We've probably all had a lot more coffee than we should have. At least until we get more food in our stomachs. A few more cups and we'll all be manic."

It was rather strange, Isabel thought, how sick Darla looked and obviously felt, but she just shrugged it off with indifference. As if it didn't concern her at all. The woman was too stoic for Isabel's liking. The only thing in her life that seemed to upset the woman was worrying about her research. She did act odd when she heard about Joe's death, but she didn't appear to be feeling any real grief. She realized some people didn't have the capacity to feel the emotions other people felt.

Scooter kneeled down beside Darla and whispered something to her that Isabel couldn't hear. Darla gave him a slight nod of her head. Scooter got up and looked over at Charles.

"Charles, Darla has some meds in her lab she says she needs to take. I'll go down with her and get them. We won't take long."

"Why do *you* need to go, Darla? Just let Scooter get them for you." Charles said.

"I am the only one who can open my cupboard." Darla said sharply. "My work is so—" she hesitated, an odd look on her pinched face. "Well, anyway, he would not know what to bring

140

back."

"Yes, well okay then. You both go. We can't play it too safe," Charles said.

Isabel glanced over at Darla and saw how peculiar she looked. It did appear she needed some kind of medicine. Her color was still off. She hoped it wasn't going to become a medical emergency. This was not the time or the place for something like that to happen. However, the storm had quieted some, so maybe they could get a chopper in if it was necessary. She was thankful Scooter had a lot of medical training.

Darla unexpectedly got up from the table. "I'm the one who is going underground to get my meds," she announced in a louder voice than usual. Scooter can come with me, but he has to stand outside the door to the stairs."

Charles gave everyone around the table a curious look. "Okay then, just get yourselves back here fast. And take a flashlight. Remember, no lights are on in the stone stair area"

Scooter motioned to Darla who walked a little unsteadily over to him. "I can carry you, darlyn, if need be." He turned to Charles. "We'll be as fast as possible."

"I can walk just fine," Darla said.

Darla and Scooter made their way out of the kitchen. Travis and Danny looked at one another as if questioning each other about the problem of safety. Charles got up from his chair and began to pace the room.

Isabel tried to think of something to say to help break the tension. "Ummm," she started. "Maybe I could make us a very early breakfast," she finally said. "Not sure what's here, and I'm not much of a cook. But I could try."

"A good idea, Isabel. I saw some meat patties and a few other things in the freezer. Anything would do. Anything at all,' Charles said. "Is your foot up to it?"

"It's better. The ice helped." She gave a little feigned laugh. "But the rest of me feels as if it went through a meat grinder!"

"Okay, if you're sure," Charles said.

Isabel looked over at Danny and Travis who were busy talking to each other. She got up from her chair and deliberately made her way to the cupboard instead of the refrigerator. Not much there. They had already pirated most of the canned goods. However, there was still some bread and a few cookies left. She set it on the table and then opened the refrigerator, which looked as if it would echo, being so empty. When she opened the freezer, she saw the pack of meat patties. There were a few other things there, some veggies and fish sticks. There wouldn't be a whole lot for everyone but it would have to do. She wasn't sure, but she thought that Charles wanted her to start cooking as a distraction, so he could go check out the flash drive. That had to be what he meant.

When she turned to look at Charles, he lifted his eyebrows in a questioning manner. She gave a curt nod, pulled the meat patties out of the refrigerator, and moved to the stove. She didn't turn back to look at him again. You are going to make beef patties, and toast, she instructed herself. It would do for the three men seated at the kitchen table, as well as Scooter. Certainly Darla wouldn't want any, as sick as she had been. She took the meat patties and set them on the counter near the stove in order to thaw them out some before cooking them.

Unexpectedly, an unwanted thought flashed into her mind like a blinding light. "Oh my God!" she said aloud, not meaning to. She turned and looked at the three men who looked back at her with concern in their eyes. "What if . . . ." She frowned and shook her head.

"What if, what?" Charles asked, a slight questioning frown on his face.

She looked at Travis, who was tapping on his hearing aid, then at Danny whose creampuff hands were neatly folded in front of his little round belly, and then at Charles whose mouth was now slightly open, his right eyebrow tilted upward.

"What if . . . I mean is it possible that Darla . . . could she be having . . . morning sickness?" she said in a breathless voice which sounded as if she had been running. "I mean, could she possibly be . . . *pregnant?*"

142

The three men stared wide-eyed at her as if she had just said, "What if Darla is really a creature from outer space!"

Chapter Eleven

Charles sucked in his breath, held it for a moment, and then let it out slowly, his eyes closed, his mouth tight. Isabel's words were oddly delayed by his unaccepting mind. Then with a cracking sound inside his head, her words hit him. Good God, was it actually possible Darla was pregnant? If so, who was the father? And why hadn't she said anything? Darla's work seemed to totally consume her, and she gave the impression she was extremely close to success. He didn't remember her leaving the place more than once or twice in months. Could she have snuck out to a fertility clinic? Or to meet a man? Questions kept bouncing around in his head like ping pong balls. It made him feel giddy for a few minutes. All he needed was another complication. Everyone else sat silent, looking from one to another.

Finally, Travis said, "Isabel, what gives you that idea?" He frowned. "Darla's never had a male friend I know of. Or a woman friend for that matter."

"It's just . . . well it sounds just like morning sickness which I've heard can last all day for some women." Isabel hesitated, and then said, "I mean, it is possible isn't it? She's still young enough to have . . . or want a child."

"She never mentioned she wanted a child. Never talked about it at least. Her work was her family," Danny said, reaching for a slice of bread Isabel had set on the table. He tore off a piece and put it in his mouth.

Charles watched Isabel as she slowly opened the pack of frozen meat patties, a becoming pink flushing her cheeks. She kept shaking her head obviously not understanding the weird situation she had stumbled into. She no doubt wished she'd never done what Joe had asked. That was for certain. In addition, he imagined she hoped to never again find her way to the Hotel Grande and a bunch of nutty scientists. This was the awful place where she discovered her once dead husband was dead again. It was enough to make anyone collapse in a nervous heap. As he had thought earlier, he saw just how strong this woman really was. For one fleeting moment, he wondered if she could, in any way, be involved with whatever was going on. Then he reminded himself she had turned over the one thing that Jorge had asked her to find. If she was involved, wouldn't she have kept it a secret?

He craved another cup of strong coffee, to fight the need to sleep, but he didn't give in to the urge. He had to get control of himself, and begin putting the things he needed to do, in order. More coffee wouldn't help.

He sat there for a moment praying to God that Darla wasn't pregnant. That couldn't be possible! He tried to take a deep breath, but his throat and lungs were so tight he wondered if they were going to accept any air. He began numbering things in his mind that he needed to do. The very first was to see what was on Joe's flash drive. Second was to find out what the unusual pieces of equipment he'd discovered in Joe's lab were being used for? Third, he had to find out what Darla was keeping in her locked cupboard.

He needed to slow things down, not make any assumptions, and begin thinking in straight forward logical thoughts. After all, science was going to continue creating new things, thousands of them, no matter if some people objected, or were frightened by them. There was no way he could do much to control that. He was only one individual, and one who did not have much education in the type of science that he feared others might be doing. With those thoughts cleared, he began to breathe much easier. Now he needed to quickly get a look at Joe's flash drive. Number one on his list.

Isabel put a skillet on a low flame on the stove, and placed the frozen meat patties on it. While waiting for the meat patties to cook, Isabel sat down and leaned forward with her elbows on the table and her head cradled in her hands. It was more comfortable than sitting up straight. She needed a little comfort right then. She had a feeling she was right about Darla. That she *was* pregnant, which would explain her odd mood swings. Danny and Travis didn't appear to believe it. She wasn't sure if Charles believed it. She looked over at him, but couldn't read his face. Tense one minute, thoughtful the next.

It seemed like hours before Scooter and Darla arrived back in the kitchen. Darla's cheeks were back to their normal persimmon color. It made Isabel feel more comfortable. Hopefully Darla just had too many things to deal with, and then some Brandy on top of it. Or maybe she *was* pregnant but had not yet told anyone. She watched as Scooter pulled out a chair for her, and then sat down next to her.

"All's well," Scooter cried out like a night watcher in days of old.

"Are you okay," Charles asked Darla.

"Yes, yes, yes, it is nothing to worry about," Darla barked.

"So when is Isabel going to fix us a little something to eat?" Danny asked, grinning.

Isabel stood up and smiled gently, "Yes, yes, I'm cooking something."

Darla nodded her head. "Is it breakfast or lunch time now, or what?"

"A very early breakfast, Darla," Isabel said.

"Doesn't matter to me," Danny chuckled. "I'm starved. I hope there's a lot!"

"Just a few meat patties, Danny," Isabel told him.

Charles looked at Isabel. "I thought I also saw a few fish sticks in the fridge."

Darla sat stiffly upright in her chair. "No! No! The fish are for my . . . my kitties. They need feeding." She cleared her throat. "After I eat, I need to feed my kitties."

"Where do your kitties usually stay, Darla?" Isabel asked, thinking about what had felt like a strange cat that had come close to her in the dark cavern. The one that had hairless skin.

Darla looked confused for a moment, then recovered. "In the underground. I keep telling you there is a tunnel leading up and out

146

of the underground. They go inside to get out of the frigid weather."

Charles shook his head. "Darla your cats can wait awhile. We've already had two terrible incidents down there. They'll get along until you can feed them outside."

"I will feed them when I damn well please!" Darla shrieked. "Just try and stop me!"

"Okay, calm down Darla, "Charles said. "We'll work it out."

Isabel checked out the meat patties which were pretty well close to being cooked. "So, does anyone want some gravy on their meat? I think I saw a jar of it in the cupboard." She glanced over at Charles, and he gave her a knowing smile.

"Don't fix mine yet," Charles said. "Get the others done first. I am going up to my room for a few minutes. I want to see if my computer is running and if the router is broadcasting any wi-fi. "

Isabel saw Travis and Scooter both give a questioning frown. "So, which one of us should go with you?" Danny asked

"I'm breaking my own rule. All of you get busy and eat something. If there is someone else loose in this place, I'll confront them. I've got a baby Glock in my room."

"Charles, are you sure? It could be dangerous!" Travis said.

"A Glock?" Isabel asked.

"A gun," Danny informed her.

"I won't be long. Eat. Drink and be merry!" Charles dashed out of the room before anyone could say anything more.

"Oh no, he shouldn't go alone," Darla said, unusual concern in her voice. "But then I suppose he will be okay."

"He'll be okay. He's got a gun," Danny remarked. "Maybe he'll come back and shoot all of us with it. Anyone think about that?" He pulled one hand away from his pillow-like stomach and pointed at one of them after another. "Bang, bang, bang."

"Knock it off, Danny," Travis insisted.

Isabel looked around at everyone and decided Danny was trying to be droll, in a rather stupid way. Especially with everyone's nerves on edge. She quickly filled a small pot with water and set it on the stove. She pulled the veggie package out of the refrigerator, opened it, knowing that with Danny there, they would need more food. She dropped them in the pot filled with water." The thought of Charles having a gun in his room gave her a jolt. She hated even the thought of guns.

Despite his exhausted legs, Charles made it upstairs to his room in record time. He always kept his personal computer in his room so he could do things he didn't want done on the computer in his lab. He had turned it off the day before, so he was certain the batteries were up and good for at least an hour, maybe more. He was unable to send out any email since the router for Wi-Fi wasn't connected to the backup generator. But he could check the contents of the flash drive which was all that mattered to him.

He opened the computer, switched it on, and in less than a minute it started up. He checked the battery power which said it was about half charged. He would only spend a few minutes using it right now, or someone might come looking for him. Just a quick look at the flash drive was all he needed. He pulled it out of his pocket, inserted it into the computer, and waited until the computer recognized the new drive. Before he went any further, he thought about the fact that while he was in his room alone he would be vulnerable to whomever it was that had killed Joe.

He got up, went to a little chest next to his bed, reached behind the back side of it, and felt for his gun. There it was, taped to the wood back of the chest. He quickly removed the tape and pulled it out. He had checked it every night. A safety routine. The compact Glock was small enough to be unobtrusive, was self-loading, and was just the right weapon for self-defense, in most situations. He set the gun down next to him near the computer, feeling considerably safer.

He clicked on the new drive, and only one folder came up. The caption on the folder read:

The Gray Green Underground

COMPLETED EXPERIMENTS.

Inside that folder it said: Human Experiment number 4 (four)

After that a heading said: COMMENTS: *The rewriting of code inside the required molecules and placing them into the cell is expected to allow the DNA to duplicate and morph as it should. The new linctus should totally solve the problem of rejection. It has done so in all feline and simian experiments to date.*

What he read gave him pause. He pretty much understood it, but his mind did not want to accept the implication that it made. Unfortunately, his degree was not in molecular biology. Far from it in fact. His usable scientific knowledge was restricted to limited methods of improving vegetables by natural means. However he continued to extended his research in order to help uncover Bertrand's problem. He understood that the process of producing recombinant DNA for the altering and controlling of genotype and phenotype of organisms was being done profusely lately. It surprised him to discover that the process was rather easy. Restriction enzymes were introduced into a DNA molecule to break it into fragments and then genes from another organism were inserted into it. However, the more he researched that type of work the more he discovered about the risky side of it. Of course, it wasn't all dangerous. In recent years, there had been some really exciting discoveries. He'd read about sheep being implanted with genetic markers from black Widow spiders, which forced them to produce the protein in their milk that created spider Silk. Stronger and more flexible than steel, spider silk offered a lightweight alternative to carbon fiber. Who would ever have dreamed that part of a sheep's DNA could be successfully mixed with that of a spider's?

Looking at the computer screen, he focused on the next page which was blank at first and then suddenly a flood of letters began slowly flowing across it. He stopped the flow by hitting the control key. He looked at the strip of letters.

CACTTCTAACCTAGAGGGGGGCCAGGCCGAGGTCCC(G-A)

Dorothy McMillan

He suddenly realized that there were only four letters, repeated over and over. ACTG The chemical letters that made up the language of genes. The flash drive was apparently filled with someone's genome sequence! So, who was the human experiment number 4? Was it Joe? If Joe had nothing to do with it, then why did he have it on his flash drive? Or had he stolen the information, and then been killed because of it?

During the past ten years, he knew that phenomenal strides had been made in the field of human genetic engineering. In some of the science journals, he had seen a number of private companies who offered the process of complete genome sequencing for anyone who wanted it done. The price of the process was going down considerably because of better and less expensive sequencing machines. The major reason someone would have this done was that if a person's genome sequence could be read, it might possibly reveal mistakes in the recipe which made them human. Misspellings and mutations in the four letter code. Mistakes could mean a person had some physical or mental problem. It would take specialized diagnostic testing of the entire sequence to let someone know if they were prone to such things as heart disease, cancers, alcoholism, and many other health problems. It might even reveal how long they could expect to live.

Charles didn't have any desire to learn these details about himself. Nevertheless, he imagined a lot of others might. What concerned him the most was that maybe one day every baby would have to have their genome sequence done at birth. It would then become public record. Employers could use these records to determine who to employ and who not to. Insurance companies would no doubt deny risky people coverage. It seems Aldous Huxley may well have had it right when he wrote *Brave New World*.

He shook his head, trying to wrap his thoughts around the sequenced genomes on the flash drive. And why were they there? He knew that in order to hold a whole person's genome the flash drive had to hold terabytes. Or maybe even petabytes! This flash drive was certainly not the kind one could pick up at Best Buy.

150

Then again, he'd only looked at a little of the genome sequence. Maybe it was only a sample portion on the drive. The main thing that concerned him was the idea that someone, possibly Joe, might have been fooling around with the deliberate manipulation and cross mixing of genetic material. Otherwise, why would he have kept it so secret? Why would he have tried to get it out of the underground Lab without anyone knowing? Unless he was doing something illegal. Maybe even immoral!"

Such words as hybrid, or chimera, gnawed at his mind. The idea of mixing animal DNA with that of a human troubled him. He did know, however, that it had been done successfully in certain instances, such as creating insulin, but it remained extremely risky. Adding human DNA to an animal such as a pig, so doctors could use their heart valves, was one thing, but adding an animal's DNA to a human was quite another.

He hated the mixed feelings that rattled around inside his mind. It made him feel as if he was on a run-away horse.

Isabel felt uncomfortable having Charles gone for so long. Everyone had finished eating what little food they had. Darla sat near the lantern light reading a book she had obviously picked up when she went to her lab, her eyes blinking as if questioning something. She looked better, and it made Isabel feel silly for having suggested she might be pregnant. After eating, Travis found a bottle of dark Dos Equis beer and was drinking it slowly. Danny had gulped down his food in less than three minutes and now sat with his eyes closed, looking remarkably comfortable in his kitchen chair, his fingers latched together underneath his Santa tummy as usual.

Just looking at Scooter, who was still wearing a pair of summer shorts, made Isabel shiverish, even though the room was quite warm. He'd produced a deck of cards out of thin air and was playing solitaire on the kitchen table. What a group, Isabel thought. Like something out of a comic book. She gave a giggle, born of tension, and then swallowed it, almost choking on it. She shouldn't be thinking about people like that. After all, these were eminent scientists, not objects of humor.

She wished she had a book to read, like Darla. She wanted to sneak away to the entry room where there were several shelves of books. Of course, they might all be way over her head. What she would give for a good suspense novel, or an historical saga. She needed something to take her mind off of Jorge's death, which continued to haunt her in an odd way. No sympathy for him. Only for herself. Hurry up Charles, she muttered under her breath. I need you here!

She heard a heavy thrumming and looked up at the bent glass windows where she could see the rain once again coming down in huge lead colored drops. "Oh great!" she said aloud. "The storm is getting worse again!" The room around her was shadow plagued and made her feel uncomfortable.

Travis must have heard her because he glanced up at the windows. "Some days I think we are caught in a storm vortex up here in the wilderness."

"How long . . . ." she said, but then hesitated, not sure she really wanted to know. "I mean, how much longer do you think it will be before we can get out of here?"

Scooter looked over at her and shrugged. "No idea, Sweetcheeks. Might as well settle in and make the best of it." He gave her a crooked grin. "I wish my lady girl hadn't gone home last night. She would sure as shooting keep me from being bored." He paused for a moment then said, "Want to play poker?"

"Oh, I don't think so Scooter," Isabel replied. But maybe when Charles gets back, we can all play."

Scooter looked at his watch. "He's been gone too long. I wonder what he's up to. Maybe he decided to abandon us and walk his way off the mountain."

"Oh, you don't think—"Isabel started to say.

"Nah, Sweetcheeks, just joking. Don't take me seriously. I always joke when a situation gets a bit dicey."

"Not much of a joke, however, now was it?" Danny said, giving Scooter a disapproving glance.

Charles walked into the kitchen with the oddest expression on his face. He appeared extremely upset about something, but was trying to cover it with a jaunty but crooked smile. Only Scooter looked at him, the others continued with what they were doing.

"What's up Chucky?" Scooter asked, no doubt noticing the odd attitude. "You look like a bad case of indigestion."

"Nothing," Charles said. "And cut the Chucky crap!"

Isabel wondered if Charles had found something really disturbing on Jorge's flash drive. She didn't like the way he was acting. It didn't seem native to him. What the heck had he discovered?

"Come on, what's wrong Charles?" She hoped he didn't take offense, but she wanted him to clear the air. If there was more trouble, they all deserved to know about it.

Charles looked around the room, cleared his throat, and then gave a wide yawn. "Nothing's wrong. It's just my lack of sleep! Sorry about that." He walked to the sink and poured a glass of water. After drinking about half of it he said, "I went to see if the computer in my room had any battery power. The ones in the radio won't last much longer. With the computer I thought we could email and keep track of how long it might be before they can get the road clear."

"Ah, good idea," Travis said.

"Nope . . . wrong idea." Charles shook his head. "I hadn't thought about it, but the router isn't connected to the backup generator, so no Wi-Fi. Can't get any information that way. So, we need to be sure not to use the radio unless we absolutely have to. At least we've already notified everyone and hopefully they are working on solutions to our dilemma."

Isabel was convinced Charles had gone to see if he could open Jorge's flash drive. Did he or didn't he manage it? She would have to see him alone if she wanted to find out.

It wasn't long before Charles made it possible. He took a few sips of coffee, walked around the length of the kitchen table then

153

stopped and said, "My legs are about dead, but I need to go below and see how my grapes are doing. I haven't checked them since the blackout. The generator has the lights on, but I'm not certain about the air mixture."

Scooter quickly got up from his chair. "Okay buddy, let's go."

Charles shook his head. "No, you stay here and keep an eye on Darla. Isabel can go with me. She needs something to keep her mind off . . . everything."

Isabel felt her eyes go wide at his words. "Oh, I . . . well . . . sure."

"Charles, what about her injured foot?" Travis asked.

Charles looked down at her. "You up to it, Isabel?" he asked.

"Yes, I think so. I actually was getting really antsy just sitting here with nothing to do. The foot's better, the swelling is almost gone, thanks to the ice packs."

Darla looked up from her book, tilted her head a little, and went back to reading.

"Okay then," Charles said. We shouldn't be gone long." Charles motioned to Isabel to follow him and strode toward the door. Because of her foot, Isabel had trouble keeping up with him until they reached the stone stairs. Then she stopped. She really didn't want to get near those awful gray-green stones again. They stretched down below her into the darkness; the area as black as crow wings. The little white lights on the green walls were still not working. .

She hoped he had a good reason for wanting her with him. He must have felt her fear because Charles said, "Not to worry, I have two flashlights." He pulled them out of his jacket pocket and handed her one. Relief flooded over her like warm water. With some light, she was fairly sure she could make it to Charles' lab. Then he said something that spoiled her sense of relief.

"Isabel . . . we are not going to *my* lab," he told her suddenly. "We are going to Darla's. And possibly Joe's."

"Why? I don't understand." Charles gave her a long serious look. She stared back, wanting to read the expression in his eyes. "Charles, why are we going to Darla's lab? And what did you find on Jorge's flash drive?"

"Before we go down there," he said, ignoring her question. "I have two questions to ask you."

She gave him a frown and said "What questions?"

"Are you familiar with the word Transhuman?"

"Trans . . . what? I'm not familiar with the word. What does it mean?"

He looked at her for a moment, indecision flickering in his eyes. "Transhumanism with a plus sign after it. Do you know what that is?

"I said no! But the prefix trans means . . . well I think it means *across* or *past*, or something like that. So the word could mean past or beyond humanism."

He narrowed his eyes and looked at her, obviously pondering her answer, finally said, "Okay, than I need to ask . . . can I trust you Isabel? I really need to know that you weren't involved in something with your husband. That you didn't come here as a . . . well, to put it bluntly, as a spy."

She stepped back almost as if he had hit her. "A what!"

Charles reached out and came close to putting his hand on her mouth, obviously wanting her to be quiet. "Listen to me! Your husband is, or was, involved in something serious. I need to know if you are also involved with it."

Isabel turned first one way, and then the other, wanting to get around Charles. He stopped her both times. Frustrated, she raised her voice even more. "What the hell are you talking about?" The result was this time he did clamp his hand over her mouth. A trickle of panic cascaded from her head to her feet.

"All I need is a truthful answer. If you are involved, just say so, and we'll go back. I won't get into it again with you until we are able to get out of here." He pulled his hand back from her mouth, straightened his shoulders. He looked at her with what were usually soft green eyes, but right now, they resembled hard, polished marbles.

"I have no idea what you are talking about. What I told you about Jorge asking me to meet him here is it! It's the whole damn balloon! The fucking balloon that burst like a bomb and propelled me

155

into this fun fucking vacation I'm having! I gave you the one thing he wanted me to get for him. What the hell more do you want?"

Charles actually smiled them, and gave a tight little laugh. "Okay. All I needed to know is if I can trust you. Completely." He laughed again. "Some language!"

"I usually save it for my students," she growled. "Listen to me Charles! Jorge warned me that *you were not to be trusted.* I'm beginning to wonder if he was right!" She felt her breath coming in hard little bursts as she talked.

"Of course. He would have, wouldn't he?" Charles gave her a broad smile. "I'll tell you why later. But right now, I need us to see what all we can find in both Joe's and Darla's labs."

It took a minute for Isabel to figure out what she should say. Then she knew, trustworthy or not, Charles was the only person in the grotesque stone castle she had gotten to know, even a little. Maybe she shouldn't trust anyone. But if she had to, then Charles was her best bet.

"Yes," she said quietly. "You can trust me. I swear to you I am not involved in anything Jorge may have been doing during his four dead years."

"Thank you." He let out another small laugh. "Part of the reason Joe said about not trusting me was because he had no doubt learned somehow that I'm here as a watchdog for Bertrand. They are suspicious that some of the research being done here might be beyond legal limits"

"Ah, speaking of spies!" Isabel said a little cryptic. She gave him a narrow look, as if measuring him. "Okay then. I can live with that."

"Good. So let's get on with what we need to do."

"What do you expect to find in Darla's lab?"

"We just need to look, and I'm sure we'll know when we find it."

"Does it have anything to do with what you found on Jorge's flash drive?"

"It has everything to do with it," Charles said in a grim tone.

"Then it must be something very important."

"Isabel, you have no idea!"

156

Chapter Twelve

Charles helped Isabel down most of the steps, keeping her injured foot from too much pressure. Isabel was certain she would never have made it without his help. She wondered why he had insisted on her going with him, instead of Scooter, or maybe Travis. One answer could be that he didn't trust any of them and didn't want them to know what he was looking for. The other might be that he was, as some point, going to toss her down the steps and make sure she was dead, like Joe. She quickly brushed the second answer out of her head. After all, Charles had rescued her. If he wanted her dead, he would have finished her off then.

When they reached the metal door that was the entrance to Darla's lab, Charles handed her his flashlight. "I'll need both hands to get rid of this bar across the door. Darla is so damn guarded. Makes me think she's up to something more than making medicines. Shine one of the lights on the combination lock on the left."

Isabel wondered how the heck Charles could open it. She watched as he worked quickly, turning the lock's dial back and forth quickly. Then the lock slid smoothly open and he dropped it to the ground. The metal bar dropped downward and hung loose on the right side of the door, held by the second lock. With a twist of a latch, he opened the door into Darla's lab.

"Quickly," he urged Isabel. "Get inside." The two of them moved into the brightly lit room and Charles closed the door behind them and slid its dead bolt into place.

She looked out at the rows and rows of special soybean blossoms in front of her, like a sea of pink. She heard Charles take in a long breath and let it out with a burst, as if releasing a lot of pent up tension.

"Now," he said, "we need to get the bar off of Darla's cupboard. If she's into something she shouldn't be, I think this is the only place we might find it."

157

"Do you have the combination numbers for these locks?"

"I know them." Charles said with a smug little smile, "It's easy. You just pull up on the shackle, rotate the dial counterclockwise, pull hard and you'll feel the hinge lock, Then write down the number it locks on. I learned how as a kid. Don't ask why. I was kind of a jokester." He looked a little self-conscious when he said it.

"Okay, then *why* did you learn her lock numbers?"

"Safety. In case we ever needed to verify to the insurance company there was nothing dangerous inside the cupboards. Or, in the event that something was reported stolen. Darla and Joe are the only ones who lock their cupboards. So I made sure I knew the combinations. This is the first time I've invaded them, however"

"Because," she said. "You didn't have a serious reason to until now."

It only took a few more moments for Charles to get the lock open on Darla's cupboard. The cupboard's metal door was a tight fit and difficult to open. Isabel attempted to pry open the bottom section with her fingers. Charles worked the top of the door. With a sudden loud snap, the door popped open, swung wide, and the two of them jumped back from it.

Both of them stood there staring into the cupboard; Isabel with her mouth open and Charles with his hand over his mouth.

After what felt like forever, Isabel said, "Oh my dear God!"

In front of her stood rows and rows of glass jars. Large jars and small jars. Each jar was filled with some sort of dingy looking liquid. Blobs of something Isabel tried to recognize, but couldn't, floated aimlessly in each large jar. Some sort of odious looking creatures . . . animals . . . but not animals. Some with giant marble-like eyes set into globs of greasy looking white skin. Some with fins or maybe they were horribly shaped legs covered with stiff pin-like protrusions. The two largest jars contained a flaccid white masse with something resembling oval mouths that were shell pink, along with wide open pale eyes. Eyes that stared at Isabel as if they were alive. Imploring eyes.

She looked away from the horrible sight, and grabbed hold of

Charles. He put his arm around her. "What in God's name are these things?" she asked breathlessly.

"They were not made in God's name, that's for certain," he said. "But they aren't alive, so there's nothing to be afraid of."

"Yes, but what the hell are they?"

"Man-made creatures of some sort, I'm afraid."

A jarring thought made Isabel looked back at the jars. "Charles . . . ," she began. "What if . . . ." She still couldn't get the words out.

"What?"

"What if that cat I think was in the cavern with me where I came to, was something like these. I couldn't see it, but it did feel like some of these things look."

"You mean one of Darla's kitties?"

"Yes."

"Oh Christ! Don't tell me she let some of these abominations live! There are strict laws concerning this kind of thing! The results of genetic engineering of animals require they be put down within a short period of time after developing. I don't know the full details, but I can't imagine what could happen if Darla let some of these things loose outside." He looked down at her, his eyes so penetrating she felt trapped by them. "Isabel, can you understand the unbelievable dangers of unknown genetically altered creatures proliferating in the wild?"

The two of them stood there for several moments. Isabel kept looking away from the jars, but then she couldn't keep from looking back. "What in the hell kind of genetic splicing or engineering was Darla involved in, anyway?" she finally said.

Charles sighed and stepped closer to the cupboard, inspecting each of the jars. "I have no idea. If what you thought was in the cavern with you was like a cat, then maybe felines were a major part of her projects. It's impossible to actually tell from looking at these monstrosities what mixtures they are."

"Why would she do this? What about her soybeans and incredible new medicine?"

"I suppose they could be some part of these experiments."

159

"So what do we do now?" Isabel gave him a questioning look. She was too stunned at the situation to think about what effect it could have on her, because of Jorge. "Do you suppose Jorge . . . Joe was helping her with all this?"

Charles swung around and looked at her. "You bet I do! He has a locked cupboard too. Christ! I hate to think what might be in there. And what about all his new equipment. Add to that, the two of them working together a lot of the time. His not wanting Bertrand to see his results. In addition, there's all the genetic information I found on his flash drive. Someone either wanted to stop him, or else wanted a part of whatever they were into."

The thought of Jorge being dead again grabbed Isabel like a giant rough hand. She shook off the thought. "Enough of this! Can we go back upstairs now Charles? Please!"

Charles stood looking at the jars, as if he was trying to convince himself he wasn't actually seeing such awful things. Then he backed away, closed the cupboard doors, and replaced the bar and the lock. "I'll check out Joe's locked cupboard later. I should have done it first. But I think I am afraid of what I'll find. Now it appears that Darla is also involved. At least I have a good idea now, what some of that new equipment of Joe's might be. He obviously forged the receipts for them, so Bertrand would have no idea what he was up to."

"Let's get to the stairs," Isabel said, feeling a full body shiver from either the cold or the fear of what they had found in the cupboard. "I need some of that hot coffee." She started toward the door, wanting all of this to be over.

"Wait!" Charles said. He stopped at what appeared to be Darla's desk. He looked it over slowly, and then pulled open one drawer after another.

"Charles," Isabel pleaded. "Please, let's go. Darla could possibly show up here any minute, if we're gone too long."

Charles pulled out what looked like a booklet from one of the desk draws. An odd grimace took hold of his face. He flipped through the booklet, and then held it up for Darla to see. On the cover, she saw what looked like a large letter H and a plus + sign. "Okay, "she nodded. "Whatever it is, take it and let's get topside."

"Right, of course. I'm sorry. I'm just so—." He slipped the booklet inside his jacket as they headed to the doorway. He closed the door behind them, replacing the bar and the lock. Then, he moved beside her as they began the climb up the stone steps. He used his arm again to help her avoid too much pressure on her injured foot.

"So what is that thing you took from Darla's desk? Before we came in here, you mentioned that H thing on the cover."

Charles stopped their climb for a moment and looked down at her. "H plus is the logo of a group of people called trans-humanists."

Isabel frowned. "Is that something bad?"

"No, not at all. But finding it in Darla's desk changes the whole complexion of what's going on here. I'll explain more later." He started them climbing again.

"How are you going to handle all this?" she asked, her legs feeling the burn again as they moved.

"Not sure yet. I need to think it through. Those things in Darla's cupboard are definitely not something that Bertrand would have imagined she'd be doing. So please, do me a favor and don't say a word about what we did or what we found."

"I hate secrets, but I won't say anything about all this, until you are ready to." Isabel said. "But who do you think killed Jorge?"

"Don't really know, but Darla maybe? I swear they are . . . were involved in some work together. She's so tall, she might have been able to manage it. Took him off guard. And maybe she struck you too, and left you for dead."

"No! I can't imagine that!" She shook her head. "She's strange, but I don't think she's homicidal. I think we should just keep quiet, and let the police take care of everything."

"You're probably right. Come on, only a few more steps and we're out of here I think I'm ready for some of my 100-year-old Brandy! How about you?"

"Better not. I might not be able to keep the secret about what we just saw!"

161

Charles gave a long deep sigh. "What a mess! I just hope we don't end up drowning in a sea of dark secrets."

They reached the last of the stone steps and headed for the kitchen. As they entered, Isabel plastered a slight smile on her face. She moved quickly to one of the chairs and plopped herself down with her foot throbbing some, but not as much as it had earlier. She pulled over one of the empty chairs and propped her injured foot on it. The burn in her legs lessened. Thank God for Scooter's pain pills which were still giving her some relief? Looking around, she suddenly realized Darla was missing.

Before she had a chance to ask about her, Scooter gave her an uncharacteristic pained look and said, "Darla's sick again. Right now, she's tossing her cookies in the bathroom for the second time since you two left."

Charles pulled out his Brandy bottle and set it down on the table with a loud thump and looked at it longingly. "Great!" he said in a low but gruff voice.

"Okay, everyone, *listen,*" Scooter said, getting their attention with a clap of his hands. "Since Darla is feeling so ill, I have to break my trust with her, and tell you . . . Isabel was right."

"About what?" Isabel asked, surprised by his words.

"I have to tell you . . . that Darla *is* pregnant!"

The silence in the room made the air around Isabel feel colder than the stone stairs and the raging winter storm outside combined.

162

Chapter Thirteen

The silence seemed to freeze everyone in the kitchen motionless. Isabel looked at the expression on Scooter's face. She couldn't determine if it was one of anger, or frustration. Then again it could be one of relief, being able to tell everyone about Darla's pregnancy. Finally, to break the frigid silence, she said, "How do you know that, Scooter?"

He gave her a slight lift of his shoulders, sighed and said, "First, she came to me, asking questions about childbirth. Then a little later, she told me that she was planning to have a baby, by artificial insemination. She asked if I would do the insemination. I was stunned, and said no. But then she said that she had just received the sperm packed in dry ice. It had to be done quickly. So I acquiesced against my better judgment." Scooter shook his head. "I made her sign a consent form I drew up relieving me of any responsibility if it didn't go well. I was totally shaken when it actually took, and she found herself pregnant. I just hope she can handle it."

"My God!" Charles bellowed. "I don't believe it!"

"Neither do I, "Scooter went on. "At this point, she's feeling pretty bad as some women do in the early stages of pregnancy. Nevertheless, she's so stoic that until now she hardly let on about how bad she felt. If I figure it right, she is about four months already. Her morning sickness is still hanging on, as it does sometimes. But she's not showing much yet, because she's so tall."

Charles got up and began to pace around the kitchen table. His expression unreadable. "Why didn't you tell me, Scooter?"

"Because she asked me not to. It was her business, so I felt it was up to her to let people know, when she began showing."

"Damn it!" Charles said. "I wish I'd known before this."

"Sorry, Chucky. It was up to her. I did try to get her to go out and see a doctor, but she kept putting it off."

The cold silence imploded suddenly when everyone started

talking, and Isabel couldn't keep up with all of the conversations going at once.

Charles sat back down at the table, and closed his eyes for a few moments. When he opened them, Isabel was surprised to see how deep their green was, and how different he now looked. It was if he had been waiting for something, for a long time, and it had finally arrived. She wasn't at all sure, however, if that was a good, or bad thing.

She began to wonder where Darla got the semen. From FedEx? she asked herself, starting to laugh at the idea. Get pregnant through the mail? She hadn't heard if that was possible. But then you buy all sorts of impossible things via the mail. She gave a little coughing laugh, trying to cover it with her hand.

She looked at Charles who did seem somewhat upset now. If the semen didn't arrive by FedEx, could it possibly be his? No! God no! That idea would not jell with her. She looked around at the men sitting at the table. Certainly not Danny with his little Santa tummy, nor Travis who she thought might be too old to father a child. However, what about Scooter? He was young, apparently straight, and enjoyed the company of women. But with Darla? She just couldn't put the two together.

Charles picked up the Brandy bottle he'd set on the table and looked at it. Then he looked at first one person, then another around the table. "I don't think we can fix any of our problems around here with the contents of this bottle, but if anyone is feeling extra anxious, please help yourself to just a small amount. We don't need anyone tanked-up, do we?" He took the lid off the bottle and set it back on the table. As he did, Darla came out of the bathroom and moved quickly to her chair at the table, and sat down heavily, as if exhausted.

Isabel suddenly felt sorry for her. The poor woman, having what was probably her first child and maybe only one, and then all this turmoil going on, what with the murder and the storm. She looked up at the windows above, and the rain pelting down on them, and wondered what time it was.

"Are you okay, Darla?" Charles asked in a quiet voice.

Darla looked around at everyone, a puzzled look in her gray eyes. "Yes, of course. Just an upset stomach. Not to worry."

Scooter gave a little cough and said, "Darla, I told them. I had to."

Darla turned to him, her pinched cheeks turning their usual persimmon color. "You did? Why would you do that? I am doing just fine. No business of anyone if I decided to have a baby." Her voice was measured, halting, yet clear and loud.

Charles gave her an understanding nod. 'No, of course it's not our business. But with everyone concerned about you not feeling well today, Scooter thought we should understand why."

Darla blinked nervously for a few moments. "Just morning sickness," she said, then looked at her watch and frowned. "It's close to morning, isn't it? But I read that lots of women have continual nausea sometimes, for a while. It will pass."

"We're happy for you, Darla," Charles said.

"Yes," Isabel joined in. "I'm happy too."

"Would you like to go to your room and try to sleep?" Scooter asked. I could stay with you for a while, if you like."

Darla glanced around, "Well, that might not be a bad idea. If the storm stops, or slows, we should have some help here by daylight."

Scooter got up from his chair and headed for the kitchen cupboard. "Let's take some soda crackers with us. They often help the nausea," he said, pulling a large package out of the cupboard along with a jar of peanut butter. He grinned. "The peanut butter is for me. Dinner was a little light."

Darla began feeling around in the pocket of the pants she was wearing. She pulled out a small bottle, and gave a sigh relief. She grinned. "Just my meds my . . . ah, doctor gave me. Some . . . well, prenatal vitamins I suppose."

Isabel saw Scooter's eyes narrow as he said, "I didn't know you went out to see a Doc. Good girl, Darla. I was worried about that."

The room turned silent again after the two of them left. Charles was leaning back in his chair, his eyes closed. Isabel wondered what

165

he was thinking, or was he just exhausted? Travis had his mouth pinched forward, almost as if he was whistling. Danny had his shiny pink fingernails tapping on the table's surface.

"Boy, I wish I'd known that we had some peanut butter. I love peanut butter," Danny murmured.

"Listen," Charles said. "I'm sure we are all tired and could use a little sleep. Maybe we should take watches, and have two of us sleep for an hour or so. Travis, you and Danny could sleep first, then Isabel and I."

Travis leaned forward and gave Charles a thumb's up. "Just an hour or so?"

"That would bring us up to about five or six a.m. With luck, the police and company officials might be here by then. That is, if they get the road cleared enough. Or if the storm's over so they could bring in a chopper."

"I'm good with that," Travis said with a brittle chuckle. "Although there's still the chance that you or Isabel might be the murderer, and kill us both in our sleep.

"Yeah, well that goes two ways," Isabel replied. "And would be difficult to explain to Scooter and Darla. As well as the police." She surprised herself by being so glib in such a tense situation..

"Okay, since Scooter took the peanut butter, then I'm gonna sleep." Danny yawned.

"How about you, Isabel?" Charles asked. "Are you good for a while?"

"I'm not at all sleepy right now," she said.

It took only a few minutes before both Danny and Travis were snoring lightly, their arms stretched out on the table, and their heads resting on small stacks of paper napkins.

Charles gave a small laugh. "Didn't take them long, did it?"

"Aren't you exhausted," Isabel asked him.

"I feel like a dead man," he replied. "Dead and just walking around like I wasn't aware I'd died." He yawned. "But it's more the tension of our situation than the lack of sleep.

"Well, look, I had a good nap in my room, and one on the table,

166

so I'm really not sleepy at all. Why don't you sleep while those two sleep?"

"I don't think so; I need to be on guard."

"Believe me, if anyone does anything they shouldn't I'll scream you awake." She watched him as he yawned again. His eyelids were bunched into folds like little curtains ready to close down. "I can wake you in just an hour, or maybe two, if you want."

He looked at her, blinking to try and keep the eyelids from closing. "Okay then. One hour. No more!"

She looked at her watch. "One hour it is. Even a little should help."

Charles went to the stove and picked up several hot pads and carried them back to where he'd been sitting. "Nifty little pillows," he said, his voice beginning to fail. He stretched out his arms on the table. "Nighty night," he whispered and laid his head down on the hot pads.

Isabel looked at the three sleeping men. "What," she said in a quiet voice, "am I doing here with three men sleeping with their heads on a kitchen table? With one of them possibly being a murderer. Here she was in a giant stone castle with green mold oozing all over the stone walls in the underground, and metal lined caverns filled with some sort of vegetation growing underneath her. She wondered what her students would think about their biology teacher sitting there in a such a bizarre and dangerous place having the most unusual time of her life.

She moved her foot off the chair where it had been propped. It felt better, but it still ached some, and she wished she had a book to read, or even a newspaper, to take her mind off of everything. The kitchen was too quiet, but at least she could hear the storm through the windows above her. It did sound as if it might be slowing down some. She looked around to see if Scooter's playing cards were there. To her surprise, she found them sitting on the counter only a few feet away from her. Well, at least she could play Solitaire for the hour before she woke Charles. That is if she could remember how to play. It had been years since she'd played it. She shuffled the deck and laid out the cards. It wasn't long before she became completely absorbed with trying to win.

When she finally became bored with playing solitaire, she checked her watch and to her shock, discovered it had been almost an hour and a half since Charles had gone to sleep. "Damn!" she said. "I hope he isn't mad when I wake him?" When she looked around the table she realized something even more shocking. Travis was not there. She looked around the kitchen but he was not there. She got up with a start, wondering if he had gone to the bathroom. But it was empty.

"Charles!" she yelled. "Wake up!"

Charles sat up, one of the hot pads clinging to his cheek. "What!" he said, pulling the pad off.

"It's Travis. I was playing Solitaire and when I looked up, he was gone! He's not in the bathroom. I didn't hear him, or see him leave. I should have kept my eyes on the two of them, but I was playing cards to help myself stay awake. I didn't hear anything. I'm sorry; I just didn't hear him get up." She felt tears beginning to well up. "I am so sorry!"

"Don't get weepy on me," Charles gave her a soft smile. "He probably went down to check out his lab. Or, maybe went to his room where it's more comfortable to sleep."

"Oh, God, I hope that's what happened. But he should have told me!"

"Yes, he should have told you." Charles got up from his chair and went to the stove, picked up the coffee pot, and touched it gingerly on the side, obviously trying to see if it was still hot. Apparently, it was. He poured a cup full and took a sip. "Good. Would you like a cup, Isabel?"

Isabel shook her head. "No. But I do need to use the bathroom. And clean up some. I feel pretty grungy."

Charles nodded. "Yes, of course. I'll keep watch. I'm sure Travis will be back soon. Danny over there is still snoring like a mini volcano trying to erupt."

"I feel so terrible about not noticing that Travis left, I could just bite myself!" Isabel grumbled as she made her way to the little bathroom and closed the door behind her.

It was only a few minutes later when Charles heard a sound of shoes smacking against the wood floor in the hallway.

Travis came dashing into the kitchen looking first at the darkened hallway behind him with his scrunched eyes, and then at Danny and Charles. Then he bent his tall stick of a body over and shook Danny vigorously to wake him up. He admonished both of them to be quiet. A finger to his lips. Danny, still stunned by sleeping soundly, got up from the table, a mystified expression on his face, and almost tripped over one of the kitchen chairs. Charles thought he might take a tumble if he tried to move too fast in such a state.

"What the-." Danny started to holler.

"Quiet," Travis whispered hoarsely.

Charles hesitated, wondering nervously what in the heck was going on. Cautiously, he picked up his coffee cup and took it to the sink, setting it down quietly on the counter.

"Get over here," Travis said, motioning to Charles, his voice barely loud enough for him to hear. "There's trouble!"

Charles hesitated. Isabel was still in the bathroom. He went to the door and gave a little knock. "Isabel, I'm going to go check on something. I'll be right back."

"Okay," Isabel replied.

"Okay Travis, what kind of trouble?" Charles asked quietly. "I haven't heard anything, or seen anyone. Scooter is still upstairs with Darla. Isabel didn't say anything about noises, or arguing. She just said she looked up and you were gone! Why didn't you tell her when you left?"

Travis raised his voice slightly, "Frankly, she'd dropped off to sleep, her head resting on the playing cards, and some of them still in her hands. I don't think she'd been asleep long. So I just went to investigate on my own."

Charles wondered if Isabel wasn't aware that she'd dropped off to sleep. That was easy to do, under the circumstances. If it was true."

"So if we are all accounted for, what was it you heard?" Danny asked.

Travis gave the two of them a grim look. "I think it was whoever blew up our generator."

"What makes you think that?"

"I heard some banging, and voices arguing down under. I don't want to go down there alone, so come on, let's check it out."

Charles thought about it. Would Isabel be safer here in case there really was some danger down below? Probably best to leave her here, he decided.

"Okay, let's investigate," he said, really dreading the idea of using those damn stone stairs again.

They quickly made their way into the hallway and walked to the still dark stone stairway. Travis suddenly turned on a bright flashlight and illuminated the area in front of them. "You two go first, and I'll keep the light on you so you don't fall," he insisted.

Charles, his legs already starting to burn at the thought of using the stone stairs again, turned to look back at Travis. Something was wrong about this whole situation. He tried to ferret out what it was, but couldn't.

Chapter Fourteen

The three men strode down the huge steps in the underground, checking all of the locks on the lab doors. The first three were locked up tight, with two padlocks on each one.

"I think this is a fool's errand," Danny said, rubbing his legs and making a little moaning sound. "Let's go back up, find something to eat, and wait out the rest of the night."

Charles shrugged. "Danny's got a point, Travis. There doesn't seem to be any kind of trouble down here."

Travis narrowed his eyes and flashed his light on down toward the last lab in the underground. "We got this far, let's at least look at Joe's lab. Maybe someone tried to break into it."

"I doubt it." Charles shook his head. "It's pretty well locked up."

"Well, you never know who might have managed to get in. We should check inside, even if it's locked."

"I don't have the combinations for Joe's locks," Charles lied. "Bertrand doesn't want anyone in there until their people get here."

Travis grinned. "No problem. I have them."

Perplexed, Charles growled, "How did you get them? I'm the only one who has permission to open these locks."

Travis didn't answer, and quickly went about opening the lock on the door to Joe's lab. After that, he pushed the door open, but Charles managed to peer cautiously inside before Travis did.

"Okay, nothing looks disturbed," Charles said, wanting to get back topside and make sure Isabel was okay. He was sure she would be disturbed by being left alone.

Travis flashed his light around inside the room. "I know Joe had a lot of new equipment brought in. We should check and make sure no one got hold of some of it. Expensive stuff."

"A waste of time," Danny said, rubbing his short chubby legs again. "I'm hungry, and I want some of that peanut butter Scooter had."

"Just a quick look," Travis insisted. "Then you'll get peanut butter."

With a sigh, Charles followed him inside the lab. The bright lights were on, so the one power generator was still working okay. That was encouraging. "It looks like Joe's corn is still growing great," he said. "Even without Joe's help." He gave a slight laugh. "Mother nature really doesn't need us, does she?"

"Yes she does! To grow corn this good, it takes man to create the right atmosphere," Charles insisted.

Danny went to some of the new pieces of equipment in the room and checked them over. "Holy moley!" he cried. "Look at all this! Where'd he get the money for all new stuff?"

"What's all this stuff for, Danny," Charles asked.

"All GE stuff. For genetic engineering." Danny patted several pieces of equipment. "A Minicentrifuge. And an electrophoresis apparatus. What I'd give for new things like these."

"Eat your heart out, Danny. Never gonna happen." Travis's voice held an odd snarling sound.

"Yeah," Danny replied. "I know. But I can dream."

"Come on Travis. We need to get topside." Charles said.

"I need to, but you two don't." Travis had an odd look in his scrunched eyes.

Charles cocked his head, wondering if he'd heard right. "What did you say?"

"I said, I'm going topside, and you two are staying here in Joe's lab." Travis reached into his jacket for something.

"Are you crazy? Why would we stay here?" Danny asked.

"Because I want you to."

Charles made a move toward the open lab door, but Travis moved in front of him. "I said you two are staying here."

"And who's going to make us do that?" Charles asked angrily.

From his pocket, Travis slid out a hand gun. A drab olive-colored baby Glock. Charles closed his eyes and realized that he'd made it known he kept a gun in his room. And Travis had found it. How stupid of him. Now he was faced with his own damn gun!

Danny squealed, and backed away from Travis. "Hey, you, where did you get that? Guns aren't allowed in the underground . . . are they?"

"It's mine," Charles said in a steady but fierce tone. "He stole it from my room."

"It was nice of you Charles, to let me know you had a gun handy. So now, I think you know that the two of you will be staying in here. Locked in, of course. So that I can take care of some things that are necessary."

"What's this all about, Travis? This doesn't seem like you. I'd bet you don't even know how to release the safety on that gun of mine."

"You'd lose that bet, dear Charles" Travis lifted the gun for Charles to see. "It's a standard Glock isn't it? Probably a 17, self-loading, with an auto safety after each firing. But that's easy to turn off. "

He was right, Charles had to admit. He wasn't about to rush Travis, even if the gun did have the auto safety. He couldn't imagine what Travis thought he was doing, or why. It made no sense.

"It's perfect for killing someone you *want* to kill. However, I don't plan on shooting either of you." He pointed the gun at Danny. "I just want you both to move over there and sit on Joe's cot."

Danny looked at Charles, then at the cot. "What's going on? I'm not about to sit on Joe's cot."

"Right now, Danny, me boy. And you too Charles. I said I don't *want* to shoot either of you, but I will if I have to."

"Travis, what the hell are you doing?" Charles asked angrily.

"Just sit the fuck down, and I'll explain. I'm not unreasonable." Travis waved his gun toward the cot. "Now do it!"

Both men slowly walked toward the cot and sat down stiffly. Charles patted Danny on the arm. "It's okay Danny. Just let him explain."

Travis began pacing the room, walking back and forth in front of the two men. To Charles it seemed like hours before Travis began to talk. Then his voice came out with a peculiar cadence, as if his

173

tongue was a little drum, beating out the words. "The first thing you should know is that Darla's getting pregnant was her idea, and she convinced me that she was on to something with her work which might make it possible for her to have a perfect child. Or a near perfect one at the least. One who might live twice as long as most people do now. She expects her child to be a genius. From what I've seen of her genetic technique, she may be right."

"How . . . I mean, what has she done to make you both so certain about that?" Charles asked.

"First of all, her soybeans. They are not for creating some sort of medicine. That's just her front."

"So we aren't going to get a cure for one of the world's worst disease," Charles said, hoping to keep Travis revealing more information

"What's she's managed to do with her precious soybeans, is to make a substance that keeps the human body from rejecting her genetic experiments," Travis bragged. "Lots of other scientists are working on what some call Transhumanism. There's even an organized group that supports her kind of work."

"Trans . . . what?" Danny asked.

"Where have you been buddy? It's on its way. The man of tomorrow. One day we can look forward to a thousand years of life, maybe more, baring accidents or wars."

"Yeah, sure," Danny said. "Good idea. No one ever dying! That ought to give over-population a nice boost!"

"But Travis, an H+ group is one that advocates caution and strict adherence to the laws of the country where the experimenting is being done," Charles interjected. He shifted his weight on the cot so that if possible he could lunge at Travis should he get the chance. The man was obviously going bananas! "What Darla is doing is dangerous. I mean by actually trying it out on herself, without knowing the consequences."

"Charles, it has already been tried on animals, tons of them. We're not that different from the other animals on this world. The most recent animal experiments have been one-hundred percent successful." Travis kept lifting the gun in his hand, pointing at something, and then saying a soft "bang" before pointing it back at the two of them.

"I have to say, I'm relieved. I was thinking it might be something . . . worse . . . like creating a Chimera, or something of that nature. " Charles said, forcing what he hoped looked like a friendly smile.

Travis gave Charles a wide-eyed look. "Ahh, I see. So you thought she might be working on hybrids?"

"Yes, when we saw all those strange . . . animals or whatever floating in jars in her cupboard." Charles paused, desperately thinking about how he could get this hazardous situation under control. "Tell me Travis, does Darla's baby have a father? She'd have to start with some decent DNA, wouldn't she? Or was it all a random thing done at a clinic?"

Travis gave a loud chortle, waving the gun around, which he now pointed at the ceiling. "Oh, it has a father. A strong, extremely smart, perfect body, all the necessary parts, father."

"Is it *you*, Travis?" Danny interjected. "You're smart. But I doubt you have all the necessary working parts!"

The look on Travis' face startled Charles. He wasn't sure if he was angry, or stunned by the answer.

"No! Of course it's not my DNA. It belongs to the only person around here who would qualify."

"Joe? Is it Joe's baby?" Charles asked, knowing that would make even less sense.

"For God's sake, are you brain dead!" Travis was quite angry now. "It is obviously *Scooter's* baby!" His scrunched up eyes jumped open in a hot, glaring look that make his eyebrows peak up like tiny mountains.

"Please Travis, tell me that Darla did not fool around with splicing God knows what when using Scooter's sperm. Is she trained enough to do something like that?"

"As you may have noticed, Joe has been Darla's lab partner. He's a genius when it comes to genetic engineering. Growing corn has just been his cover. He ordered the equipment. He helped run tests. Smart lad, that one. Too bad about him." He gave a little sigh.

Charles had never seen Travis this way. Surely he had gone over the edge for some strange reason. How did he think he could get away with any of this? What kind of reward was he expecting?

"Before this project is rid of you two, I just had to tell you about all this." Travis gave a little excited laugh. "Some time ago Darla and Joe started creating embryos using Darla's and Scooters DNA. Extensive testing was done so they could eliminate any life threatening disease. A major problem showed up in Darla's Mitochondrial DNA which had errors. She feared they were the cause of her being bi-polar, not autistic. So they had me find a woman who's mitochondrial DNA was okay and was willing to donate it.

"So after four years of work and finally creating an embryo they felt was as close to perfect as it's possible at this time, Darla had what she prayed was a flawless embryo implanted. It took, and is growing normally so far."

"You do know that what you've been involved in is totally illegal in most countries in the world, don't you Travis?"

Travis paused and waved the gun about now, wildly. "Yeah, yeah, but if the baby proves the science works, then the details on how to make this baby will be worth billions!"

"Can you give us more details?" Charles asked. "This is all so . . . interesting." He hoped he could keep Travis talking longer. He had to find a way to get the gun from him."

"Nah, that's about it. It's not my science specialty you know. But I did learn a lot working with Joe and Darla. And I finagled some of the stuff they needed from our supporters at Bertrand. But I'm sure Darla has kept a record of everything. She said it was all on a flash drive she has somewhere. The flash drive to prosperity." Travis's laugh had a strong edge of irrationality to it. "To everlasting life!"

"Listen to me Travis. Just tell me there was no cross-species in the splicing," Charles demanded.

"Why Charles, I can't tell you that!"

Charles felt his heart banging heavily in response to that. "Was any animal DNA used?"

Travis gave a slightly lopsided grin. "Yeah, well, I can say that among other things, the baby does have a tiny bit of one non-human in it. The Turritopsis nutricula it's called."

"What! Are you talking about the immortal jellyfish?' Charles said, aghast.

"Yep. It's DNA has a process called transdifferentiation. I can't even pronounce it much less understand how it works," Travis said, shaking his head. "But that dang fish actually lives forever! So who knows maybe the baby will too. I only know that Darla claims she studied it every which way, and made the decision to add something from it to the embryo.

"Oh great, a Frankenbaby!" Charles said, angrily. "Just what the world needs"

"It's a Frankenbaby that will make some of us rich beyond imagination!"

"Does Bertrand know all about this?" Charles had trouble accepting that idea.

"Well of course . . .but only a very few.. Only the *right* someones. But it's on the hush hush, mind you." Travis's hand holding the gun began to shake a little.

Fatigue? Or Fear? Maybe both? Charles wondered . "So you got rid of Joe, because that way you don't have to share the billions with him."

Travis gave a sharp laugh. "Don't be ridiculous. He had to go because he turned on us. He changed his mind and said it wasn't the right time to create a super human baby. Can you imagine? I ask you, what better time is there to enhance mankind?" Travis looked thoughtful for a moment, slowly waving the gun in his hand back and forth. "But I didn't believe him. Especially after he blew up the generator. He wanted it all for himself."

"It was *Joe* who blew the generator?" Danny said. "Why?"

"He wanted the power out so he could get all of his specs out of his lab. He blasted one generator, but missed the other." He gave a

177

little laugh. "Then we had a lightning strike that missed too. I got to him before he set off a second bomb, and made sure he wouldn't be able to do it again. Then I dropped him off in the underground."

"So then you tried to kill Isabel." Charles said. "But it didn't work."

Travis just gave him an odd look.

"I get it. You think she knows where Joe's specs are." Charles said.

Travis backed away from the two of them, gun in hand. Then he tapped on his hearing aid. "Someone rescued her before I was able to find them."

Charles closed his eyes for a minute, and then looked up at Travis with questioning eyes. "So are you going to split up the money, even though Darla is now the one brain behind it, and she's going through childbirth for it. You really think that's going to happen?"

Travis gave a little snort. "It's not going to be split at all. Especially with Bertrand's fuckers." Then, he let out a melodic high pitched laugh. "The funny thing is . . . that Scooter has no idea the baby is *his*!"

Charles and Danny exchanged dumbfounded glances and then looked back at Travis who had walked away from them and was fiddling with something on one of the unusual pieces of equipment, and then backed away. With the gun still in hand, he pulled out a cell phone from his pants pocket, nodded his head and said softly, as if caressing his words. "So now you know what all we've been doing here. We've talked enough. So now it's time for you two to move on. I'll ask God to make sure you have a longer, better life . . . next time. Maybe he'll make you an immortal jellyfish!" Travis's voice was turning to a slight cackle.

Charles jumped to his feet but Travis pointed the Glock at him. "Oh no Charles, a bullet is really painful. There's a better way. So I'll say goodbye to you both now. I need to get back to Darla and make sure she and the baby are okay." Travis gave a deep sigh, and then backed up to the door that led to the old steps. He stepped out of the room, but leaned in, the gun pointed at them, and said. "This will only take a minute or two. I won't use my phone to detonate the pod I planted here, until I'm safely topside in a safe area. So you two have a short while before the gas fills the room" Travis looked a Charles, with hot eyes and quivering lids. "I'm surprised that you didn't notice it Charles. That I had a bag of organophosphate pesticide in my lab, for quite some time now. You know full well that underground crops have no insect problems. My pesticide concoction works exactly like GB, only better, and faster."

Charles was too stunned to react. His mind whirled like a gyroscope. Travis slammed the door shut and the sound of the steel locks being replaced, rattled around the room. "Dear God!" Charles, said, feeling his heartbeat speed up.

Danny frowned, puzzled. "We're going to die by pesticide?"

"Not exactly. We're going to die because Travis has obviously used a pesticide to create something rather bad." The idea of what might happen, made his stomach go cold.

"Oh, that's nice! GB? What would that be?" Danny asked.

"Sarin." Charles replied, in an oddly calm voice. Sarin Gas."

Chapter Fifteen

As soon as Travis locked the door to the lab, Charles jumped to his feet and ran to look at the piece of equipment that Travis had been fiddling with. He couldn't see any possible way to take it apart and safely remove whatever was going to detonate the metal pod Travis had put there.

He knew that several dangerous materials could be made using pesticides, including Sarin gas. He still remembered newspaper articles about how someone had released a deadly nerve gas, ricin, in the London Underground. If Travis had actually made something like that, it gave him the shakes just thinking about it. Ricin was made from castor beans. He wondered if Darla might have grown some of those among her Soybean plants. "Jesus!" he said in a husky whisper, trying not to upset Danny more than necessary.

"So what do we do," Danny asked. "Are we dead men?" He didn't sound as panicked as Charles expected him to. He had an almost acceptance tone in his voice.

"Not if we hurry. Come on. The Sarin can't get out through the insulation around the door to the stairs. Unfortunately, neither can we since Travis bolted it." Charles raced to the door that led to the dressing room of Joe's lab. On one side of the door, he saw the metal box, reached into his pocket and pulled out his ID card and swiped it across the box. He heard a soft sighing sound and the door slowly slid open. "Thank God," he said. "The generator has kept the ID box on, and the positive pressure working. It might be a barrier for the Sarin gas, or whatever the hell it is." He stepped out into the short hallway and checked out the elevator doors. Danny followed him. "Get to the dressing room, Danny, and put on as many lab coats and as you can. Latex gloves, and face masks too."

"Will that help?" Danny asked as he began walking toward the dressing room.

"As far as I know that type of gas can be inhaled and I think

180

Sarin can paralyze ones lung muscles if inhaled. It's also absorbed through the skin, so bundling up might help."

With that, Danny took off as fast as his little bubble of a body would let him.

Charles swiped his card again to close the lab door. He heard the whoosh of the positive oxygen machine, which made him feel calmer. He had no idea how much deadly gas Travis was going to let loose, but at least there was some hope that it wouldn't get out of Joe's lab. Then he turned around to the elevator and put his card in the slot, praying it would also open the elevator doors, and he'd find the elevator at their level.

His heart sank. Just like when he'd tried it to see if Danny was stuck in the elevator, it didn't work. He tried it a second time. No luck. So, they would have to find a different way to get topside and hope to find Isabel before Travis got to her. He then raced after Danny, grabbed a lab coat, some latex gloves, and a face mask. If the positive pressure kept the gas at bay, he wouldn't need them. If it didn't . . . well, the extra material might help. He handed Danny one. "Just in case," he said.

"So, now we take the elevator topside, right?" Danny said.

Charles puckered his lips for a moment, not knowing what to tell Danny.

"Oh, oh," Danny said. "If I read you right, it's not working. The elevator, that is."

"You read me right. No power. But we should be thankful that we are at least this far away from whatever it is that Travis has concocted" Just as he said it, he heard a jolting roar coming from the inside of Joe's lab. He felt it jar the floor under his feet "That shit actually *did* detonate something," Charles said.

He looked around frantically. They needed to move away as far as possible in case the explosion jarred the pressure door loose, and the gas was able to get through. The dressing rooms were only a short distance away. No protection, really. He looked at the elevator and realized that there might be a way. If the elevator was at their level. If they could get to the top of it. If Bertrand had put some metal climbing bars on the walls around the elevator, in case they had to service something on the elevator, they could climb up. Too damn many ifs!

He looked over at Danny. His rotund body and short legs were going to be a handicap, but if he could just get him up on top of the elevator, maybe he could climb as far as the next floor up. He could leave him there. He felt he should be safe from the gas there because the gas would probably sink downward to the unknown depth of the building. He wasn't sure how long it would hang around, but he felt it was probably a number of hours. They'd need Hazmat for sure.

If they could just force the elevator door open enough to see if the elevator was at their level, and if it was, then with enough effort they might be able to force the doors open enough to get inside..

Danny kept eyeing the door into Joe's lab, as if expecting any minute deadly gas would come seeping out of the corners. "If the gas leaks, would we be able to smell it?" he asked.

"I don't think so, not if it's a Sarin type of nerve gas. Charles took his arm and pulled him toward the elevator doors. "How strong are you?' he asked. "Do you think you can help me wedge those doors open?"

Danny looked puzzled. "What good would that do? Or do you think we'd be safer from the gas inside the elevator. Seal ourselves inside?"

"I don't even know if we'll find the elevator there. It may be topside." Charles gave a little growl. "I just want us to get as far away from this area as possible. But you're right, the enclosure might help. But I've got a better idea. So give me a hand with the doors." The two of them began tugging on the narrow space between the two doors of the elevator. It made a sound like thick rubber being over-stretched.

"Harder!" Charles demanded and he pulled as hard as he was physically able to. The door let out a loud raspy complaint, and then moved open. Slowly. As soon as it was as far open as they could get it, he helped Danny struggle to wiggle his Santa tummy into it, muttering some obscenities not usually heard from Danny. Charles followed. "Now, let's close the doors" he said.

Charles struggled to close one door, but Danny had difficulty with his. The doors were synced, obviously. They had to close at the same time. "Come on Danny, get some of your testosterone surging. We can do it. More protection like you said."

Danny nodded, gave his tummy a pat and then said, "I'd have more energy if we'd had more to eat." With that, he grabbed the edge of the door and pulled so hard the veins in his neck began to bulge. Then the doors suddenly closed with a small thump. The inside of the elevator went dead dark.

Charles heard Danny slump down and sit on the elevator floor. "I really didn't think I could do it," he said giving a slight laugh.

"Well, buddy, you did it! Good for you. Now, get up. We have to do one more thing."

"Ah, Christ, no! Let's just lie down here in the dark and sleep until someone finds us."

"Sorry. But I have to get out of here. I need to find Isabel and Scooter. And I need to be there when help arrives. If it hasn't already." Charles heard Danny let out a long pained sigh. Then a second one.

"Okey dokey," Danny said. "So how do we get out?"

"Escape hatch. I'll boost you up, you open it, and crawl out on top of the elevator. I'll see if I have any muscles left from the last time I worked out at the gym. Hopefully, I can get myself up enough to get my arms free up there, and then hoist the rest of me up and out." Charles felt around each of the elevator walls, gauging where the center of it was. The escape hatch should be in the middle of the elevator roof.

Danny was more agile than Charles thought he would be. With great effort Charles boosted him up and Danny felt around for a minute, then he easily opened the escape hatch. Dim light slipped into the elevator. With some effort, he forced his head and shoulders through the opening. Charles prayed that Danny's tummy wouldn't get stuck, but much to his surprise, Danny was able to suck it in, and with some struggle, was finally sitting on top of the elevator.

183

"Okay Danny! I'm going to try now." Why the heck did I stop paying for my gym membership, he asked himself. It was only a short jump to get his hands onto the edge of the hatch. He quickly tried to chin himself like he often did at the gym. But the hatch edges were not the same as a bar, and he lost hold and fell to the floor of the elevator. "Damn, damn, damn!" he growled.

"Charles! You okay?" Danny yelled.

"Only my pride got broken." He looked up, took several deep breaths, hoping to God none of the gas had leaked out of Joe's lab yet. He stood up and made another jump, grabbing the edge of the hatch. This time he slowly lifted himself up. Danny was there and grabbed at his wrists and helped pull him up further until his shoulders and arms were free. He was then able to use his arms to get the rest of his body out and onto the elevator roof. The two of them sat there for a few minutes, Charles just resting aching muscles, and getting his bearings. Finally, he said, "Thanks, Danny. I wouldn't have made it without you."

"Nah, you would have. I just wanted to give you a little help." Danny looked up and around the inside of the elevator shaft. "Now what?" he asked.

Charles had assumed that the elevator shaft would be dark. But to his relief the emergency lights, obviously connected to the emergency generator, were making it possible to see the walls of the shaft. Even better, he saw a row of metal climbing rods that reached, no doubt, to the main floor. He looked at Danny, who seemed to be sweating from his unusual exertion and wondered if he could possibly make it to the next floor, much less the top level. If he left him there on the elevator roof, he couldn't be sure some of the gas might somehow escape and get to him.

He leaned forward and closed the hatch cover, just in case. However, he reasoned, if the gas was escaping it might just slip down the walls to the bottom of the shaft. Not totally safe, so he couldn't decide what to do. He looked at Danny. "Do you see that row of metal bars up the shaft wall," he said, pointing. "Do you think you could climb up to that third light next to the bars? That's where

Darla's lab is. You might be safer there."

Danny frowned. "What if Darla is there? What if she couldn't find Travis, and went to her lab to see if he was there. So no, just leave me here. No gas yet. So I think it's safe."

"No guarantee." Charles said.

"None asked for. Just be sure when things straighten out topside, you'll come get me.

"No problem."

Danny stuck out his hand. "It's been nice working with you. Oh, will ya bring some peanut butter, when you come back."

"You bet!" Charles shook his hand, then stood up and headed to the metal climbing rings. He took hold of one, and then looked back at Danny. "Nice place to take a nap," he said. As he began to climb the elevator wall, Charles heard Danny chuckle. After passing Darla's lab doors, he began to wonder if he would be able to make it to the ground floor. And if he did, he wondered how he would be able to get out of the elevator shaft there. He took in a long deep breath and continued to climb.

Isabel took her time in the little bathroom off of the kitchen. She was so tired, and it was so late she had to do something to perk herself up. She washed her face with cool water, using a small piece of soap that had been sitting on the edge of the sink. After washing she dried her face and hands, and then spent some time finger combing her hair. All that made her feel better, and she was ready to face the others for however long it would be necessary. She opened the bathroom door and walked out into the kitchen, forcing a smile on her face.

What greeted her erased the smile. Charles had told her he was going to be gone for a little while, but he didn't mention that the others were going with him. The kitchen was empty. She was alone. The look of the empty kitchen made her heart take off, beating fast and erratically, pounding in her chest like a base drum.

Where had they all gone to? And without her! She'd stood there alone for some time, trying to fight the shock. She called out all the missing people's names, but only heard her voice echo off the blushing brick walls of the kitchen. "Damn it to hell! What's going on here with everyone disappearing?" she asked the empty room. She looked over at the kitchen counter and saw the cup of coffee that Charles had been sipping when she'd left for the bathroom. She moved to the doorway and peered out into the hallway. No one there, as far as she could see. No noise. No voices.

She was alone in an ancient stone castle, eerily dark except for a few dripping candles here and there. She shuddered. It seemed like a scene out of some horror movie. She turned and moved back into the kitchen, walked to the counter and picked up the cup that Charles had been drinking from. Cold! She had no idea how long it was that she just stood there, praying that someone, anyone, would show up. Finally, she gave up and sat down at the table, the playing cards in front of her. She decided the best thing to do was not to panic. She would just sit there and play solitaire until someone, anyone, showed up. She shuffled the cards and began to play.

Time went slowly, as she waited. Then she heard a slight noise but didn't turn around until it was too late. A large strong hand suddenly covered her mouth, so tightly it was painful.

"Don't make a sound," a raspy voice whispered in her ear. "If you want to live, then do exactly as I say."

She didn't have time to react before someone grabbed her from the chair and held her forcefully with hands that felt like two iron clamps.

"Believe me, if you want to live, you won't make a sound," the voice whispered again.

She struggled to see who it was that was holding her. When she finally saw his face, and realized who it was, she couldn't accept it could be him. He was the last person in the world she would believe would grab her, and hold her so skin-tight she could barely breathe. She could scarcely get in enough air to keep from passing out, much less scream for help.

The man carrying Isabel set her down in a totally dark corner of the main hallway. He quickly put his hand over her mouth again. "Like I said, not a sound." They stood there for a few minutes. Isabel heard someone walking in the hallway, some distance away from them. The sound of his shoes faded into the distance and she could no longer hear them. He took his hand off her mouth.

"Scooter, what the hell are you doing?" she said in a pale whisper. She didn't know if he heard her or not. He looked down at her, his arms holding her in an agonizing grip. Then his eyes began darting around erratically, as if looking everywhere, for heaven knows what. She sucked in a breath and said it again. "Scooter, what's going on? You're scaring me!" She couldn't believe that the man, who had cared for her wounds and injured leg so gently, was the same man who was now holding her like a prisoner.

"Okay, let's go," he said. To the stone stairs. "Quietly."

"Why are we going there," she whispered.'

"No questions, no answers until later. Now move it, or I'll carry you."

She looked at him. His face still had a tight, hard look to it. It was as if he wasn't seeing her, his mind was somewhere else. "My foot still hurts, Scooter," she said in a pleading tone.

"Okay then," he said as he effortlessly hoisted her up and over his shoulder, her head bobbing against his back. "Keep your mouth shut," he whispered, and pulled out a flashlight from his shirt pocket and moved out of the dark corner toward the stone stairs. He began moving down them with incredible speed. She hoped to God he didn't miss one, or trip and fall. She already had too many bruises.

She couldn't believe what was happening to her. She couldn't understand why Scooter was doing this. It made no sense at all. She closed her eyes and tried to think of something else. But found that impossible. Was he taking her to the underground to kill her? Did he kill Jorge? She found it difficult to think of him as a killer, when he'd spent so much time helping people with his medical knowledge. She wanted to fight him, free herself, but she knew his arms and hands were a hundred times stronger than hers.

Suddenly Scooter stopped and slid her off his shoulder. "You can

187

talk now. There's no one here. This is the bottom end of the stone stairs. Look over there," he said pointing the flashlight at an opening in the gray-green stone wall. "That's where we can get out of this place."

Isabel remembered Darla saying there was a path or a tunnel from the bottom of the stairs that went up to the pine forest that surrounded the stone citadel. "Why are we going outside? It's freezing, and probably still raining, or maybe snowing. Neither of us has a coat." She shuddered even then from the cold inside the stairwell, and couldn't imagine how cold it would be outside. She was being kidnapped and she had no idea whatsoever why. If Scooter was going to kill her, wouldn't he have done it in the underground? Or did he want to hide her body in the woods? A painful wave of fear roared over her and she began to shake. Her eyes, without permission, began to flood with tears. "Scooter, why are you doing this," she cried.

"I'm sorry. But I have to get you out of here. When we're out and a distance from here, I'll explain. Okay?"

Through some gulps of tears, she said, "Okay."

"It's a steep climb, but not all that difficult." He put both his arms snuggly around her and steered her to the opening. They started to climb upward. Scooter stopped now and then to let her rest. The higher they got, the colder it was. "I can carry you the rest of the way," he said. "if you can't make it." She shook her head no and they kept going.

The first blast of the outside air hit her like flames of ice. She sucked in her breath, feeling as if it froze her nose and throat solidly. She tried to say something to Scooter but couldn't. Her body's shaking got harder.

Scooter turned her and pulled her against his chest, and wrapped his arms around her again. "Come on Sweetcheeks, you can make it. I know you can. You're strong, or you would have cracked up by now".

The warmth of his body helped to slow her shaking. He held she for a few minutes and then she turned around and together they made

188

their way to the thick stands of pine trees. Inside the tree area, it wasn't so horribly cold. And then she realized that the rain had stopped. The trees still dripped, but it was a relief to find the night sky showing patches where stars shone through.

"Just a few more yards and we're there," Scooter said.

"What? We're where?"

Scooter didn't answer, but a few minutes later they entered a small clearing. Isabel saw what looked like a tiny hut made of pieces of pale rough wood. He hurried her over to it and pulled open what didn't look like a door, but was. As small a door as it was, they both managed to get inside quickly. Scooter flashed his light around and Isabel saw that it was just one small room, with no furniture, a wood floor, and sad looking walls. At least the floor was dry.

"I'm sorry it's not much, but at least it's a place to stay until daylight. Just a short while now. With the rain gone, I'm sure help will be here first thing."

"What is this place? Did you . . . build it?"

Scooter sat down on the rough floor and pulled her down beside him. "No. It's been here a long time. Someone told me that when this was a hotel, some kids managed to build this little place so they could hide from their parents. I found it one day when taking a jog through the trees. I've enjoyed a cold beer here, on hot days, when I wasn't in the mood to be sociable."

"Well right now I'd like to enjoy a large cup of hot coffee!" Isabel said, continuing to shiver, but not as much as before. The small enclosure helped a lot. Scooter looked down at her, put his arms around her again and snugged her close to him.

"I'm not trying to take advantage of you, Sweetcheeks," he said. "I've got a steady lady. I'm sure glad she went home when she did, before all this shit happened. Anyway, I just need to help keep you warm."

"Thanks. It helps a lot. But, why in God's name did you drag me all the way out here? You owe me an explanation."

"Because I felt you were in danger. I am not sure about what all is going on in that old stone place, but it's not good, I can tell you

189

that." Scooter sucked in a long breath and let it out, the warmth of it flowing over Isabel's chilled face. "I was sitting with Darla in her room," Scooter went on. "She finally dropped off to sleep, poor baby. I decide to check out the others, and let her sleep. Just as I started out of her room, I saw Travis leave Charles room, a gun in his hand. No doubt the gun that Charles had mentioned earlier. I was sure that Charles hadn't given him permission to take it.

"I had the key to Darla's room, so I locked her door so she wouldn't wander around feeling so sick. And no one could get in. Travis didn't see me. I hung back and followed him. The gun wasn't showing by then. I saw him, Danny, and Charles come out of the kitchen and head for the stone stairs. With Travis having a hidden gun, I felt something was wrong. I waited around in the shadows, and it was awhile before Travis came up from the underground, without Charles and Danny. Darla was safely locked in, so I decided to go take a look in the underground. I was only a short way down the stone stairs when I heard some sort of muffled explosion, but I couldn't tell where it came from. So I thought the worst. If Travis had done something to Charles and Danny, he'd probably be looking for you. That's why I went back to the kitchen, found you there, and grabbed you. I felt I had to get you out of that place, and somewhere safe until we get some help here."

Isabel sat there for quite a long time, trying to sort out everything she'd been through. She tried to make sense of it. She leaned her head against Scooter's chest, fatigue flooding her whole body like a tsunami. Without a fight, she let herself fall into an exhausted sleep.

Chapter Sixteen

Charles couldn't believe how much his arms and legs hurt, as he continued to climb up the metal bars inside the elevator shaft. If he managed to get out of whatever the hell was happening in this stone prison, he sure as heck was going to get back to the gym and get in better shape. His legs were already beat from his numerous climbs up and down the stone steps, not to mention the regular stairs that went up to his room.

Every few yards, he stopped climbing and just clung quietly to the bars, letting his muscles lose some of their painful burning. He had to reach the top. However, if he stopped short of that, he might be able to crawl into one of the labs along the way up, but then he would have no way to get out of even his own lab, since the doors leading to the stairs were all bolted on the outside. If he made it to the top, he might be able to get to the hallway next to the elevator doors. The thought cheered him. He'd find Isabel and get the two of them someplace safe for the night. He prayed that Travis hadn't harmed her. The gas explosion might be explained away by Travis as a scientific accident. But explaining Joe's and several other deaths, wouldn't be so easy. The word death made his stomach go cold. He kept telling himself that Travis would realize that the more dead bodies he caused, the worse his chances were of getting away with whatever he was up to.

His thoughts about the whole thing gave him a rush of adrenaline and he found himself climbing faster. He could actually see the last set of elevator doors at the very top of the shaft.

He began counting the metal bars as his feet hit each one of them. His breath became labored. His heart felt as if it was going to burst. Despite the fact that it was bitterly cold inside the elevator shaft, sweat dripped from his face. He wanted to stop and take off some of the extra lab coats he'd put on, but it wasn't worth the chance of losing his grip and falling. He was glad, however, that

191

Danny had wrapped up in several of them. Also, since Danny had a lot of fat padding, the cold might not hit him as hard, as it might for other people.

Looking up, he saw that he was only about ten steps from the last of the metal bars. One step, he told himself, lifting his foot. Now, another step. He slowly counted until he was even with the last set of elevator doors in the shaft. He hadn't thought about how difficult it would be to force open the doors while standing on the metal bar steps which were next to them, but not quite even with them. And a miss-step could send him tumbling down to the bottom of the shaft.

He made sure his shoes had a good hold on the metal bar. Then he stretched his arm out sideways and just barely reached the center of the doors. He forced his fingers into the small area where they opened and began to pull. It took every ounce of energy he could summons up to make the doors part. He finally got them open just enough for him to get his shoulders through sideways, and then he lifted his feet off the metal bar. With one last burst of energy, he pulled the rest of him inside all the way through. Freed from the doors, he dropped to the hallway floor like a lump of soft dough. He would have kissed the floor beneath him, but he didn't have enough energy.

He stretched out on the floor and let every muscle in his body go limp. It felt so good! "Home sweet home!" he said, hardly able to make more than a whisper. He lay there for quite a long time, wondering if his legs would allow him to stand. He wasn't so sure they would. He looked around the hallway but didn't see or hear anyone.

With concerted effort, he managed to stand on trembling legs and slowly made his way down the hall toward the office. He approached it cautiously. He kept his flashlight off as he scanned the darkness of the room, trying to make sure Travis wasn't there. With relief, he found no one in the small room.

He ran his fingers around the side edge of the door, and was glad to feel a lock there. He closed the door behind him, and clicked the lock on. Quietly he made his way to where he could just barely make out the leather sofa. He lifted a tired arm and looked at his watch but he couldn't see the time in the dim light. But it couldn't be much more time until daylight

He suddenly remembered something. He reached his hand into the pocket of his pants. Was it still there? The flash drive! The one with all of Joe's and or Darla's information on it! Was it the formula for Darla's baby? *A designer baby?* He was positive it was. The shock of that possibility hit him again, and gave him a prickly sensation all over. Then he felt it, the flash drive was still there. What the hell should he do with it? From what Travis had said someone with Bertrand was also involved in the project. Joe had died because of it. He had absolutely no idea what he should do. Even so, he realized that it was more important for him to rest and survive.

He plopped down on the sofa and a rocket of unbearable pain climbed up his body. He desperately wanted to go and find Isabel, praying she was still alive, that Travis hadn't used the Glock. However, he knew his body would not work anymore. He'd be useless to help her, until he let his body rest. He tried to remember how long it had been since he'd slept. He couldn't recall when it was. He didn't care. The soft leather sofa felt like a mattress made out of clouds.

He pictured Isabel in his mind. A little humming bird of a woman, with rusty hair and a scattering of freckles on her checks. She'd been so strong, just by coming here, when he knew she really hadn't wanted to, and then she had gotten through the shock of her husband's death, for the second time.

The last thing Charles had thought about was how, when he could finally move again, he would be able to cope with Travis, and all the unbelievable things that had been going on. He prayed that Travis believed he and Danny were dead. And if he did, what would his next move be? That is, if they weren't able to find him. And then there was Darla who Travis claimed would give birth to . . . to a new age baby? Or maybe a monster of some sort? Darla was brilliant, but was she brilliant enough to tear apart and reassemble DNA so that it would work exactly the way she intended to? The god-awful possibilities were too much to think about yet.

Charles gave a sigh. He needed to sleep, but something inside him refused to let him. Something that kept telling him that he should be like a movie hero. The kind that spend twenty minutes fighting the evil entities, and once he'd won the battle, he only showed a little sweat, fast breathing, and a few fake cuts and bruises, before moving on to doing something else. It just didn't happen that way in real life. He looked up at the bent glass windows, narrowed his vision on them, and tried to relax his fiercely aching muscles. He would start moving again the moment the dawning light erased the night sky.

Isabel's sleep generated a plethora of dreams. In them, she sat by a fireplace, hearing the crackling of wood burning. She heard church bells ringing melodically in the distance. A flock of chattering birds flew slowly by. Then, her dead husband, Jorge, took the advantage to visit her trance-like world, declaring his love for her. She tried to shoo him away, but he turned into a hairy wolf and growled at her, baring his teeth. At that point, her dreaming felt like an emerging nightmare. She awoke with a start, relieved to find it was only a dream. She sat up straight, causing Scooter to lose the tight grip he'd kept on her. Her memory was numb, and she tried to remember how on earth she'd gotten inside what looked like a rough little shack. Her mind was still dazed with sleep.

"Good morning, Sweetcheeks," Scooter said with a thick throaty sound in his voice. He yawned, got up, and stretched his long arms. "I'm glad you slept. It's just beginning to get light, and the rain has stayed away. "We should get some help here in a short while." He moved away from her, opened the hut's odd little door, and looked out. "Couldn't ask for a better day to help get us off of this mountain," he said turning to her. Then his face went tight. "Jesus! I hope Danny and Charles are okay" he said with a sound of desperation in his voice."

Isabel got up and looked out the door. The light was dim, but she could see the far edge of the pine forest a short distance away. Then

194

her mind cleared, and she abruptly remembered how Scooter had roughly dragged her from the kitchen, down the steps, and out to the little hut in the forest. Thankfully, she no longer feared him. If he had intended to kill her, he would have by now.

The wind was up a little, whispering in the pines. Over that sound, she heard a motor throb, like that of a helicopter. She looked up through the trees at a small part of the sky, faint blue and cloudless. She couldn't see anything else. "Do you hear that, Scooter?"

His eyes narrowed. "Yeah!" He looked up. "It's a chopper, I bet cha." He looked down at her and smiled. "Thank God!"

Isabel felt a dozen questions rattling through her head. She looked up at him, catching his eye.

"What is it, Sweetcheeks?" he said quietly.

"Scooter . . . is it possible that Darla's baby is yours?"

"*My* baby?" he gave a chortled laugh. "I don't think you could call it my baby, just because I helped with the implantation."

"Implantation?"

"Yes. It seems that she had discovered some sort of DNA error in her own DNA that she was certain had caused her bi-polar or autistic disorder so she somehow had another person donate some part of hers and . . . ah, I'm not sure what it was all about. I've got some medical training, but don't have a toothpick size bit of education in all that genetic engineering stuff. But the implant worked fine, as far as I know."

"In any event, you're not the father?"

"Hell no. What would I do with a kid? Maybe in a few years."

"So whose sperm did she use?"

"Heaven only knows. She may have had it sent from a lab, packed in dry ice, or something like that."

"Well, I suppose it's possible that one of the other guys . . . maybe Charles?" Her voice trailed off.

"Ah, no, I can't imagine that."

"So it definitely wasn't you."

"Isabel, I did not impregnate Darla, nor did I give her any of my

195

sperm. Why would I do a thing like that? She just told me she really wanted to have a baby; she didn't have a fellow, so she managed to get some sperm probably from a fertility bank. Once she had the altered embryo created, I did the implant."

Satisfied with the answers, Isabel stepped outside the hut and looked around. The air smelled sweetly of early morning. "Well then," she said to Scooter, feeling more refreshed than she felt she had a right to. "Why do you suppose at her time of life, Darla's having a baby? She has to be in . . . what? Her forties?"

"It's about a lonely woman wanting a child. I'm really happy for her. But I didn't donate anything except what I knew medically." He let out a deflated sounding sigh.

Isabel ruffled through her short hair, finger combing it. For some reason, she wanted to tell Scooter about the flash drive she tried to take out of the underground. Since Charles was the only other person there who knew about it, she would feel better if someone else knew about it too. If, God forbid, something happened to Charles, it might be because he had the flash drive she'd given him. She only knew a smidgen of the info on the drive, but was convinced it was something significant. Charles reaction to it had been strong but odd. She didn't want to be the only one to know about what she'd given him. She let out a little unexpected moan.

"What is it? Something you want to say?" he said, as if reading her thoughts.

"I don't know exactly how to say it."

He was silent, forcing her to organize her thoughts.

"I found out that my twice dead husband . . . you know him as Joe, had me meet him here so I could smuggle out . . . a flash drive for him."

"That sounds like Joe."

"I didn't think I could do it, but I somehow managed. That's why I was on the stairs when I fell . . . or when someone knocked me out."

"So you found where Joe had stashed it and I bet you gave it to Charles?"

196

"Yes."

"Good girl. You did the right thing. Did he find out what was on it yet?"

"He took a quick look when he went to his room. From what he said, it was something unusual and . . . well, an alarming type of genetic engineering. The whole thing had him troubled. He didn't go into it much, but I could tell how concerned he was."

"Do you think Travis found out about it?"

"I'm not sure, but I don't think so."

"I'm glad it got to Charles. He is a special type of person. He'll know what to do with it."

"What do you mean by *special type* of person?"

Scooter blanched slightly. "I shouldn't have said anything. But, well I'm sure you'll find out before long. Not to worry. It's a good thing."

"Scooter!" she yelled. "Tell me—"

Scooter looked up at the sky. "Hey, look there! That's a Bertrand company chopper about to land.

She heard the rotor-throb of the chopper as it was descending a distance away, probably in the parking area in front of the stone building. For the first time in two long days, waves of relief washed over her.

Charles was still awake when his watch alarm went off. Even so, he felt much more rested than he had before lying down on the leather sofa. If only he had some of Darla's thick, black coffee it would be wonderful. It took him a few minutes before he could coordinate his thoughts.

Travis had come close to killing both him and Danny. Too damn close, the son of a rat! Now, Danny was stranded on top of the elevator. He had no idea where Isabel was, or if she was safe. He hoped Scooter was still watching over Darla. He felt calmed that Travis had not tried to get into the office. He was no doubt convinced that he and Danny were dead. He heard a rumbling sound in the distance and prayed that it was some help that had finally arrived.

197

He managed to convince himself to get up off the sofa. His legs actually worked, but felt like two wobbly twigs. At least some of the pain had ebbed. He made his way to the door and cautiously turned the lock without making any noise. He opened the door only a slight bit. The hallways were still quite dark, and most of the candles that were lit after the blackout, were melted masses of sour looking wax. He stepped out slowly, checking every dark corner. All he wanted was to get to the front door. The rumbling he heard grew louder, obviously a chopper. Bertrand's or the police? He wondered if what Travis had said about them was true, that a least a few of the son-of-bitches at Bertrand were in on what was going on.

He reached the front door and opened it, letting in the sweet breath of a storm-less day. Only a few bruised clouds hung around the tops of the pine trees. He moved out onto the porch and looked at the cars in the parking lot. Travis' pickup was still there. Was he was still inside the building? Or, maybe he'd taken off through the woods during the night, meeting someone who was in on all the stuff going on.

The rumbling rotor-throb grew louder and when he stepped out on the porch and looked up, he saw a huge bullet-shaped chopper landing a short distance from the building in the wide grassy area. The word BERTRAND was printed in giant letters across the body of it like bright slashes of brilliant blue paint. Cautiously he stepped out on the stretch of muddy grass, and headed toward the chopper. The blades on the chopper slowed, and stopped.

In the distance, Charles heard the faint sound of sirens. He hoped it was the police. Once they were there, he hoped that Travis wouldn't be able to cause any more deadly problems. He just prayed that if Travis was still inside, he wouldn't use the Glock to blast away at everyone.

A short man, with a fifty-dollar hair style, climbed out of the Bertrand chopper and looked around. He spotted Charles and gave him an awkward wave and a rather grim smile as he made his way across the grass toward him. "David Manning." the man said. "I understand you people have been having an uncomfortable time of it," The man extended his hand, his long tapered fingers looking like pale round sticks. They matched the man's tapered body, which was wearing a pale gray suit with a crisp white shirt and of course, a red power tie. He was certain the man had never been anywhere near dirt in his entire life, until now.

"That," Charles said, "is the understatement of this century." He shook the man's hand, which had fingers neither warm nor cold, and almost mannequin like. "Charles McGraw. I'm the acting supervisor here, but it looks as if I haven't done such a great job of it."

The man gave him a strange nod, by lowing his eyelids down and back up. "We'll get it all straightened out. Just give us the details and we'll take care of it."

Charles looked past him at another man who was now climbing out of the chopper. A familiar face, an old friend, and a giant of a man with a thatch of premature silver hair. Thank God someone human! "Gray!" he called out. Grayson McCurdy was such a welcome sight.

The man looked up, his face blank for a moment and then recognition flooded his features. "Charles! They didn't tell us you were here." The man lumbered over to him, his long, heavy legs apparently slowing him down. 'It's been . . . geeze, how long?"

"Too long, Gray." Just seeing his old friend lifted the helpless mood he'd been in. "I'm so glad they sent you." Charles saw that his old friend, as usual, resembled a rebel, in direct contrast to the David person. Gray had on a rather ragged leather jacket with a turtleneck black sweater underneath, and a pair of ill-fitting but comfortable looking jeans. He actually towered over Charles's six-foot three-inch frame.

"So, how are the crops? The lights in the labs still working?" Gray asked. "Especially for your grapes. They'll make fine wine." he said, smacking his lips.

"We have something much more serious here than grapes or corn. How much did corporate tell you?"

Gray shrugged. "Just that there was a furious storm and some kind of problem in the generator area."

"Is that *all* they told you?"

"That's about it. They said to go take stock of the damage. We brought along a crew to fix whatever." Gray gave him a perplexed look. "What didn't Bertrand tell us?

"How many are there in the crew?" Charles asked.

Gray shrugged his thick shoulders and looked over at the huge chopper. "About twenty. That should help, right?"

"It sure won't hurt." Charles said impressed . "That flying insect is a big mother!"

"A military heavy lift mother. Refitted for Bertrand's needs."

"Impressive."

"We flew in heavy since we brought equipment and a new generator, just in case."

Charles wondered how the hell he was going to explain to Gray about what all was going on. He looked at the man, at his dark inquiring eyes, hoping the man wasn't involved in whatever was happening. He'd known Gray for a long time. He just couldn't imagine him being involved with anything illegal.

Gray turned to David. "Maybe you should go on inside and go through the office files. See how things check out."

David nodded and started toward the stone step entrance, his pair of what looked like $200 Italian shoes squishing in the muddy grass.

Charles raised his hand, alarmed. "No David! Wait! Don't go inside yet. I need to explain." He turned to Gray and said, "We've got an insane idiot here somewhere with a loaded gun. You know him. It's Travis Emerson! Last night when Danny and I went with him to one of the labs, he set off a fucking nerve gas bomb. He locked the two of us in Joe's lab, and then set off the bomb remotely. He's probably convinced that Danny and I are dead. But we managed to get out of the lab in time, and right now poor Danny's hiding on the top of the elevator. I'm praying he's okay"

"No way!" Gray said. The shock in his eyes made them look like two black marbles in the sunlight. "That's insane! And shit, we're gonna need a Hazmat team!"

"Sorry, but it's true."

200

"And it was Travis? That old stick of a man?"

"He claims he's in on something being done here that's worth several fortunes. And he obviously doesn't intend to share it with anyone."

"Jesus, man, what kind of fortune can you make out of the crops growing underground here?"

"Gray . . . I hope you're not a part of it. I hate deadly surprises."

"Never!" Gray said. "My word!"

Charles didn't say anything for a few moments.

"Serious stuff." Gray sounded as if he were short of breath. "You're positive of this?"

"We just experienced it, Gray!" Charles looked over at David, whose face had bleached to a pale white. "And did they mention that we have a dead body in one of the labs below. Joe Watson's. There would have been two more dead bodies if Travis had succeeded with his nerve gas. And then there is Darla, who is somehow a part of all this too. Add to that a batch of weird cats, and horrifying unnatural things floating around in jars inside Darla's lab." Charles put his hand in his pants pocket, fingered the flash drive there, but pulled it back. He was not going to reveal Joe's flash drive yet. At least not until he trusted that the tight-assed David guy wasn't involved in the whole frigging mess!

"I did hear from someone that Joe took a bad fall down the old stone stairs," a stunned Gray said. "I wasn't told he was dead, for God's sake!"

"But you did hear about the explosion that took out our main generator? Right"

"Ah, damn it! I didn't hear a word about any explosion. We were told that it was damaged by the storm. Lightning possibly."

"Who was it that told you about all that?"

"On the short-wave radio. It was . . . oh my God, it was Travis!"

"And right now he may still be somewhere around here, with my Glock in his hand."

Gray closed his eyes, and Charles could see his pulse throbbing on his forehead. Then Gray said, "Okay David, get yourself back to

201

the Chopper. Radio for Hazmat ASAP. Tell everyone to stay outside for now."

"That's not protocol, Grayson," David said, his pinched-mouth face looking arrogant. "I have to inspect the place, inch by inch," His nostrils flared slightly. "That is my job."

"Good God, man!" Charles said. "Inch by inch in that place would take a lifetime. And some of the nerve gas may still be around. Better relax in the chopper until we get things checked out around here." He didn't think that the young man had ever relaxed.

David looked at him, and then at Gray. "This is a ghastly looking place," he said, giving them a slow reluctant nod, then turned on his muddy expensive shoes, and headed back toward the chopper.

"And don't touch the radio except for the Hazmat call," Gray yelled after him. "Not one word about anything you've heard here until I say so. If you do, I'll toss you out of the chopper at a thousand feet!" Gray watched him go. "Tight assed little snot, that one. But I have to admit he's good when it comes to putting details together."

Charles listened for the sound of sirens, but didn't hear them anymore. "I wish the police or sheriffs, whatever they call them, would hurry and get here. Your crew can work on the generator. Once Hazmat says we're safe, then we'll need a lot of armed police to help us find Darla, as well as our visitor, Isabel Warren, and get poor Danny off the top of the elevator." He gave a mirthless grin. "And do all this without getting shot by Travis."

"Yeah, well, the road into this area didn't look too good yet from the air. ' Gray said. "The river looks a little too high, and only part of the trees are cleared.

"Oh, Damn." Charles felt like a slowly deflating balloon.

"I'm sure they'll get enough done before too long." Gray shook his head. "All this is going to take quite a while.

"I pray Travis hasn't gotten to anyone still inside." He didn't say it, but Isabel was his main concern. The urgency of his finding her overrode all of his other concerns.

Gray put his hand on Charles shoulder. "Okay then, do you have any idea how long the gas Travis used would continue to work?"

"I think it can stick around about as long as water takes to evaporate. But I'm hoping it hasn't seeped out of the lab."

"So if Travis is still inside, he's not our only problem."

"Right."

Grays eyes went to the chopper. He let out a long sigh. "So we can't start inside until Hazmat gets here and proves it safe. Hopefully, we'll have a hell of a lot of police by then." He paused and appeared to be looking where David was standing outside talking with the pilot. Then he turned back to Charles. "So, tell me, what is it that Travis is so entranced by that he's willing to commit murder. This road to riches he's talked about."

"Did you know Bertrand hired me to stay here and to keep a watch on some suspicious things they thought might be going on? To trouble shoot something. Only they didn't say what the hell it was. My understanding was that they didn't know. They just had suspicions."

"I had no idea you were on a new case." Gray shook his head. "I just thought you wanted to learn about growing great grapes. Considering your usual work, I did think that was kind of odd. Do you still have your private detective license?"

"Yes, but no one here knows about it. Bertrand hired me to troubleshoot an unknown but suspected problem in their company. So I had to learn about the grape growing from scratch. Plus a ton more about genetic altering and all that. At least I now know what's been going on here. And Gray, I suspect that some high up Bertrand mucky mucks may be involved in it."

"Charles, my friend, Bertrand is huge, and has a lot of broken chunks. And one or two of those chunks may be the problem. Not the entire piece. But we'll find the chunks! Take my word for it"

A sudden howl of a police siren pierced the air as a motorcycle roared into the parking area, followed by two others. All three of them over-ran the parking cement, and ended up in the muddy grass a short distance from Charles and Gray. Their tires spewed up muddy rainwater which made Charles and Gray dash to the porch. George realized that they were three California highway patrolmen.

203

"If the road's closed how did these guys get through?" Gray asked.

"Probably using the hiking trails in the woods, along with a small wood bridge over part of the creek"

Gray yelled out to David who was standing just outside the chopper. "Get with those three coppers. I'll be right there."

"Coppers. Jeeze, I haven't heard that word in a long time," Charles said.

"Once a great Brit, always a great Brit," Gray laughed. "Are the generators still on the right side and back of this ridiculous shack?"

"Yep. At least they were before the explosions."

"Okay, I'll check with the cops and see if we can expect any more help soon." Gray stepped off the porch and made a quick dash to where the three highway patrol men were looking around a bit puzzled as to where they should go.

That's when Charles spotted Scooter who was making his way around the far side of the building, his arm around Isabel. He had never felt anything like the liberation that overwhelmed him at the sight of the two of them. Two found, and three to go, Travis first, and then Darla and Danny.

Chapter Seventeen

At the sight of Charles standing on the porch Isabel couldn't help but cry out his name.

In return, Charles gave her a wave and indicated for her to join him on the porch. She looked up at Scooter.

He gave her a grin. "Go on, Sweetcheeks. Chucky looks relieved to see you."

"Because of you, Scooter. I don't know how to thank you."

"No need." He pulled his arm from around her waist and looked over at the three policemen who were still trying to position their bikes upright in the muddy ground. "I've got to talk with the police. These bikers can't be all they sent."

She gave Scooter a hug, then turned and made her way toward Charles who stood on the edge of the porch, waiting for her. Her one shoe was soggy and covered with mud. It made a squishing sound with each step she took. Her foot still hurt but not as bad as it had. When she reached him, Charles took her hand and helped her up the giant step onto the porch.

"Thank God," he said in a low whisper. "I had such terrible pictures of all kinds of things that might have happened to you."

She shook her head, trying to dislodge the memories of everything that had happened. "Last night Scooter grabbed me and carried me outside through the tunnel at the bottom level of the building. I was terrified at first because I thought he was kidnapping me. But when he finally explained everything, I realized he was really just trying to help. We spent the rest of the night in a little . . . well, a sort of little shack a short way into the woods." She explained to him what Scooter had told her about Travis skulking about with a gun. "He wasn't sure what was happening, but he felt it best to get me out of there." she said.

"He was right," Charles said. He reached for her and hugged her. "I'm so thankful you're okay."

205

Charles's warm arms made Isabel feel safe. She felt her face flush and right then she didn't ever want to leave Charles's arms.

He kept his arms around her for quite a few minutes, then sucked in his breath deeply and said, "Unfortunately, the police, except for those CHPs on motorcycles, haven't gotten across the road block yet. And here we are with a murderous idiot who may or may not still be inside." With that, he slowly removed his arms.

"They'll find Travis. I know they will," she said already missing the safety of his arms. "Scooter said he thought Travis was carrying a gun. Do you think he killed Jorge . . . I mean Joe? Not with a gun, I know. But even so . . . ."

Charles sighed. "I'm afraid so."

She paused, and finally said, "But he seemed like such a nice old man."

"Things aren't always what they seem, Isabel. Last night that nice old Travis tried to kill me, as well as Danny."

She blinked and swallowed hard. "So maybe I didn't fall. Maybe he did try to kill me also."

"Very likely." He looked around the parking lot. "At least the rain has finally stopped. I hope Hazmat gets here soon. I have to get inside and find Darla," he said. "And poor Danny has been lying on top of the elevator all night." His words were machine gunned, his face flushed. He took in a long shuttering deep breath, then another. "Sorry. Way too little sleep." He yawned and closed his eyes. "I'm really beginning to feel the effects of it."

"So, did Travis shoot at you? With your own gun? Obviously he missed. And Danny—"

"No, it wasn't the gun he used."

"Scooter said he locked Darla in her room last night," she asked. "So she may be okay, if Travis didn't know where she was."

Charles looked thoughtful, as if trying to organize his thoughts. "I'm afraid that Darla is a part of what all is going on here. But she may not realize the danger." He shook his head looking like he was unable to get rid of the random thoughts that were probably racing through his mind. "We are waiting for Hazmat before we can get inside,"

"Hazmat?"

"Oh, I forgot that part," he yawned widely and closed his eyes. "The gas I mentioned. Travis had gas."

"Gas?" Isabel tried to make sense of what he was telling her. "Was that unusual?"

Charles gave a jerky laugh. "I mean the deadly nerve kind of gas. That's how he tried to kill Danny and me. In Joe's lab. And you two were lucky. Travis set off a blast of deadly gas and you and Scooter must have gone past it not long after it went off. Thanks to the security door to Joe's lab, the gas evidently didn't get through to the old stair area."

Isabel felt herself go pale. "Oh, dear God, I'm glad I didn't know about it!"

"Now, he probably thinks that Danny and I are dead. And he's still got my gun.'

"Oh, holy mackerel! What next?" Isabel felt a shiver running through her blood. Charles put his arms around her again, which greatly helped to reduce her discomfort. He leaned his head down and rested it on top of her head. "Despite all you've been through, Isabel, you still have the sweetest scent of honeyed perfume. I've forgotten how much I loved the scent of a woman, and the feel of her in my arms."

"Yes Charles, I understand." She knew he was just acting out of a desperate need for sleep. Even so, she felt her lips curl into a very small smile at his words.

"I want to keep you safe and warm next to me." He yawned again and put his other arm around her.

"Charles, let's you and I just sit down here on the porch until we are allowed to go inside. Or when they want to talk to us. I'm shell shocked, and you're sleep deprived. We're both apt to shut down and fall over."

"Good idea," he said.

She felt his legs buckling and together they collapsed onto the stone porch, Charles with his back against the side wall. She snugged her back against his chest and he wrapped both arms around her. She heard his breathing change and settle into a soothing rhythm, and she knew that he had fallen asleep almost instantly. His arms, however, continued their warm hold around her. She closed her eyes, hoping she would stay awake, but she relished the soothing sense of shelter his arms gave her.

Isabel had no idea how long they had been sitting together on the rough stone porch. She didn't know if she had slept or not. All she knew was that someone was patting her on the shoulder and saying in a throaty voice. "Wake up you two." She looked up to see a giant of a man leaning down over her.

"You must be the visitor Charles told me about," Gray said. "Isabel is it?"

"Um, yes," she said looking up at him. "And you?" She rubbed her eyes with her fingers, trying to get them to focus. She must have been sleeping after all. Charles didn't move.

"Just call me Gray. A long time buddy of Charles. I'm from Bertrand. We now have a big crew of Los Angeles sheriffs on the scene, and three highway patrol guys. Seems the latter were chasing a car that spun off the 210 freeway, took out a road sign, and then sped off up the main mountain road. That's when they heard our radio call for help." Gray paused, and then said, "It seems that the gravel road into here is finally open. My guys have checked the damage to the generators. The backup one is going great. But the other one sure is a piece of trash. We're gonna get the new one we brought installed ASAP.

She felt Charles moving behind her, removing his arms and making grumbling sounds. She forced herself to her feet, and looked down at her wet, muddied shoes. "Gonna need a new pair," she said, not knowing why it was necessary to say that.

Gray gave a subdued laugh. "Gonna need a lot of new things around here. Shoes are easy."

"Oh!" Charles said, struggling to his feet. "Sorry! How long did I sleep?"

Gray looked at his watch. "Over two hours. As I just told your

208

friend here, we've checked the backup generator which is fine, the main one is trashed, and then we carefully looked at everything around the outside of this so-called house. There's no other damage that we could find. Except for that bent and twisted thing hanging over the edge of the roof."

Charles frowned. "What?"

"I think it used to be a TV dish."

"Oh, that thing. It's useless even when it's working."

Isabel looked around. Close to the chopper she saw several dozen officers wearing heavy duty gear. A swat team maybe? Talking with David were two men in business suits. The suited ones looked uncomfortable and out of place there in the wilderness area. Detectives maybe?

Charles stretched several times, and then gave Isabel a more relaxed look than he had before sleeping. "Let's go see what the sheriff procedures are," he said. He gently took her hand and helped her step off the stone porch, her muddy shoes still making a slushy sound. Gray followed slowly behind them.

Charles continued to hold Isabel's hand as she struggled to step through the muddy area. "We can't go inside until it's cleared by Hazmat," he said. "Feels like we're inside a slow clock."

Isabel nodded. She was thinking about how comfortable she would have been, had she not agreed to help Jorge. She'd be snuggled on her sofa watching a good movie, or maybe sitting with friends at a local restaurant having lunch. If she had it to do all over again, she would make totally different decisions. Then again, she would never have met Charles. It was interesting how one decision could totally change a person's life.

Before the three of them reached the crowd of sheriffs, a huge truck, and several cars suddenly arrived, and parked on the road in front of the stone building.

"Great!" Charles said. "Hazmat has arrived. They have the equipment to get inside and make sure it's clean and safe." He waved his hands over his head to direct them his way. Two men from the truck began to trot toward them.

Isabel wondered how long it would take them to check everything out, and hopefully things would begin to settle down.

"What's up?" one of the men asked as he got close to Charles.

Charles quickly told them, in detail, what had happened and where to find the lab which had been gassed. She listened as he explained to them about the nerve gas release, and where the location was when it was set off. He also informed them that Danny was stranded on top of the elevator. The team went into action lightning fast, which impressed Isabel, and she felt easier when she saw the tightness on Charles face relax.

While the hazmat team checked out the entire building, the sheriff officers finally began questioning everyone. They started with Scooter who talked with them for quite a while. After that, they spent even more time with Isabel, making profuse notes on small pads. Charles was thankful when they finally got to him. He was reluctant; however, to get into intricate scientific details about the work that Joe, Travis said Darla may have been doing. He still wasn't sure about their individual involvement. And was it really a new age baby? Even if that was so, Charles knew the chance of it working was almost zero. And that the laws about that kind of thing were rigid and strict and could land anyone involved in prison if they weren't careful. So he gave the Detective only a limited generic rundown. He explained that detailed information on whatever they were working on would have to be given to them by someone who knew more about the subject than he did. He showed them is private detective ID and explained that he was not an regular employee of Bertrand.

Another uncomfortable thought hit him after they finished questioning him. What if some of the Bertrand people who were in league with Travis, discovered that Travis had spilled the information about their plans for a hybridized baby to him as well as Danny? Having knowledge of those plans might make it dangerous for the two of them. He carefully pushed those thoughts as far away from his

210

mind as possible. There were too many other factors to cope with first.

After what seemed like hours, The Hazmat crew finally emerged from the building and gave Charles a thumbs-up.

"All clear," one of them shouted.

Immediately, a flood of uniformed officers entered the building, guns drawn. Charles prayed to God they would find Travis quickly, and bring him out. Dead or alive.

"Do you really think Travis is still somewhere inside?" Isabel asked.

"I have no idea," Charles said, shaking his head. He looked down at Isabel who with her shoes coated with mud, her clothing wrinkled and mud splattered, and her rusty colored hair in little semi-curled tufts. "You look like little Orphan Annie," he said with a slight chuckle.

She looked up at him, blinked a few times, and then pinched her lips forward for a second before saying, "Yeah, well you look like Indiana Jones! All you need is his hat!" Her words made both of them laugh.

"Come on," he said. Let's get back to the porch and sit down again, until they allow us inside. It's getting cold out here, and some dark clouds are threatening to close in again." He took her hand and helped her rescue her feet from the sticky mud. They sat down to the far right side of the porch so as not to obstruct any of the police action. This time Charles didn't feel the least bit sleepy. Tired, yes, but not even drowsy. He might actually make it through another day.

"I keep wondering if we're going to hear gun shots," Isabel said quietly.

"If so, I hope it's aimed at Travis, and that they've put him down. What an insane idiot!" The thought of almost having died from the nerve gas spiked him with a sense of rising anger beginning way down inside him. He suppressed it, as much as possible, but refused to let it go.

The large front door that led into the stone building opened and a tall stout officer motioned to them. "The big entry room has been

211

cleared and checked for any evidence concerning what happened here," he said. "If you would be more comfortable, go inside and find a better place to sit. But you are not to go anyplace else until it is Okayed. We have six armed men in that room, for your safety. It's going to take a century to check out the rest of this crazy place."

Charles let out a relieved sigh, helped Isabel to her feet, and led her inside the large entry room. She settled down on one of the leather couches framing the huge fireplace, mud and all. He looked around the room where the six armed sheriffs had taken their place around the sides of the room. The wood bin still held several logs so he quickly managed to start a fire. The large room was damply cold so he figured it was a good idea. Isabel sat quietly on the couch with her muddy shoe off and her feet curled up, her head laid back against the top of the sofa. When the fire was going well, he sat down beside her.

"Are you okay?" he said quietly.

She gave a light smile. "As okay as anyone could be in such an unbelievable situation."

Her expression told him that she was coping quite well. "It will be over before you know it," he said trying to be encouraging.

Isabel looked around the room, and then looked directly at him, her eyes penetrating his. "It will be over, when it's over," she said in a smooth voice. "That's life, isn't it?" Then she frowned, her eyes looked away from him and she let out a little sigh. "I'm worried about Darla. No matter what part she has in whatever is going on here. She's not that young, and she's pregnant. That might cause a serious problem, physically, for her."

"There's more to all this than you know," Charles said. He would tell her later, when all of this was over, about the possibility of a designer baby, but now wasn't the time.

Scooter suddenly joined them, plopping his muscular body down on the small sofa. "What a mess all this is," he grumbled and then looked over at Isabel. 'How you doing, Sweetcheeks?"

Isabel sighed and said, "As good as possible. What about Danny?"

212

Scooter grinned. "The Hazmat team found him still on the top of the elevator like Charles left him. They said he seemed fine,. He just kept saying he was hungry and that he wanted peanut butter. They should have him back here before too long."

"Sounds like Danny," Isabel said with a slight smile.

"They've checked all this main floor, and are working the upstairs bedrooms."

"What about Darla," Charles asked.

"Still locked in her room upstairs, I assume," Scooter said. "I told the guys where to find her. I gave them my keys."

"And Travis?" Isabel asked.

"One of the detectives told me they've started with the labs and the empty caverns down below," Scooter said. "Although the Hazmat guys got to those first. No sign of lingering gas, but in Joe's lab there was evidence that there had been a detonation of some sort. So the detectives are searching now, for evidence as well as for Travis. So it's a slow progress." Charles frowned and then said in a low soft voice, "They took Joe's body out through the service area of the kitchen instead of through here. They claimed that he was probably the one who blew up the generator as he had the smell of explosive material on him."

Charles looked at Isabel to see if that information had upset her. Her face was not bright, nor dark. She drew in what sounded like a shuddering breath. She sat next to him, huddled against the sofa's soft leather, her arms crossed. He hoped her four years of accepting her husband as dead had hardened her some. He was certain the deception of his faking his death would be hard to forgive. Isabel looked up at him, her eyes showing some sparks, which he felt was a good sign.

"Charles," she said in a rather whispery voice, as if wanting her words to be kept a secret. "If Jorge . . . Joe thinks I'm going to give him another funeral and place him at Brighter Day Memorial park next to an angel spraying water out of its mouth like a mist of tiny white diamonds, then he's got another damn think coming!"

For some reason Charles found her words extremely funny. He

213

had to choke back his laughter, but he knew she saw it. Her lips barely twitched, but it was obvious she was also trying to reign in her sense of the absurdity considering their situation. All this isn't going to break this woman, he told himself with relief.

She looked away from him and began checking around the huge room. "I hope Darla is okay. Even if she is in on all this with Travis. She's rather a tragic character in all this drama."

Almost as if they had called her name, Darla suddenly appeared. She came walking into the room beside two armed Sheriffs. Startled, Scooter got up and went to her.

"How are you doing?" Scooter asked. "Feeling okay?"

"I could be better," Darla said an odd snarl to her voice. "Some son-of-a-bitch locked me in my bedroom.

"The baby!" Scooter said, "Everything okay? No bleeding or anything?"

"No," she said, her cheeks turning their usual persimmon color. "Things are just fine."

Charles still wondered if Darla had any idea about what Travis had planned for her, or the baby, and all of her research. Had she been an active part of it with Joe? Or just the brilliant scientist who figured out all of the details on how to do it. If so, how many laws had she broken if she'd done what Travis had claimed she did? Or was her research actually legitimate? Questionable, but not illegal. Charles realized he still wasn't up to many organized thoughts or answers. It would take more than a few hours of sleep before his brain would function properly again.

Isabel got up and walked over to Darla, and then asked the officers, "Where are you taking her?"

"Outside," said a tall man whose uniform seemed way too large for him. "For questioning."

"I think you need to take her to a hospital, to make sure she's okay. She's pregnant," Scooter insisted. "She's had a bad nausea problem."

Both officers looked Darla up and down, frowning. "Doesn't look it," the tall one said.

"I am only four months," Darla said. "And what is going on around here? I was in the bathroom throwing up again when these two men jacked my bedroom door, and dragged me out of there."

"We want to question her," one of the men said to Scooter. "But to be safe, we'll take your advice and have her checked out at a hospital when they're done."

"Good," Scooter said.

Darla's mouth twisted tightly as she said, "You should be concerned, Scooter. After all, this is *your* baby."

Scooter blanched and then his forehead pinched itself into a puzzled frown. "Darla, just because I did the implantation it does not mean it's *my* baby."

The smile that spread across Darla's face made Charles cringe. He wasn't used to Darla smiling and her smile had a strange craziness about it.

"Well Scooter," Darla said in a quiet, measured voice. "You should be more careful what you do with your used condoms when you toss them away. Especially on the nights when your bitchy girlfriend goes home."

Scooter appeared to attempt saying something, but he didn't get out a word.

"Once she left, you always fell asleep immediately so I could retrieve the condom" She nodded knowingly. You are such a good specimen. Your DNA sequencing showed no errors, no sign of inheritable diseases or disorders. As close to perfect as we can tell these days. So you and I are going to be parents. Do not worry. I will not ask for child support." she said giving him a hard tight smile. "I will take care of him myself."

Scooter opened his mouth, and then closed it again. Charles could hear his breathing quicken. "Him?" he finally said.

"Yes. I know it's a boy." Darla said, her strange smile widening on her face.

"You won't be able take care of him, Darla, since you'll be in jail forever," Charles said, realizing that Scooter was totally incapable of comprehending the situation. He was, after all missing the most important information. That the baby was a composite of DNA, and who the hell knew what it would turn into, if it actually made it into the world.

"I'll be enjoying my Nobel prize, that's what I'll be doing." Darla's strange smile faded and she turned to the policemen with her and said, "Let's go."

With that, the officers escorted her across the large room to the front door Before Darla left, she turned and gave Isabel an offbeat look, almost as if she wanted her help. Then the room was silent for a few minutes. Charles knew he had to tell Scooter, as well as Darla, about the ominous claims Travis had made. It was pretty evident that Darla was not just a pawn that Travis was using. She was probably chin-deep in the whole thing.

Isabel went back and sat on the sofa next to Charles. "I kind of feel like Dorothy lost in Oz. Charles is the lion, and Scooter the tin man."

"So who is the Strawman" Scooter asked, happy with the more lightweight atmosphere.

"Danny, of course," Isabel said. "Kind of an overstuffed Strawman." She started to grin, but then stopped and said, "Oh, dear. I'm sorry. That wasn't a nice thing to say.'

"Not to worry, Sweetcheeks, Danny would be the first person to laugh about it."

Charles held up his hand. "Listen you two, I hate to break up the relief we're feeling. But remember, they haven't found Travis yet. And I want to fill the two of you in on what Travis claims has been going on here," he said. "Alarming things!"

Oddly, Scooter ignored Charles words, got up and went to the fireplace, looked down at the crackling flames for a moment, and then turned around and said to them, "Holy shit!! Am I actually going to be a father?"

216

Chapter Eighteen

Isabel looked up to see Danny's arrival, along with a stocky woman sheriff with polished silver hair. It kept Charles from starting his explanation about the serious problems. Danny almost ran to where the three of them were sitting. The woman walked to the back of the sofa and stood there looking around at the four of them.

"Got room for me on the sofa?" Danny said. "I need something soft to sit on. That damn top of the elevator is like lying on metal.'

"That's because it *is* metal, Danny," Scooter said with a slight laugh.

"Yeah, yeah, I know. And I know I'm starving. He shook the watch on his wrist as if it wasn't working "Fer crying out loud! We didn't have any breakfast yet. So, when are we going to eat?"

Charles moved closer to Isabel, leaving some room for Danny to sit. "We can't fix any food, Danny," he explained. "It's going to take a long time before the police get through with their investigation. They are going to need to talk with you like they did with the rest of us."

"Yes," said the silver haired Sheriff. "We do need a statement from him."

Danny slumped down on the sofa and then burst into tears. "Oh, God, I really need to eat something first. Anyone have a candy bar?"

Scooter gave him an understanding look. "What Danny didn't say is that he's hypoglycemic. Low blood sugar. That's one of the reasons why he's always hungry. He can't help it. And I don't have a glucose tube on me."

"Oh Danny, that must be difficult," Isabel said. She turned and looked at the silver haired woman who was still standing behind the sofa. "Is it possible for someone to go out somewhere and find us some take-out food?" she asked her. "None of us has eaten since last night."

The woman looked at Danny. "I think maybe I can get that

217

done," she said, reaching over the back of the sofa and gently patting Danny on the shoulder. "I think food is urgent right now. For all of you."

"Oh, thank you," Isabel said. "That would be really helpful."

"It will have to be burgers or something."

"I'd like three, with fries, if possible," Danny said in a pleading voice. "No onions"

The women gave a nod and a gentle smile. "I'm sure we can handle that. We'll get something for everyone." She patted Danny's shoulder again, and then jogged to the front door, closing it quietly behind her.

The large room took on an empty silence as the four of them looked at each other. Then, Isabel's gaze went to the flickering flames in the fireplace. She wanted to say something, but had no idea what."

Scooter stretched out his arms and legs and gave a moan. "God, I'll be glad when I can get down the mountain and have a steak and a beer. Yesterday feels like a year ago, but yet all of this impossible stuff seems to have happened just an hour or so ago. Sort of like it's clinging to me. How's that for being schizoid?"

"Scooter . . . ," Isabel hesitated. "I've been wondering how you feel about what Darla said. That you're the father of her baby."

Scooter took a few moments to consider the question. Isabel was glad that he didn't just give some sort of flip answer.

"First things first," he finally said. "It will take a DNA test to prove it. And if it's true, then I'll need to know what kind of herculean child Darla feels she's carrying, and what she's done to try and make that happen."

Charles cleared his throat. "I think I may have a flash drive in my pocket that has some answer on it."

Isabel blanched. She realized that meant Jorge was definitely a part of all this mess. She got up, feeing restless from sitting so long. She moved to the fireplace, still feeling chilled, and hugged the warmth there. "So, tell us more, Charles," she said, wanting to get everything out in the open. She wanted to face what was going on, and then get the hell out of this horrid stone prison. She glanced up at the plaque of slightly rusty metal hanging on the stone wall above the fireplace hood with the words WELCOME TO POOLE'S GRAY-GREEN UNDERGROUND stamped on it. "A fine welcome all this is," she told the plaque in a clipped tone."

"What?" Charles asked.

She turned to him. "Oh, sorry. Just thinking out loud." She quickly returned to the sofa and plunked herself down next to Charles. She heard him clear his throat again, and then got up and begin to pace for a few moments. Then he faced the three of them and sucked in a deep breath and let it out with a puffing sound.

"Okay then, here's what I know, or at least suspect so far. Danny knows too. I'm in no way an expert concerning altering human DNA, so all I can do is give you what little info I have." He reached into his pocket and pulled out the flash drive. "This," he said firmly, "appears to be filled with Joe's, and probably Darla's, DNA work. Travis has no skill in that area. Darla had some literature on Transhumanism. Something called H+, which seems like it's a very well-intended international movement that supports the transforming of the human condition by creating technologies that will eliminate aging and improve human's physical, intellectual and psychological capacities. However, it appears Joe and Darla went off on their own and experimented with changing the genetic code of a human being to that end. God only knows what they've already created with it. With her cats. With jars full of macabre life forms floating in a dozen jars in her cupboard. And from what Travis said, she used DNA from another species, not human, for the baby. From something Travis said never dies!"

"But that's impossible!" Scooter's voice was sparked with anger. "Haven't most of the experiments with that kind of thing failed or been catastrophic. Not to mention against the law! I'm just a medic, but since I work here I've read a lot about things like that."

Isabel heard Danny give out a low moan.

"What is it Danny?" Charles asked.

Danny twisted himself around on the sofa, nervous energy

219

obviously making him uncomfortable. "Whenever I've had lunch with Darla, or visited her in her lab now and then, she has always been adamant about what can be done to create humans who would live as long as Methuselah.. She said to me a dozen times that we can now take any part of another creature's DNA that will prolong and enhance life, and splice it into the DNA of a human. And, without any chance of rejection as there has been in the past. She says the drug she's created from her soybean plants will stop any rejection, and increase the efficiency of the virus which carries the foreign material into the DNA."

Scooter got to his feet. "The devil you say!"

"I swear!" Danny insisted. "I didn't tell anyone because I just thought she was exaggerating. Boasting that she would find a way to do that. Not that she had already done it!"

"So all of her talk about creating a vaccine that will cure some horrible disease was just a front." Isabel said, stunned at the thought of what Darla may have done.

"Oh my heavens!" Isabel said. "The question she asked my students to answer but that she didn't tell me the answer to—"

"What question?" Charles asked.

"What is the worst disease everyone in the world eventually gets?"

Danny frowned. "So what is it? What disease?"

"Death, Danny," Isabel said softly. "Everyone gets it." The room around them went eerily silent for a few moments. Not even the fire crackled.

"So is what she's trying to do actually possible?"

"That's not my field, but I did give it a try at one time. It turned out to be too much of a risk for me." Danny grimaced. "However I did learn that because of the universal genetic code, it is absolutely possible to splice a gene from another organism into the human genome. However, I understand the outcome is most often unpredictable."

"What's the worst?" Charles demanded.

Danny looked away from him. "I'm starved! Where's our lunch?"

"Danny, what can happen?" Scooter said.

"Well, Darla has also been fooling around with technologies that could be used to rewrite the genetic code of a living cell, allowing them to make large-scale edits to the cell's genome. MIT and Harvard researchers have made progress with this. I don't know how far Darla has gotten."

Isabel had an alarming thought. "Couldn't putting any genomes from one species into a different species possibly create a whole different species," she said.

It was a relief when Isabel saw the silver-haired lady sheriff arrived carrying a number of bags of what smelled like food. That didn't take her long, she thought. Thank God! Some food would make all of them feel a lot better.

"McDonald's," the woman said laughing. Got the police chopper to run down to somewhere in Altadena." She quickly sorted through the bags and made sure everyone had plenty to eat and drink.

"Hamburgers! Cokes! Fries!" Danny exclaimed. "He opened his bag and sniffed, as if it was filled with some kind of fine wine.

Isabel got up and put her bag, which held two fat hamburgers and a wrap of French fries, down on the sofa. "Charles, is it possible for me to go to my room before I eat? They said they checked out this floor."

Charles looked at the Sheriff who was getting ready to leave. "Is that possible?" he asked her.

She shrugged and said, "I don't see why not. However, have one of the armed men go with you. He can wait outside the door.

"Charles, would you go with me too?" Isabel asked.

Charles got up and put his food bag on the sofa next to hers. "Of course."

"I would just feel kind of . . . creepy moving around here alone considering what all has happened."

"No problem. I need to stretch my legs. They're cramping up from all the climbing I did last night."

They walked across the room to the hallway, and Isabel asked the sheriff standing there to please go with them. It made her feel much safer having someone there with a gun, just in case. She badly needed to go to the bathroom and she hoped she would make it. It had been far too many hours since she'd been able to do that. "You two stay out here. I won't be long."

Charles gave her a smile, and then hugged her. "No one is going to get by us," he said.

Chapter Nineteen

Once alone inside the bedroom Isabel let out a giant sigh. The window was open a slight bit. She closed it after taking a look around outside. Several armed men were there standing guard. Maybe now that they had questioned her, they would let her go home. If so, she hoped she would be calm enough to drive safely down the rugged mountainside. Maybe Charles would offer to drive her. But then one of them would have to leave their car here. Besides, she was sure he would have a million things to do here after what all had happened. She had to admit that she would miss Charles. He really made her feel safe and as if he cared for her. However, what Jorge had said, that she shouldn't trust him, kept creeping back into her mind.

She looked over at the bed which was terribly inviting, but she quickly made her way into the bathroom. After using the toilet she decided to freshen up a little. Then Charles could use the bathroom if he needed to. She turned on the water and, not waiting for it to warm up, she splashed her face with it several times. Even though her room was chilly, the cold water felt wonderful. She tried to use the one towel on the rack but found that due to the stormy weather, it was still too damp from when she'd taken a shower yesterday morning.

"Damn," she muttered and went into the bedroom where she remembered that the polished wood hope chest held several clean folded towels. She raised the chest lid and grabbed one of the white towels and began drying her face. She heard a thump and when she turned to see what it was, something flew up, hitting her in the face. A sharp riveting pain sliced across her forehead. "Good Christ!" she screeched. All she needed was another injury. Her foot still throbbed from the last one. That was when she felt a strong arm grab her around the waist. "Charles?" she asked in a weak tone.

"No, I'm not Charles," said a deep raspy voice. "And I'm not Christ, and I'm not good."

223

Isabel turned her head to try and see the person that was holding her. But as she did, she saw a gun in the man's other hand. The hand pressed the tip of the gun barrel against the side of her neck. The cold metal bit at her skin like a sharp piece of ice. All she could see was the faint image of a man's face. A face she recognized!

"Travis!" she screamed. "Oh my god!" Somehow he had managed to skirt all of the armed men searching the building by hiding out in the hope chest. She realized that the clean towels had been lying on a removable shelf inside the chest. That must have been what hit her. The pain on her forehead escalated and her heart hammered inside her chest.

"I didn't hit you hard enough when you were snooping around in the underground. I did a better job with Joe though, didn't I Isabel?"

The mention of Jorge caused her to close her eyes tightly and pray that Charles and the armed Sherriff had heard her scream. The bedroom door gave a sudden rusty shriek which caused Travis to lift the gun and fire at the door. Isabel heard a howl. Someone in the hall had been hit! Moments later the door burst open and Charles charged into the room. Travis fired the gun, and Charles grabbed at his right side. After that, it looked as if his legs just crumpled under him, and he dropped to the floor

"Charles!" Isabel screamed.

Travis quickly put the gun back against her neck. "Stay down, Charles." he growled. "One shot and she's dead. I rather hoped you were already dead. Too bad the gas didn't work. Is Danny alive too?"

"You fucked up Travis!" Charles said attempting to scramble backward to the doorway.

Before Charles could get out the door, Travis fired at him again. The bullet hit him in his right shoulder. Isabel saw a trail of dark blood beginning to run down the right side of his shirt. "No! Charles!" she screamed, her voice going hoarse as she did. Where the hell was the armed guy who was supposed to be just outside the door?

Once more the gun was planted firmly against the side of her neck. The noise from the gunfire gave Isabel a ringing numbness in

224

her ears. She hardly felt it as Travis backed up and dragged her with him to the widow. He used his elbow to push the window open as wide as possible. He turned her around to face him, holding her painfully tight, obviously to use her as a shield. She looked up at his eyes which were marble shiny and had a demented look to them. Then with one quick thrust, he tumbled the two of them out of the window. They landed with a painful smacking sound on the ground below the window with Travis underneath her. Isabel frantically tried to break away from him, yelling for help which could hardly be heard as her breath was pretty much knocked out of her because of the fall. His free arm quickly retrieved her and held her so constricted her ribs felt like long sharp pins were jabbing them His other hand still held the gun. She couldn't believe someone his age could be so damn strong! Desperation no doubt.

The only morsel of hope that Isabel had was that because the grounds around the building had several armed men guarding the area, surely at least one of them had heard the shooting, or saw them fall from the window, and would somehow save her from Travis' insanity.

Charles still on the floor, his shoulder bleeding and his side injecting him with incredible pain, looked up and saw Scooter rush into the room. Behind him, peering into the room, were two more men holding firearms. "It's . . . about . . . time!" Charles said with a choked voice.

"Good God Almighty!" Scooter cried as he knelt down beside Charles. "You're bleeding like a leaky boat. Let's get that stopped."

"Doesn't matter," Charles insisted. "Get Isabel. Travis went out the window with her."

Scooter yelled at the men standing in the doorway. "Let your guys know that the murderer they are looking for just took off out that window with a hostage. And have them call and get a medevac chopper ASAP."

One of the men nodded and took off running. Scooter removed

his shirt and rolled it up tightly and then pressed it hard against the area of Charles chest that was bleeding. "Are you breathing okay?"

"No problem."

"Good. We've got one of the sheriffs in the hall who was also hit. Not too bad. Two shots in one leg." Scooter ran his hand around Charles chest. "Ah, looks like a second bullet went all the way through the side of your ribs. Didn't hit your lung. Cracked the ribs no doubt. Not bleeding much. But it's gonna be painful."

"Forget about me, damn it! Find Isabel!" Charles demanded, taking the bundled shirt from Scooter and pressing it against his shoulder. He felt a tremor, a shivering, that spread across his whole body. Scooter must have seen it because he put his hand on Charles hand.

"Okay Chucky, relax. I don't want you going into shock. Was Isabel okay when she went out the window?"

"Yes, I think so. But it's quite a drop, and Travis still has the gun"

Scooter gave a scowl. "If he hasn't hurt her yet, it's probably because he wants to keep using her as a shield until he can get away. Or maybe he thinks she has something he wants. . But until he gets what he wants, Travis probably won't hurt her."

It took a minute before Charles realized what it was that Travis wanted. "Of course! The information on Joe's flash drive! "Damn it!" he said. "It's my fault he came after Isabel."

"What makes you think that?" Scooter said, taking Charles pulse for the second time.

"Because Joe absconded with Darla's information about how to make a designer baby. Put it on a flash drive."

"And he didn't find it on Joe, so he figures Isabel has it. Right?"

"Exactly," Charles said, leaning forward to ease his pain.

"And the designer baby is the one that Darla and I are apparently having. That is if what we've been told is true."

"It should all be on the flash drive," Charles said. Now please, go help get Isabel away from that maniac. Please!"

"I'll go and check with the detectives to see what happened with

226

the two of them after they went out the window. There are a number of armed men around the place. Maybe they've rescued her." Scooter motioned to the policeman who was still in the room. "Help him onto the bed. He needs to stay warm and rest. How is the guy in the hallway doing?"

"In pain, but okay. Paramedics should be here soon."

The policeman helped Charles to his feet and settled him on the bed. Jolting throbs of pain ravished his shoulder and side. He bit down on his lip to keep from crying out.

"Rest easy, Scooter said. "You need to be in good shape when they get Isabel back here. She would never forgive me if I let ya die."

"*If* they get her back," Charles said with a throb in his voice. He lay his head back against the pillow and discovered it smelled of the honey sweet scent of Isabel's perfume. Just the scent of it made him feel better.

"With all the police around this place, Travis isn't going anywhere," Scooter assured him.

Charles suddenly found a peculiar thought nagging at him. "Two bullets in you 0and two more in the wounded man in the hallway."

"Right, Thank God there weren't more."

"Four bullets!" Charles cried out. "I only had five bullets in the gun. I used the others when I went to target practice awhile back. I hadn't replaced them yet. So Travis only has one bullet left."

"He may not realize that!" Scooter said.

"But one is enough, if he fires it." Charles said, feeling the tremor in his body increase.

"If he fires the gun just to frighten her, then he's out of luck," Scooter said. "No matter what, I'll go do what I can to help us find Isabel"

"Thank you," Charles said, gritting his teeth against the pain.

Scooter started toward the door but Charles called to him, "Wait!" He fumbled in his pocket and touched the flash drive. Should he or shouldn't he give it to Scooter? After all, if it was information about the baby, and the baby might be his, then maybe he should have it.

"Patience! The paramedics will give you something for the pain," Scooter said.

Charles pulled out the flash drive, cupping it in his had so the policeman wouldn't see it. "I think you should have this." He extended his hand to Scooter.

Puzzled, Scooter took what was in Charles hand, gave it a quick look, and then obviously realized what it was. He quickly shoved it into his pocket. "I'll take care of it," he said, then quickly made his way out of the room.

Charles relaxed against the softness of the bed. He took a minute to look up at the ceiling where he saw the multitude of grotesque carved faces. If he remembered right, they were traditional images made to scare off evil forces. He prayed that they would do a successful job of it.

To Isabel, Travis' arm felt like a strand of thick steel wire wrapped tightly around her waist. He was much stronger than he looked to be. After the rough tumble out the window, and by the time the two of them had gotten to their feet, the police on guard there had all their guns pointed at the two of them. Travis continued to keep his gun tight against her neck, and began yelling "Back off or I'll kill her!"

"Travis, if you kill me, they will shoot you," Isabel said as he forced her along the side of the building toward the back of it. "I'm sure they are all dead shots." She tried to sound as calm and undaunted as possible.

"Shut up!" Travis tightened his grip on her even more.

One of the policemen began yelling at Travis. "Turn her lose you coward. Hiding behind a woman! Come on, give it up, chicken. Be a fucking man!"

Travis ignored him, and tightened up his hold on Isabel.

Isabel began searching her brain trying to remember some of the moves she'd learned some years ago in a self-defense class. She sure as hell wasn't going to go down without a fight. She thought of a few actions she could take, and then concentrated on watching Travis for any weak moment. He didn't seem to be that good of a shot. If he wanted to kill Charles, he had missed hitting a crucial spot. She just hoped he wouldn't bleed out.

They passed the end of the building with the police not far behind them. She wondered if he was taking her into the pine forest. Not a great idea during daylight. But a few yards away he suddenly stopped. His breathing became a little labored. Leaning over her as he was, she could feel his hot damp breath on the back of her neck. Was he exhausted? Had he slept at all during the night? She hoped not. The more exhausted he was the better her chances.

Sound overhead caught her attention: the rotor throb of a helicopter. She tried to look up but because of the pressure of the gun against her neck it was difficult. She hoped it was another police chopper. The sound of it made Travis jumpy. His grip on her tightened even more.

He suddenly stopped their movement, looked toward the mass of pine trees, and then back at the stone building. He then moved toward a deeply sloped area of the grounds. An area that looked familiar to Isabel. Then she realized why. It led to the underground, the way that Scooter had gotten her out of the building and into the forest last night.

Travis quickly pulled her toward the area where Isabel knew the slope inside went down to an iron gate and the entrance to the bottom of the underground. It only took them minutes to reach the gate. Isabel hoped that Scooter had replaced the lock on it before they had left. But it was wide open, the lock dangling. He tugged her inside and ordered her to close the gate. She tried to appear clumsy, slowing the progress. Irritated by her slowness, he slammed the gate shut and tried to close the lock, finding it impossible while holding the gun and Isabel.

"Lock the damn thing," he thundered at her. Reluctantly, she managed to do what he asked. She heard him cough and then sigh after the gate was finally locked. He then pulled her down through the narrow tunnel to the bottom area of the underground.

229

"I don't think they've completely searched this underground area yet, Travis," she told him. "They'll find you!"

"Won't be here long. Just until I get the information I need from you."

"What information?" Isabel asked, seriously not knowing what he meant.

"Joe's information. I know he put everything about the process that Darla has pioneered, on a flash drive. He didn't have it on him when I killed him. I'm betting that he gave it to you. Otherwise why would he have gotten you here? So what have you done with it?"

"Jorge . . . I mean Joe never gave me anything. He knew I wouldn't understand much about those kind of things." She realized then, that was the only reason she was still alive.

"I started to search you, after you were unconscious and I had dropped you in the same cavern as I did Joe. But the damn stair lights went out and I heard noise up top. Went out to investigate and thought I'd better get myself outside. I knew I could always get back to you later."

"Well you're wrong, Travis. I do not have any flash drive."

"Darla wiped her computer." Travis said. "She then melted the hard drive. That flash drive is the only record of what we did. I know you have it. So give it to me!" Travis gave her a jolting shake and Isabel actually heard her bones rattle. It hurt like crazy but she wasn't going to give him the satisfaction of knowing he was hurting her. "Go ahead and search me! You've trapped yourself in here, don't you know?" she said.

Travis let go of her and slowly backed away, pointing the gun at her. Without his tight wire-like arm around her, Isabel felt a renewed sense of courage.

"There's another way out and Darla is meeting me there. We'll disappear and take the golden baby with us. Once we can show the remarkable results of Darla's work, all will be forgiven. We just need that damn flash drive so the results can be created again without taking a lifetime to remember the process, and not make any errors. Darla might be able to recreate it perfectly, but she night not."

"How careless you've been, Travis. You'll never get away with it."

"Yes I will. Darla will get us to another country where none of this will matter."

Isabel thought about what he said. "They were questioning Darla the last I heard. I don't think they will let her go. They will realize she's totally involved in all this."

Travis gave a pinched frown. "No. They have no proof. She'll be there for me, mark my word."

What about Bertrand? Are they involved?"

"A few people. They'll be pissed about being left out." Travis lifted the gun and looked at it, then pointed it at her. "But fuck them!"

With her heart skipping beats in her chest, Isabel took a few slow steps toward him. "You don't want to do this, Travis."

"Actually I don't. You're a nice woman. But Darla and I can't leave any loose ends. Once you're down, I'll no doubt find that damn flash drive on you."

"No, you won't." Isabel continued to move closer. "If you're going to shoot, do it up close. You're a rotten shot. Don't just wing me and leave me to bleed out."

"Stay back!" he yelled at her.

Anger overcoming her fear, Isabel leapt forward, caught her left foot behind his right leg and gave it a herculean tug toward her. Losing his balance, Travis flipped backward and ended in a lump on the stone floor. When he hit, the gun flew out of his hands. She dove for it, grabbed it and pointed it at him. She heard a clanging sound and realized someone was trying to open the locked gate at the bottom of the tunnel. She heard a voice shouting instructions. Would they get to her soon enough?

Travis began to force himself up off the stone floor.

"Stay down, Travis," she yelled at him.

Instead, he kept moving, and managed to stand up. "You won't shoot me, Isabel. You're not the killer type, like me." He took another step toward her.

231

"One more step," she said. "One more step and I shoot. Remember, you tried to kill me, and you killed my dead husband. Then you wounded Charles and a policeman." Her finger felt for and found what she hoped was the safety. She had heard Charles say it had an automatic safety. She just hoped she had taken it off, not turned it on.

Puzzled, Travis hesitated for a moment. Then with an apparent surge of energy he took one long step toward her. She felt the hair on the back of her neck stand up. He took another giant step, a malevolent grin on his face. Isabel pulled the trigger.

She only vaguely felt the warm spray of his blood and the stinging flick of bone fragments as they struck her.

She stood there holding the gun, frozen to the spot where she was standing. She didn't move during the five or more minutes it took a number of police to get the gate open, and reach where she was. She had just killed a man but she felt a sense of liberation, rather than guilt. One of the policemen called out to her and asked if she was okay. She nodded. "I need to clean up," she said. "I really do need to clean up"

"Yes, of course you do." The policeman came and stood alongside her. He smelled of a musky aftershave, the kind Jorge used to wear. Such a strange thing to notice, she thought. She slowly handed him the gun.

"We could hear you as we were coming up that tunnel," he told her. "You were amazingly strong, standing up to him that way," he told her. "Now, let's get you out of here."

"I have a hamburger to eat. And I bet it's getting cold," Isabel said, wondering why on earth she said that. Then it hit her! "Charles! Is he okay. Travis shot him!"

"As far as I know, he's going to be okay. Nothing vital was hit." The policeman took her arm and began urging her to start walking. "One of our guys was hit too but he's also doing okay"

Isabel was amazed how easy it was for her to make her way up the tunnel to ground level now that she knew Charles was okay. When they reached ground level, she felt something odd touching her ankle. Something rubbing softly against her jeans. She looked down, and there was a cat. The color of pale clay. A very peculiar looking cat with no fur, no tail, and ears that lay flattened smoothly against its head. It rubbed its head against her ankle, gave a raspy meow and then looked up at her. It looked at her with the queerest eyes. They were identical to human eyes. The sight of it made Isabel gasp. She took one moment to give it a pet, hearing it begin to purr. Then she moved on.

When they reached the entry room, Isabel was grateful to see Scooter there. "I need to clean up she said," a pleading tone in her voice.

"Tell me all that blood isn't you." Scooter looked her over, his face draining its color. "Who?"

"Travis. I shot him."

"He's dead?"

"Yes."

Scooter reached for her and pulled her to him, ignoring the blood and bone on her. She started to cry then. He held her as long as it took for her crying to ease. A lot of her sense of fear flowed out of her with the tears. She felt better. "I need a shower, but I don't have a change of clothes."

"Not to worry. You go shower, and I'll find you something to wear."

"Ah, I see," she said. "You're a cross dresser." At that they both burst out laughing. Another form of getting rid of unwanted feelings, she realized.

"Actually, they are a former girlfriend's things. She moved to Chicago a year ago, and said she didn't need them back. "So, get to the shower. A long and hot one."

"Charles! Where is he?"

"Asleep in your bed. Don't wake him. Shower first. Then you can talk to him before Medevac gets him to a hospital. They gotta get the bullet out of his shoulder. One on the side went right through. "

Isabel could hardly keep herself from waking Charles the minute

233

she arrived in her room. But he looked so peaceful, and was breathing easy, with his color good, so she let him sleep. She'd talk to him once the Medevac team was ready to take him.

Arriving back in the entry room, in a pair of too long jeans, a purple sweater with little white metal hearts sewn all over it, and a pair of plastic flip flops on her feet, Isabel was so glad to see Danny sitting on one of the sofas next to the fireplace with a genuine smile on his face.

"It's a good thing you got back," Danny said. "I almost ate your hamburger and fries." He gave a little laugh.

Isabel returned his smile. "You can have the fries, Danny, but not my burger. I just killed someone, I need nourishment."

"Oh yeah? Who?"

"Travis."

"Good! Nasty bugger that one. Don't feel bad about it. After all, he tried to kill me, you, Charles, and he did kill Joe. Someone had to stop him." Danny looked away as if trying to hide some tears.

Isabel suddenly heard a familiar voice coming from the far end of the room. It was the friend of Charles that he called Gray. She got up and quickly joined him and the policeman he was talking with.

Gray gave her a quick nod and then looked back at the policeman. "Where are they keeping the woman? Darla I think it is."

The policeman thought for a moment. "You mean the tall, thin one with the sour face?" he asked.

"That's her."

"She's with some guy over near your company's chopper."

"A short guy in a gray suit with a red tie?" Gray asked, puzzled.

"That's the one."

"What the fuck is David doing with her? I thought the police were holding her."

"She's not cuffed."

"Interesting." He turned to Isabel. "I need to go talk to her. I want to know who else from Bertrand was in on this baby she's having," He turned back to Isabel. "I hear you did the world a favor."

Isabel shook her head. "It was him or me. I always vote for

myself. However, I don't like the way it feels."

"Time. Time will help erase it. If you let it."

"Have they told you about Charles condition?"

Gray grinned, his eyes shining. "Just that he's going to be fine."

Isabel didn't know if she should cry for happy, or get hysterical because of all that had happened. She chose neither. "I'll go and try to eat my hamburger before Danny does." She looked up at Gray. "It's funny isn't it, the way life seems to just go on as usual after such unbelievable things happen? We can join it, or just watch from the sidelines."

"The sidelines may seem safer, but aren't nearly as interesting or as much fun." He reached out his hand and gently touched her cheek. Then he turned and quickly made his way out of the room.

Chapter Twenty

When Isabel got back to the sofa she found Danny stretched out on the short one, sound asleep. She saw he had thoughtfully put the sack with her hamburger in it on the longer sofa. The fries were gone but the hamburger was intact. She wasn't hungry at all, but thought she'd better eat something considering everything she'd been through. She did feel extremely fatigued and wanted to do what Danny was doing. Sleep. Forget about the past few days. But instead she began nibbling on the hamburger, finally finishing most of it.

Looking over at the huge entry door she saw Gray rush in and look around rather wildly. He sped over to her and said, "Have you seen Darla and my tight-assed assistant?"

She shook her head no. "Aren't they out there by that huge helicopter?"

"Not a sign of them." He kept looking around the room, as if he expected to see the couple.

"Did you look in the chopper?" she asked.

"Yes. They hadn't been in there. I checked all the cars, and asked if any of them had left. None of them were missing."

"Well, they didn't come through here.'

"Shit," Gray grumbled, turned on his heels and headed back outside.

The room turned silent except for the soft snoring sound coming from Danny. Isabel had to force herself to stay awake. Coffee! She needed some coffee. She got up and made her way slowly to kitchen. With her foot still hurting some, she walked like a beetle, her plastic flip-flops tapping with each step. She found the big coffee pot filled with some pretty bad smelling coffee so she poured it out and refilled it with water. She took out the coffee grinder, ground an adequate amount, and dropped it into the coffee pot. After lighting the stove, she set the pot on the flame and then went to the cupboard for a cup.

"Isabel," someone behind her said softly. "Will you feed my

kitties while I'm gone?"

Isabel swung around, and sucked in her breath when she saw Darla standing there. "Oh, Darla . . . Gray from Bertrand is looking for you."

"Yes, of course. But please say you'll take care of my kitties."

Isabel swallowed, her throat dry and not cooperating. "Are the police taking you in for more questioning?"

Darla's cheeks began to flush their usual persimmon color. She reached up and slowly removed the strand of pearls around her neck. "I have a favor to ask," she said quietly.

"What's that, Darla?"

Darla handed her the pearls. "These are for you."

"Oh, I can't take these. Really! But I'd be glad to do you a favor, if I can."

Darla reached out and closed Isabel's hand around the pearls. "Please, take them."

Isabel sighed. "Okay then, what is the favor?"

"Will you take care of my kitties? The two friendly ones. The others are wild however, and can get along on their own. The pearls can pay for their food and a vet when necessary."

"Yes, of course, I'll make sure they are looked after. Do they have names?"

Darla gave a tiny smile. "Tic and Tack," she said.

"Cute." Isabel said, feeing awkward with the strand of pearls in her hand. "Will you be away long?"

"I have no idea."

"Darla, I saw one of your kitties near the tunnel to the underground. His eyes were—"

"Yes, his eyes. Unique aren't they?"

"Um, Darla . . . would you like some coffee. You look beat. It's been hard night and day for everyone."

"Yes, thank you."

"Good." Isabel carefully set the pearls down on the kitchen table, and then opened the cupboard and took out another cup. "Cream?" she asked. No answer. She turned around.

"Darla," she cried and heard her word echo around the kitchen. She stood frozen in place, the coffee cup in her hand. Darla was gone!

The police detective cleared his throat, getting ready to talk to the few people gathered in the entry room of what everyone continued to call the Hotel Grande. The giant fireplace had been filled with dry pine logs and sent out long fingers of orange incandescence flames. The detective stood to one side of the fireplace, a short stout man with his jacket unbuttoned due to the fact that it was a too small for him. His skin had that drooped look of someone who was deeply fatigued and was ready to go somewhere to sip a beer or three. Isabel felt sorry for him. It was obvious he would rather have been anywhere but there in that giant stone edifice.

Danny, with his little bubble of a belly sat on the sofa in stark contrast next to Scooter and his bulging muscular frame. Gray, who was oversized for even the large entry room, sat on the other sofa, leaned forward with his eyes narrowed. His assistant, David, seemed to almost blend in with the back of the large sofa, and Isabel expected him to just go poof, and disappear as Darla had.

Isabel sat on the end of the large sofa, her whole body tensed, and her mind not sure if she wanted to hear what the detective had to say. All she wanted was to go home. To enter the real world. To abandon the absurd and dangerous world she'd somehow managed to fall into. To keep her mind off everything she looked down and carefully examined the pattern on the small Persian carpet in front of the sofa.

"Hey there Chucky," Scooter called out in a husky voice. "How you doing?"

Isabel felt her breath go thin. She looked up and saw Charles. Not more than three feet away, he stood a little wobbly, looking at her. He had a large white shirt on, not buttoned, and she could see that his right shoulder and most of his chest were wrapped in a snug bandage.

238

"I'm better than I deserve to be," Charles said as he reached down with his left hand and took hold of Isabel's. He urged her to her feet then still holding her hand, he sat down in her place.

"Oh!" Isabel said, startled. "Okay-." Before she was able to say any more, Charles pulled her down on his lap, leaning her back against his uninjured side. "Oh,' she said again in a soft tone.

"After this they are flying me out to get some medical treatment. The paramedics bandaged me very nicely. But I'm gonna need some shots, and bit of surgery. Will you go with me?"

She nodded her head firmly, and then relaxed herself into the warmth of his body. Two people with two different kinds of pain melted into one.

The detective cleared his throat again then said. "Is that everyone now?" His words were met by silence. "Well then, here's what we have."

It took the detective close to a half hour to get what was on his mind put into words.

Joe Watson, aka Jorge Warren was deceased. Travis Emerson is recently deceased. Bench warrants for four employees of Bertrand had been issued, thanks to David, Gray McCurdy's assistant, who discovered some of Bertrand funds had been unaccounted for. They are also looking for Miss Darla Dotson who appears to have disappeared. It wasn't clear yet about the unusual connection between these people. "Everything has been pretty closed-mouth about what kind of DNA research has been going on here," the detective told them in a scolding tone. In closing, he said "You are all cleared to go home if you wish. Those of you who live here most of the time will have to find other lodging until we do more investigating. You can check with us in about a week to see if it's okay to come back here." With that he gave them a wave of his hand, turned and quickly walked to the door, avoiding any chance of a question and answering session.

Silence gripped the room for a few moments, and then everyone began talking. Isabel, not wanting to hear anything more, extracted herself from Charles lap and stood up. He got up slowly, with a little groan and stood next to her.

"Well, as soon as I get patched up, Charles said. "I'll need to get a motel room I guess, since I've lived here fulltime."

Isabel looked at him. His eyes now wide and innocent, his face looking like that of a lost child. He badly needed a haircut, and she so wanted to use her fingers to straighten it out.

I don't suppose you would want me to put you up in my spare room until this place opens up again. Who knows how long it will be shut down, they said it needs more investigating." she asked, trying to sound serious.

Charles leaned forward and whispered in her ear. "Thank you so much." His smile gave her a glowing sensation she hadn't felt in a lot of years.

"In that case, you fly and I'll drive. I'll pick you up at the hospital when you've been released. What do you need from upstairs? Maybe Scooter will get them for you."

"He's already gotten them. Put them in your car. I still had the keys you gave me."

Isabel felt her face blush with impulsive color. "Oh, you are so bad!" she said while he took her hand as he had been doing often the past few days, and led her slowly out of the so called Hotel Grande for what she hoped would be the last time.

Before Charles boarded the medevac chopper she asked him, "Do you suppose they will ever find her?"

"Who?"

"Darla, of course."

"No. I don't think we'll ever see her again. Although I'd bet that Scooter will go searching for her. But first he needs to find out if the baby is his. Even if it doesn't survive, or ends up being some sort of monster. But with all the genetic crap Darla may have used on that baby, she will probably lose it early on. That appears to be par for that course. She is such a brilliant, but sad person."

"Yes, but one with such an inflated belief in her ability to change the future of mankind through remodeling one baby."

Charles gave a deep sigh. "I remember something I read that said

"I hope we can one day splice ourselves with that Immortal jellyfish. *We would be Gods!!*"

Isabel gave a laugh. "Jellyfish?"

"Yep. One special kind. It's believed to be the only living thing on this earth that never dies."

"You don't suppose Darla . . . . tried something like that."

"I doubt it would work even if she did." Charles then put his one free hand on Isabel's face. "Would it be okay if I kissed you," he said.

"It would not be okay if you didn't." Then she felt his warm full lips pressing against hers, waking up feelings she hadn't experienced in years.

With an obvious reluctance he finally ended the kiss, smiled and started to board the chopper. Then he turned back, a little boy look on his face. "Isabel, do you know why your husband told you not to trust me?" Charles didn't wait for an answer. "It's because he discovered I'm not really a biologist. I'm a licensed private detective that Bertrand's CEO hired to ferret out some problems. I spend most of my time here studying the ins and outs of genetic splicing. So Joe was afraid I would discover what he was hiding. But, hey, you are the one that rescued the flash drive!"

Feeling a little stunned, but in many ways relieved, Isabel gave a bark of a laugh. Then she sobered. "By the way, where *is* that damn flash drive?"

Charles paused and then said "I gave it to Scooter."

"Not to Bertrand?"

"Nope. I still don't trust everyone there."

With that, Charles climbed aboard the helicopter which took off with a blast of rotor-blade wind. Isabel gave him a wave and then headed to her car. "Hot damn!" she said aloud. I believe I'm going to be dating a private detective, not a frigging scientist!

Chapter Twenty One

It was Isabel's thirtieth birthday, and she had arranged for a substitute teacher to take over for her at the high school for the day. Charles had gone out for what he said was a surprise. Isabel made her special turkey and avocado sandwiches for their lunch and then sat in the living room of her condo by the picture window, waiting for him to get home. She looked at the diamond ring on her finger. In a few months, a wedding ring would be added to it. Both of them were pretty much healed, both physically as well as psychologically, from the trauma they had both gone through. Charles' detective business was flourishing and he was being very selective with the cases he would take. Isabel never wanted to hear anything, or see anyone connected to the Bertrand fiasco again. Life was now so blissfully peaceful.

She looked down at the two cats snuggled together in a large cat bed near the fireplace. She had no idea how much she would come to love Darla's kitties. Even Tack with his close to human eyes. And Tick who was the playful one who could manage to open any cupboard in the entire house. Yesterday Tick had opened a new box of Graham Crackers, ate one, and then took one to share with Tack. Isabel often worried that Darla would show up at her door and say she was ready to take the two of them back. If they were Darla's genetic creations, she'd sure done a great job of creating the two of them.

Suddenly Isabel's cell phone bleated loudly from the entry hall table. She went to the hall, picked it up, and clicked it on, hoping Charles wasn't running too late.

"Hello," she said, hearing some jangly music in the background of the caller."

"Hello Sweetcheeks," said a familiar voice.

Isabel let out an audible gasp. "Scooter! My God, we thought you fell off the end of the earth. What have you been up to?"

The background music stopped. "For months, I searched for Darla," Scooter said. "I had to know about the baby."

"Well . . . did you locate her?"

"I did."

"How was she? Did she carry her baby okay?"

"Yes . . . and no. She gave birth to a healthy ten pound baby boy. His name is Robin."

"Ah, nice name." Isabel was totally surprised to hear the baby went full term considering the circumstances surrounding its origins. "So what's the *no* about?"

"Darla . . . she didn't make it. During the delivery she suffered a severe postpartum hemorrhage. Delivering such a large baby may have caused a wound of some kind. They couldn't stop the bleeding."

"Oh my God, Scooter! So, were you with her?" Isabel asked, feeling breathless.

"Yes, of course. Every minute until she passed. I promised her I would take care of . . . our son. A DNA test proved Robin *is* my son. And despite everyone's dire predictions, he's beautiful, smart, and perfect."

"Oh, Scooter I'm so sorry about Darla. Isabel felt herself well up with tears of mixed feelings. "But I'm so happy for you! So, when can we see him?"

"Yeah, well that's why I called. I could use some advice. On child rearing. It scares the hell out of me. He's a year and a half now, and is all over the place, and into everything."

"Golly, Scooter, neither Charles nor I have any experience with kids." Isabel thought about it and then said, "Where are you Scooter?"

"I'm living in a small place in Monrovia. Not far from you"

Just then Charles came bounding in the door, a small brightly wrapped package in his hand. "Who's on the phone," he asked.

"It's Scooter," she said. "Hang on a minute Scooter, Charles is here."

"Good God Almighty!" Charles said, his face looking stunned.

243

Isabel stood there with the phone in her hand, her mouth open, both hands shaking slightly. "It's about . . . well Darla, and of course the baby." She didn't want to say the words to Charles, but knew she had to. "Unfortunately . . . Darla passed away during the delivery of the baby."

Isabel saw the blood drain from Charles face. "Oh no! The baby too?"

"No, no, the baby was a ten pound full term healthy little boy. And yes, a boy, just like Darla predicted. His name is Robin."

Charles gave a sigh and then in a husky whisper he said, "Well, that's something at least. So he's not some outlandish little monster then? Despite all the mischief with his DNA?"

Isabel shook her head no. "Listen, Scooter," she said into the phone. "Why don't you come on over with Robin and we can talk about the advice you say you need."

"Right now?"

"Yes, right now. I need to meet your little boy. Besides, it's my birthday. Bring a gift," she laughed, then gave him their address.

"I'd love that. I do need some help. I'll see you in a half hour or so," Scooter said and hung up.

Charles stood there for a moment with a stunned look, and then gave a smile. "Wow! That's some unbelievable news." he finally said. "It's too bad about Darla, but at least her son is alive."

"The boy is about two now, and Scooter is apparently learning the hard way that it's tough to raise a motherless child. We should do whatever we can to help him find a good Nanny or something."

Charles gave her a kiss. "Of course we should." He set the package he was carrying down on the hall table.

"Well then, I'm going to go fix more sandwiches." Isabel bounded into the kitchen and began pulling things out of the refrigerator.

An hour later Scooter arrived on their porch holding a bundle of toy items with one hand, and a little boy's hand with the other. When Isabel opened the door she gave Scooter a hug, and then looked down at the little boy, and smiled at him.

The boy held out his tiny free hand and said, "I am happy I meet you,"

His words gave Isabel a start. She wasn't sure how fast babies developed but Robin didn't look or sound like what she pictured an eighteen-month-old would look. His brindle eyes and a mop of black hair made him look like a miniature of his father. She cleared her throat and then said, "Hi Robin, I'm Isabel. Come inside and meet my friend Charles.

The boy stared at her for a long moment and then said. "I come inside your house?"

"Yes," she said, then looked up at Scooter, amazed by the fact that such a young child could speak so well. "You are right Scooter; he is beautiful, and smart. Darla must have done something right with her DNA soup."

As she watched, Robin marched past her and into the house on steady feet.

Inside the condo, Charles welcomed them, and urged them to go into the living room and get comfortable.

"I hope you don't mind, but I brought a lot of play things for Robin. He gets bored easily," Scooter told them.

"Good idea," Isabel said. "We haven't had lunch yet, so would you like to join us?"

"If there's enough," Scooter said

"Plenty." Isabel dashed into the kitchen and piled the sandwiches onto a tray so they could eat in the living room. Without a highchair for Robin, she thought it might be awkward eating in the dining area. In the living room Scooter and Robin sat on the pale blue sofa that faced a small coffee table. Isabel plopped down on the floor across from them, and Charles joined her. Robin pulled the turkey and avocado out of his sandwich, and gobbled them down, ignoring the bread. He then wiped his mouth with one of the napkins Isabel had set out on the coffee table.

"I ex cused," he said, and then he got up and began wandering around the room, carefully examining each item he came across.

"Look, but don't touch," Scooter told Robin.

"My goodness Scooter, you've taught him to be so polite," Isabel remarked.

"Actually, he's pretty much taught himself"

"Amazing," was all that Isabel could said.

Isabel enjoyed the three of them being so relaxed, and having time to talk about what all had happened since they had last been together. "Have you seen Danny?" Isabel asked Scooter. "I've wondered what happened to him.

"He's still with Bertrand. But I may hook up with him soon. Robin is such a handful I've hardly have time to do anything else. But Bertrand wants me back at the old stone castle. Pretty much troubleshooting the setup there. They pay well. So far we've been living on Darla's savings that Robin inherited. But I don't know what to do about Robin. I love him to death. He is so affectionate and eager to please. But he's also so dang energetic, and wants to know about absolutely everything."

"Have you thought about hiring a good baby sitter or nanny to begin with," Isabel suggested.

Scooter shook his head in a discouraged manner. "I've had two baby sitters, and both of them left because of they couldn't keep up with Robin. It's always a problem."

"Problems are solvable," Isabel assured him.

Scooter looked across the room at a lamp table where Robin had his back to them, working with something. "What is that you are playing with, Robin?" he asked in a gentle voice.

"I fix," Robin said. "You come see,"

The three of them got up and went over to see what Robin was doing. To Isabel's shock, the clock-radio lay on the table in dozens of pieces.

"Oh, great!" Scooter said. "I'm so sorry."

"Not to worry," Isabel gave a laugh. "It hasn't worked in years."

"Look at that! The little guy has his own tools. A small

screwdriver, a cutter, and other neat stuff," Charles remarked. "Did you buy those for him?"

"He won't give those up. Carries them everywhere in his pockets," Scooter said. "I have no idea who gave them to him, or if he found them somewhere. But I think he'd die if you took them away from him."

"So he took that whole clock apart with those little tools?" Charles said. "Are you sure the hospital didn't give you a much older child?"

"I am sorry. I should have been watching him closer." Scooter put his hand on the boy's shoulder. "Remember Robin, I told you not to play with things that aren't yours. This belongs to Isabel and Charles."

Robin looked up at Scooter, blinking his dark lashed eyes and said, "Robin knows that. Robin fix."

"Oh, just let him play. Maybe it will keep him busy while we talk." Isabel said. "I don't even know why I keep that old clock. No harm done at all."

Scooter gave Robin another pat on the shoulder. "Okay then, but you don't touch anything else in here."

"Robin not touch anythin else," the boy said, running his fingers through the dozens of loose pieces from the dismantled clock.

The three of them sat back down and Isbell asked Scooter, "So then, you might go back to work for Bertrand?"

"There's a whole new crew there, except for Danny. He's still like part of the furniture. And he's accomplishing quite a lot for Bertrand. Thank God all of Bertrand's bad guys are history."

They began talking about everything that had gone wrong while they were at the stone castle. As well as how all the culprits had been ferreted out. Charles asked Scooter about his grapes, and looked disappointed at hearing that the one crop had been sold, and so far no one else had carried on with them.

"Oh, my beautiful grapes!" Charles said with a little faux moan. "But at least I learned a lot about growing them. Not much help with

247

my detective work however."

Isabel enjoyed their chat with Scooter so much she almost forgot about Robin. So it surprised her when Robin came over to her and handed her something. It was her clock-radio!

"Oh my God! Look*!*" she squealed. *"He put it all back together!"*

"It work now." Robin said, giving her an impish grin. "I fix. See, it ticking!"

A hush came over the room. Robin looked up at Isabel, expectation on his face. Obviously wanting something. "Oh Robin," Isabel said softly. "You did a good job. Thank you!" The boy nodded and then toddled off, checking out the room as if searching for something else to fix or take apart.

"Oh dear God, Scooter!" she said looking at him with puzzled eyes. "You certainly do have a problem! He really is like . . . well like what Darla insisted he would be," she lowered her voice. "Some kind of a Designer Child."

"Sweetcheeks, what you've seen is just a tiny fraction of the problem. My son reads better than me, and far more than I do. He can run my computer a hell of a lot better than I can. He actually ordered me a new car the other day. A red Prius. I still don't understand how the hell he managed that. He comprehends everything better than I do. At only thirty-six months old! What on earth will he be able to do when he's fifteen, or twenty or older?" He took a breath and then in a terse voice said, "Do we know how old he will get to be? What if Darla actually did include a DNA element from the Immortal jellyfish? Could he possibly live . . . forever? So damn many questions. And no answers!"

Scooter reached into his jacket pocket and pulled out something. He held it up and Isabel saw that it was the flash drive that she had found at Jorge's insistence. She remembered Charles telling her that he'd given it to Scooter. Neither of them wanted Bertrand to have it. Too much, too soon, too dangerous, was their agreement.

"Robin discovered this in my dresser, where I'd hidden it." Scooter gave a sigh. "After Robin spent a few days of working with the contents on this flash drive and researching stuff on the computer, guess what he announced to me?"

Isabel and Charles looked at each other, speechless.

"Robin, come here please." The boy quickly came to Scooter's side. "What is this?" he asked Robin, handing him the flash drive.

Robin checked it over, grinned, raised the flash drive at arm's length overhead, and waved it around. "This is *me*," he cried. "This is **Robin!**"

The End